SERVING LIFE

Previously published by Baraka Books in the Nurse Linton, Detective Bellechasse Mystery Series:

A Stab at Life (2020)

Banking on Life (2021)

RICHARD KING

SERVING LIFE

Baraka Books
Montréal

ISBN 978-1-77186-272-1 pbk; 978-1-77186-281-3 epub; 978-1-77186-280-6 pdf

Cover by Maison 1608
Book Design by Folio Infographie
Editing by Elise Moser, Deirdre King, Blossom Thom
Proofreading by Barbara Rudnicka

Legal Deposit, 2nd quarter 2022
Bibliothèque et Archives nationales du Québec
Library and Archives Canada

Published by Baraka Books of Montreal

Printed and bound in Quebec

Trade Distribution & Returns
Canada – UTP Distribution: UTPdistribution.com

United States
Independent Publishers Group: IPGbook.com

We acknowledge the support from the Société de développement des entreprises culturelles (SODEC) and the Government of Quebec tax credit for book publishing administered by SODEC.

Société de développement des entreprises culturelles
Québec

Funded by the Government of Canada
Financé par le gouvernement du Canada
Canada

Dedicated to the staff of the Segal Cancer Centre
at the Jewish General Hospital for the compassionate
care you provide to all your patients. Thank you.

APRIL 1995

Prologue

The court clerk rose from the table where she sat with the other court staff. She called out in a practiced voice that could be heard at the back of the crowded courtroom, "Tous se lèvent pour la juge Louise Patenaude." She remained standing, staring at the audience, until they rose and fell silent. Her tone of voice and stare accomplished this in less than ten seconds. The rest of the court personnel got to their feet and Judge Louise Patenaude made her way to the bench. She remained standing for a moment as she looked out over the crowd. She was just over five and a half feet tall. She wore her grey hair shoulder length and her blue-framed glasses gave her attractive, oval face a look that combined compassion and severity. She wore a heavy justice's robe, black with long red lapels, which her father and grandfather had worn before her.

She nodded to the staff standing at the table just below and in front of her bench as she sat. The clerk called for the audience to be seated.

Once everyone was seated Judge Patenaude said, "Bring in the prisoner."

The clerk tapped a buzzer on her desk and two guards entered from a side door with the prisoner, Ian Chambers. They brought him to the defence table where his lawyer stood to greet him. The guards removed Chambers' handcuffs and he and his lawyer sat down.

Judge Patenaude looked at the prosecutor and the defence attorney and asked, "Are you ready for sentencing?"

Both lawyers, the defence and prosecution, popped up and said, almost in unison, "Yes, your honour."

The defence lawyer remained standing. The judge said, "The defendant will rise." Chambers got to his feet and stood next to his lawyer. His wife, sitting behind the defence table, started to get up, but the defence attorney gestured to her to remain seated. The people sitting closest moved away from her.

Ian Chambers was a tall, slim man who wore his hair shaved close to his scalp. He looked more professorial than criminal. Standing next to his lawyer, about to be sentenced, he showed none of his habitual self-confidence.

Judge Patenaude gave Chambers a stern look and read from papers she held in her right hand. "Ian Chambers," she said, "you have been found guilty of the crime of first-degree murder. You callously and with malice aforethought caused the death of a dozen people. Your crime is all the more heinous as you were an orderly at the Gursky Memorial Hospital charged with the care of the people you brought to death. We have heard from the loved ones of your victims, many of whom are in the courtroom. Before I pass sentence, do you have anything you wish to say for yourself?"

The defense attorney started to say, "No, Your Honour," when Chambers put a restraining hand on his attorney's forearm, cleared his throat, and said, "Yes."

Judge Patenaude's blue-grey eyes widened a fraction. "Go ahead."

Chambers inhaled, exhaled, and started speaking in a voice that trembled with nervousness, but became more confident as he went on. "I would like to offer an apology to the court for my actions. More importantly, I would like to tell the families that I am deeply sorry for their losses. I felt that at the time of the deaths of their loved ones, and my feelings haven't changed since then. As Your Honour said, I was an orderly at the Gursky Memorial Hospital. And, yes, I did have the responsibility to see to the comfort of the patients. That, Your Honour, was my motivation for doing what I did." Chambers paused and looked around him at the families of the deceased who had come to court to hear his sentence. Most of them were sniffling and dabbing at their eyes with tissues.

"Do not address the families of your victims. Make your remarks to the court," Judge Patenaude ordered.

Chambers returned his attention to the judge and continued. "Each of the patients arrived in the Emergency Department in an extremely serious state. They were elderly and in failing health. Once in the hospital they were brought to a unit we call the Resuscitation Unit. There they were attached to a variety of medical devices that kept them alive. They were probed and poked often by two doctors and as many nurses. They were robbed of any dignity they may have had before they were brought to the hospital. We all knew that the only thing keeping them alive was complex and expensive medical machinery. Family members were usually close at hand, crying and shrieking to save the patient. We often had to almost drag them from the room so the medical staff could do their work. Once the patient was stabilized, they were left alone, attached to machines that helped them to breathe and which monitored their condition."

Judge Patenaude looked up from her note-taking and stared at Chambers, indicating that she thought he was exaggerating a bad situation in a desperate attempt to make himself look good. Chambers understood her silent stare and after a pause continued. "Maybe not alone all the time, but the patient was limited to one visitor, and as I said the visitors were often in the way and in the end could do very little to comfort the person.

"I would see these elderly people in this desperate situation and it broke my heart." Chambers dabbed at his eyes with the sleeve of his suit jacket. "I was certain that each and every one of these poor souls had lived a full and productive life, working hard, raising families and so on. They deserved a better end. That is what I provided. It was not hard to slip them a little extra morphine or whatever I could get my hands on to allow these people a peaceful and merciful death. Part of what I am guilty of is caring about my patients." His confidence restored, Chambers concluded with a Shakespearean quotation he'd memorized and rehearsed in his mind over and over again.

In the silence that followed the sniffles turned to sobs. Judge Patenaude gave the families of Chambers' victims a moment or two to regain their composure before she spoke.

"Mr. Chambers, it is not your right to make life and death decisions. Your motives are not exculpatory. If you have nothing more to say, I'll deliver my sentence." Ian Chambers and his lawyer were silent. Judge Patenaude cleared her throat. "Ian Chambers, you have been found guilty of twelve counts of first-degree murder by the jury. I, therefore, sentence you to serve a term of life imprisonment for each of the counts, with no possibility of parole for twenty-five years. All the sentences to be served concurrently. And quoting recycled Shakespeare does nothing to lessen your crimes," she added. She gave a sharp whack with her gavel and said, "Remove the prisoner."

The courtroom audience was silent; the only sounds were sniffles and sobs from the families of the victims. Mrs. Chambers, crying loudly, got to her feet and tried to hug her husband as the handcuffs were again placed on his wrists. He was led away by the guards.

Ian Chambers was held in the medium security wing of the Archambault Prison.

FEBRUARY 2020

Chapter 1

Annie had an hour left in her shift in the Resuscitation Unit of the Emergency Department at the Gursky Memorial Hospital. The Resuscitation, referred to as Resus by the staff, is the service reserved for the patients in serious distress, often near death. It had been a busy day and Annie looked forward to a planned dinner with her boyfriend, Gilles Bellechasse, a detective in the Major Crimes Division of the Montreal police at the end of her ten-hour shift.

Annie decided to take a minute to slip into the Triage Unit to see if it was busy. Experience had taught her that when tirage was busy it usually meant that Resus would be busy as well. She could see the street from the Triage Unit, built like a fishbowl with windows that went from desk top to ceiling. It was not yet dark. An ambulance pulled into the bay. The driver jumped out, as did the emergency medical technician. They pulled a stretcher out of the back of their truck and rushed into the triage area. Annie observed the speed with which the EMTs moved and the fact that two Hassidic women, one old, the other young, descended from the ambulance and half-ran behind them into triage.

The EMTs barely tolerated one family member in the ambulance. The fact that there were two meant that the EMTs believed that getting the patient to the hospital was more important than arguing with family members.

It was more than likely that the patient was destined for Resuscitation and Annie wanted to get as much information about him as quickly as possible. She got to the room used for patients brought to the hospital by Urgences-santé at the same time as the ER orderly who pushed a hospital stretcher next to the one from the ambulance. Annie and the orderly were on one side of the stretcher and the two EMTs on the other side. "On my count," Annie called. "One, two, three." They moved the patient to the ER stretcher.

"What've we got?" Annie asked.

"Solomon Gluck. Heart."

"Vitals?"

"Blood pressure is low and pulse weak," one of the EMTs replied. "I thought we lost him en route."

Annie put her stethoscope to the patient's chest and said, "Mr. Gluck, can you hear me? Do you know what's happening?" His eyelids fluttered but he made no response.

"I want to get him hooked up. Do you have his card?"

The EMT nodded and held up Gluck's assurance maladie card.

"Give it to Tasso, please," she said and turned to Jean-Guy, the orderly. "Resus three is open. Follow me." Annie pulled the stretcher with one hand while the orderly pushed it.

Once in the room they were joined by Dr. Alex Rosen. Annie brought him up to date as she and Jean-Guy got the patient on a respirator and heart monitor. Dr. Rosen listened to Gluck's heart and gave Annie orders for medication. She got the meds and attached an IV feed to a vein in the patient's left arm.

Mrs. Gluck had followed the stretcher to the room and she stood at her husband's right side, holding his hand and mumbling something in Yiddish. Her lined face was white with worry and Annie feared she would have an anemic fainting spell.

"We're going to do our best to help your husband," Annie said softly. "Jean-Guy will take you to the waiting room, where you'll be more comfortable. I'll come and talk to you as soon as I can."

Mrs. Gluck stared blankly at her; Annie was not certain that she'd understood. Perhaps she only spoke Yiddish. "Do you understand?" Annie asked.

"Ich farshteyn."

"Jean-Guy, please take Mrs. Gluck to the waiting room."

The Emergency Department of the Gursky Memorial Hospital was newly built. It was at the western edge of the main campus attached to the main building, an Art Deco edifice dating from the 1930s. The department was designed so that there were four waiting rooms for the seven medical service areas.

All the hallways in the ED that led to the patients' rooms were straight and wide. This meant that those whose job it was to serve the patients, everyone from doctors to orderlies to the people who delivered meals, could move quickly and efficiently through the department without having to detour through a labyrinth of hallways like those in the older buildings.

No sooner had Jean-Guy left with Mrs. Gluck than Tasso, the registration clerk, came into the room with the patient's chart. He was followed by the second woman, the patient's daughter. Tasso handed the chart to Annie, who made her notes and passed it to Dr. Rosen so he could do the same.

"How's my father? Where's my mother?" the young woman asked.

Annie gently held the woman by the elbow and led her out of the room so Dr. Rosen could continue to make his notes and monitor the patient. "My name is Annie Linton. We're going to take very good care of your father, I promise.

Your mother is in the waiting room and it would be best if you waited with her. I'll come and talk to you in a couple of minutes." Annie put a comforting hand on the woman's shoulder. "What's your name?"

"I'm Dvora, Dvora Steiner." Dvora was dressed in modest Hassidic style. Her skirt fell to below her knees and she wore opaque beige stockings with a seam up the back. Her *sheitel*, the wig worn by Lubavitcher women, was slightly askew, which made her look confused in addition to worried.

"I'll show you where you can wait with your mother." Annie kept her hand on Dvora's upper arm and brought her to the double door that led to the corridor. "The waiting room is on your right." Annie opened the door for Dvora.

Annie went back to the nurses' station which was in front of the room that Solomon Gluck occupied. Dr. Rosen was sitting at the desk writing in the chart.

"How's he doing?"

"Touch and go. It's funny, though. The patient has no history of heart trouble." Dr. Rosen shifted the chart so Annie could see it. The patient had been in the ER six weeks previously with the flu. He was admitted and sent home a week later. It was not a serious case and, according to Dvora, he had not had a relapse. The only other information was that he was suffering from Alzheimer's, in its early stages. Beyond this he was pretty healthy for a man of his age.

"Is he on meds for the Alzheimer's?" Annie asked flipping through the chart looking for the list of the patient's medications.

"No. He's not on anything, really. Just a Crestor clone for cholesterol."

"So why a sudden heart problem? It doesn't make sense."

"These things happen," Dr. Rosen said and flipped the chart closed.

"I'm going to talk to the family." Annie left unsaid that she doubted very much that "these things happen." There had to be a reason.

Annie joined Dvora and her mother in the waiting room. Mrs. Gluck was seated on the sofa and Dvora was in the one upholstered chair. There was a table with a telephone on it between the chair and the sofa. Mrs. Gluck was holding her daughter's hand. The two women started to get up when Annie came into the room. "Please sit down," Annie said and smiled comfortingly. She pulled a chair from the corner of the room and sat facing the two women.

"Your husband had a close call." Annie looked directly at Mrs. Gluck. "We have him on a respirator and heart meds and the next twenty-four hours will be difficult. After that he should be out of trouble. For now, it's necessary to be hopeful and wait."

"Es is in Got's hent," Mrs. Gluck mumbled.

"Mama. Got vet kukn far papa," Dvora agreed. She turned to Annie and added, "You know, it's funny, the other doctor said his pills would be great for my father and there'd be no side effects."

"Doctor? What other doctor?" Annie asked.

Dvora shifted in her chair and played nervously with one of the pleats in her black skirt. "A week or so after my father came home from the hospital a doctor called and came to the house. He left some pills and said he'd be back when my father was done with them."

Annie knew the ER doctor who cared for Mr. Gluck during his hospital stay would not have made a home visit. It was remotely possible that his personal physician would drop by but Dvora gave the impression that the doctor who made the house call was someone they didn't know.

It was important to know what medication Mr. Gluck was taking. There was nothing other than the Crestor clone listed in his chart. Annie needed to know more about the mysterious doctor who made house calls.

"What can you tell me about this doctor?" Annie asked. "What was his name?"

"I wasn't there," Dvora said. "My brother Avrum was with my parents. The rest of my family will be here soon. I just called them." She pointed to the telephone on the table.

"Does your mother remember his name or anything about him?"

Dvora turned to her mother and was about to translate Annie's question into Yiddish when her mother answered, "*Ich ton nicht gedenken zeyn nomen. Es is geven epes modne vi,* Hong Kong."

"You mean he was Chinese?"

Dvora smiled at her mother's characterization of the doctor. In a less tense situation she would not have made an effort to supress a giggle.

"*Neyn, er iz geven a* blonde."

Dvora made no attempt to suppress a laugh. "I think we'll have to wait for my brother to get the information."

Annie got to her feet and asked Dvora to accompany her to the hallway. She showed her a telephone on the wall next to the double door that led to Resus and explained, "That phone is connected to the nurses' station. It's a direct line. Pick it up and call me when your brother gets here."

Half an hour later the phone on the desk at the nurses' station rang. It was Dvora. "My brother is here."

"I'll be right out."

Annie returned to the waiting room, which was now full. In addition to Dvora and her mother there was another woman and four men, the Gluck children. "This is my brother

Avrum," Dvora indicated the young man standing next to her. Out of habit Annie extended her hand to the young man, dressed in a black three-piece suit with a white shirt buttoned at the neck but tieless. His beard was black with touches of grey and his *pais* hung almost to his shoulders. He wore a Borsalino-style hat; she could see the half of his *kippah* that extended below the crown. The *tzitzit* of his *tallit katan,* the prayer shawl Hassidic men wore under their street clothes, swung as he turned to face Annie.

"I'm Annie." Avrum nodded to Annie but didn't take the offered hand. Annie realized her mistake and withdrew it.

"I'm Avrum. My sister tells me that you're looking after my father. On behalf of the family, I want to thank you for your kindness."

"You're welcome. I'd like to know a little more about the other doctor who came to your parents' house. Dvora said you were there when he came over."

"Yes, that's true," Avrum said. "He called and made an appointment and my mother asked me to be there when he came. He was a very nice man."

"It's very unusual for a doctor to visit a patient, especially one that he doesn't know. What did he tell you? Was he your family doctor?"

"No, we'd never seen him before. He asked if my father was over the flu and then"—Avrum lowered his voice—"he talked about my father's Alzheimer's. He said that because he was in the early stages, he had some pills that might help and he gave them to us."

"Did he check your father's vital signs, pulse, blood pressure and so on?"

"Yes. He did all those doctor things."

"What did he tell you about the pills—other than that they might help with his Alzheimer's symptoms?"

"Just to take them by themselves, not with any other medications. He said he could take them at lunch time."

"He didn't tell you the name of the medication? What the pills were called?"

"He did but I don't remember. It was a long name. Probably the chemical name. My father took the pills as instructed. He took the last one a day or so ago."

"Do you remember his name? Your mother said it was something like Hong Kong."

Avrum smiled and said, "Not Hong Kong, Hingston. Dr. Hingston."

Annie pulled a pad and pen from her scrubs pocket, wrote her name and phone numbers, including her cell number, on a sheet of paper and handed it to Avrum. "I've given you my phone numbers at the hospital and my cell. Please call me if Dr. Hingston calls you. I need to speak to him."

Dvora and Avrum both promised to call if and when the mysterious Dr. Hingston called them. They thanked Annie again and she returned to the nurses' station. She knew that there was no Dr. Hingston in the Emergency Department and she asked Dr. Rosen if he knew of a doctor by that name who worked anywhere in the Gursky. He didn't. Annie made a note in the chart about Dr. Hingston giving unknown medication to the patient. She wanted to find out who this doctor was and where in the hospital he worked. She figured he worked somewhere in the complex of buildings that comprised the Gursky Memorial Hospital, as he could only have known that Solomon Gluck had been hospitalized for the flu and had early-onset Alzheimer's by checking the hospital database.

Her research would have to wait for another day. It was six o'clock and Gilles was expected at her house at seven.

Gilles picked Annie up a couple of minutes after seven. Her hair was still damp after her shower. She was dressed in jeans and a V-neck sweater that showed off her figure. She stood on tiptoes to give Gilles a welcoming kiss. Like Annie he wore blue jeans, with a red-checked shirt and a navy-blue V-neck. They both wore brightly coloured down jackets, Gilles in red and Annie in cobalt blue.

"Shall we try Chinatown?" Gilles suggested as they walked to his car. "We can try to get into the Nan Qing."

Annie squeezed Gilles' right arm as they walked. He could feel the softness of her breasts through her jacket.

"Let's."

The restaurants in Montreal's Chinatown were usually very busy on Sunday nights but luck was with Gilles and Annie. They found parking on René-Lévesque near the corner of St. Urbain, a short walk from the restaurant. Gilles gave his name when they arrived but the man at the counter was looking at Annie. Her blue eyes and beautiful smile got a smile in response from the normally harried maître d' and they only had a short wait before a table for two opened up.

As they waited for their mains to arrive after the soup course, Gilles asked Annie about her day. "Well, it wasn't all that busy until late, about an hour before I was scheduled to leave. The day ended with a mystery." Annie smiled at her boyfriend.

"Really? I'm usually the one that brings mysteries to you. What happened?"

Annie told Gilles about the Gluck family and the mysterious doctor's visit.

"I didn't think doctors made house calls these days. It's hard enough to get an office visit."

"Exactly," Annie said. "And that's the mystery. Who is Dr. Hingston? He's not an ER doctor, that's for sure, and

I didn't have time to check the staff list for the rest of the hospital before I left. I'll do it tomorrow."

"Is there a possibility that he's some kind of imposter?"

The main dishes had arrived and Annie paused, holding her rice bowl with spicy chicken in her left hand and her chopsticks in her right. "You see too many movies. And how would he have known about Mr. Gluck's flu and Alzheimer's if he didn't have access to the hospital's database?"

"Yeah, I see. Still, if you don't find him let me know and I'll check our databases to see if there have been any complaints about doctors—real or fake."

Conversation turned to other topics as they enjoyed their meal. After dinner they decided to return to Annie's place. Gilles' condo was closer but if they spent the night there, he would have had to drive Annie home before heading to work.

Chapter 2

Annie was assigned to the Triage Unit when she reported for work on Monday. As soon as there was a lull in the flow of patients, she went to Resus to check on Solomon Gluck. He remained in critical condition. He had not regained consciousness. Annie found the family was still in the waiting room. They had obviously spent the night at the hospital and they looked haggard and worried.

Back in the triage area Annie checked the hospital staff database in search of Dr. Hingston. She drew a blank. She asked the doctors who were working in the ER if they had ever heard of a Dr. Hingston and came up empty. Daniella Taddeo, one of the other nurses working in triage, pointed out that the staff list that Annie had checked only included the medical practitioners in the nine interconnected pavilions that made up the parts of the hospital where patients were treated. It did not include the additional four buildings where medical research and a certain number of outpatient services were conducted. The Gursky covered the equivalent of fourteen or fifteen city blocks and Annie realized there were buildings she had never been in. She decided to continue her search for Dr. Hingston as soon as she had some free time.

Free time was a luxury in the Triage Unit of the Gursky, a luxury Annie didn't have that Monday. She had barely had a chance to get settled at her computer on her return from a quick lunch in the hospital food court when she heard an announcement over the hospital public address system: "Code blue, Emergency Resus three. Repeat, code blue Emergency Resus three."

Code blue meant that a patient was having a cardiac crisis and Resus three was Solomon Gluck's room. Annie grabbed her stethoscope and rushed to her patient. Two doctors and another nurse were working on him. The orderly, Jean-Guy St-Onge, was standing just outside the door to the room staring at Mr. Gluck. The Gluck family had heard the announcement and they were trying to push their way into the room. Jean-Guy did his best to herd the family away from the entrance to Mr. Gluck's room so Annie could enter it. Dr. Rose appeared at the patient's bedside a couple of seconds later.

"Clear!" Dr. Rosen shouted as he applied the defibrillator paddles to Solomon Gluck's chest. Gluck bounced as the electric current shot through his body. Annie felt for a pulse with one hand and placed her stethoscope on Gluck's chest.

"Nothing," she called.

"Clear!" Dr. Rosen called and shot another charge into the patient.

Annie again felt for a pulse in the carotid artery. "Nothing."

"I'm calling it," Dr. Rosen said.

"One more," Annie shouted. "It hasn't even been fifteen minutes."

"Christ, Annie."

"C'mon, Alex. One more at max voltage," Annie commanded, not giving Dr. Rosen the opportunity to argue. A thousand volts shot through Solomon Gluck. He didn't come back to life.

Dr. Rosen looked at the clock on the wall and announced, "Time of death is 2:05. I'm sorry, Annie. We did our best."

The Gluck family had been watching in horror as the doctors and nurses tried to save their father's life, and heard

Rosen call the time of death. They sobbed and hugged one another. Then, as if on command, they fell silent for a moment, then said the prayer, "*Baruch atah Adonai Eloheinu melech ha'olam, dayan ha-emet.*"

The prayer over, they tried to push into the room, but there were too many people and they had to wait outside. Solomon Gluck had only been dead for a couple of minutes when Yossel Katz, one of the religious volunteers who spent his days in the ER helping Orthodox Jews navigate the health system, arrived. Katz was not himself Hassidic, but was an adherent of mainstream Orthodox Judaism. He wore a kippah and observed the Sabbath along with all Jewish holy days but forewent *payos* and the strict rules by which the Hassids lived.

He offered his condolences and took charge of things. "I'll call Chesed," he said referring to Chesed Shel Emes, the home that handled funerals for Montreal's Hassidic communities. "They'll be here within an hour. Maybe less."

The family looked relieved that Yossel Katz had come to their aid. He called the funeral home on his cellphone and, speaking Yiddish, gave them the details they needed to come to the hospital to collect the body of Solomon Gluck.

Annie came to Yossel's side and the minute he got off the phone she said, "Listen, there's something not right here. Mr. Gluck should not have had a heart attack, certainly not a fatal one. I think there should be an autopsy. I think he was taking some kind of medication that we didn't know about."

The family heard the word "autopsy" and began to wail. "No, no, no," Avrum yelled, the word punctuated by sobs.

Yossel Katz held up his hand, "*Tsi nicht zorg,*" he said to the family. He took Annie by the elbow and moved her a little way from the family. "It's not happening," he said in a low tone. "There are all kinds of religious reasons why that's not happening. C'mon, Annie, you know better."

He was right that Annie knew better. She had been working with Yossel Katz for as long as she'd been working in the ER. There were times that she resented the fact that he found a way to get the Hassidic patients he served special treatment, but overall she liked the man. He had a sly (and very unreligious) sense of humour.

"But, Yossel...," Annie began.

He interrupted her, "I know, Annie. I've spoken to the family and they told me about the other doctor, but there's no medical or legal reason for an autopsy. You know the crises that will be. Lawyers, rabbis, you name it. In the end there'll be no autopsy and the family will suffer more. Let it be."

"But, Yossel," Annie repeated. "What if I'm right?"

"Annie, I know you're motivated by concern for your patient and his family. You did your best and they told me how much they appreciated it. Now they need time to mourn and find the comfort their religion offers."

Unhappily, Annie realized that Yossel was right. She didn't want to get into a fight that would further upset the Gluck family. But she was more determined than ever to find Dr. Hingston and find out what medication he'd given Solomon Gluck.

Chapter 3

Dr. Marcus Tiddley worked in a building a block and a half west of the ER: Pavilion L. He was director of research at the Dementia and Alzheimer's Research Group, a project that was looking into the cause and the cure for Alzheimer's and other neurodegenerative diseases.

One of the benefits of research into neurodegenerative diseases was that there was a lot of grant money available for it. Pharmaceutical companies, governments and private foundations were all keen to find a cure for the various forms of dementia that came with an aging population. There was another advantage of doing research at the Gursky Memorial: there were a large number of patients suffering from Alzheimer's whose cases Tiddley could follow.

Tiddley held informal staff meetings each Monday morning at ten to discuss progress and to set goals for the week ahead. He made notes on the work of each of the dozen people who worked at the benches in his lab and referred to information from previous meetings when talking to the members of his team. Team members learned very quickly to keep careful lab notes so as to be able to respond to Tiddley's questions about their progress.

"Remember, team, we're serving life, here. It could be your parents or grandparents we're saving from a fate worse than death." Tiddley closed all his meetings with that invocation. He thought it was motivational. He certainly believed it. He was as much motivated by having witnessed his mother's descent into the lost world of Alzheimer's sufferers as he was by money.

Later that afternoon, while working in his office, Tiddley received an email and text message that caused him some consternation. "Dammit!" He read and then deleted the messages.

Chapter 4

Two days later, Annie moved quickly through the parking lot, huddled under her umbrella, trying to hold it against the cold wind. She hadn't found a moment's free time to continue her search for Dr. Hingston. She walked carefully so as to avoid stepping into one of the many puddles that had formed due to the late winter storm that combined rain with heavy wet snow. The temperature hovered just above the freezing point but the wind blew frigid air through her clothing, right to the bone. She was working the four-to-midnight shift and she hoped the rain would abate by the time she left the hospital. She was pleased to enter the dry warmth of the ER.

She stowed her raincoat and umbrella in her locker and joined Daniella Taddeo at the triage desk. They received information from the departing nurses and hoped that the bad weather would mean a quiet night.

The bad weather did nothing to keep people away from the ER; in fact, it was busier than usual. Annie and Daniella had to forego their dinner breaks and satisfy themselves with a dozen stolen minutes to have a sandwich and a coffee from the Second Cup in the lobby, one floor above the Emergency Department.

At eight-thirty, an ambulance, closely followed by a police car, arrived with a patient. The EMTs wheeled in a white-haired man wrapped in blankets and strapped to the gurney. The elderly gentleman had a thick moustache the same colour as his hair and he hadn't shaved in a couple of days. The first thing Annie noticed was that the patient looked lost and confused. She stood close to the gurney and took the man's hand. It was damp and cold to the touch and she rubbed it with both her hands to restore its warmth.

"What've we got?" she asked.

The female cop answered. "We found him wandering around, soaking wet and freezing. We haven't been able to get any information from him. He speaks neither English nor French. Maybe Italian or Greek, I can't tell."

"Oh, the poor soul," Annie said. She stroked the man's wet hair, looked him in the eyes and said, "We'll take care of you. Don't worry. Can you tell me your name?" The patient didn't answer and looked sadder and more confused at Annie's question.

She started to undo the restraints and the EMTs followed her lead. She pulled down the red blanket that covered the man and saw that he was wearing faded blue pyjamas and an old bathrobe, a washed-out red and blue plaid. It too was drenched. The patient shivered with cold.

"OK, first thing is to get him warmed up. Then his vitals." She called to the orderly to bring her a couple of short hospital gowns and a long yellow one along with some flannel sheets from the warmer. "And a stretcher. Stat," she added.

A moment later Jean-Guy St-Onge appeared with sheets and gowns. "Help me get him out of the wet clothes and into these. On my count. One, two, three."

They transferred the patient to the hospital stretcher, stripped off his wet robe and pyjamas, and got him into the dry gowns. St-Onge cranked the back of the stretcher so the patient was in a seated position. He clutched Annie's hand and she made no move to pull away. She stroked his cheek with the back of her free hand. "Vitals?"

"Blood pressure and temperature low. I don't know how much longer he would have lasted if we hadn't found him."

"Where did you find him?"

"On Lucerne Road in the Town of Mount Royal, right where it meets Côte-de-Liesse," the female cop replied. "He wandered into a service station. One of the workers called us. Lucky for him. He could have been killed. Traffic is pretty fast on Côte-de-Liesse, especially at night."

"He was wearing slippers, but they must have fallen off in the truck," her partner added. "He must have been in bed and somehow wandered off in search of something. Totally disoriented." The EMTs submitted their paperwork and left. The cops remained.

"Right." Annie carefully removed her hand from the patient's and walked the two paces to the door of the room where ambulance patients were triaged. She called to Daniella and Tasso to help her.

Annie explained that the patient did not appear to understand English or French. Could Daniella try Italian and Tasso Greek to see if the patient responded to either of those languages?

The patient didn't respond to Daniella's question. Tasso moved closer to the patient and said, *"Boreece na mou peas to onomá sou?"*

The patient brightened at the question in Greek. He smiled and said, *"To onomá mou einai Giorgos."*

"His name is..."

"George, I get it," Annie said. "What about his last name?"

Tasso put the question in Greek but didn't get a response.

Annie took the patient's blood pressure and temperature and listened to his heart. She entered the information into the computer and turned to Tasso and said, "You can't register him unless you have more information, right?"

"Yeah. Listen, do you have an idea what meds he might be on?" Tasso asked.

"From the speed that his blood pressure shot up I would guess a thiazide-type diuretic, and a statin wouldn't surprise me. Why?"

"Where was he found? I mean what part of the city?" Tasso asked.

"Ville Mont-Royal," the Emergency Medical Technician answered.

"I'm going to call the pharmacies in TMR and see if any of them have a patient in their seventies, by the look of him, named George Something, on the meds you said," Tasso said.

"Brilliant. The Town is mostly residential so there are only about a half dozen pharmacies in the area."

"Let's hope he gets his meds at one of them." Tasso returned to his office, did a Google search for pharmacies in the Town of Mount Royal, and got busy on the phone.

Annie and St-Onge wheeled the patient to the corridor just outside Tasso's office and returned to their respective tasks.

Twenty minutes later Tasso parked himself in the chair next to Annie's desk in Triage. "I think I found him."

"Terrific, that's great."

"His name is Giorgos, George, Prodosiakis."

"How certain are you? George is hardly an unusual name."

"I would say about 90%. The pharmacist recognized my description and the fact that he had some dementia."

Annie turned to her computer and said as she typed, "Let's see what information, if any, we have." Tasso leaned forward so he could see the computer screen. A minute later a screen of information popped up. Sure enough, the patient was George Prodosiakis. Annie checked the meds listed in the file and saw that her assumptions were correct. The emergency contact listed his daughter and son along with their cellphone numbers.

"You can register him while I contact his children. Let's hope that no lasting damage was done by his night in the rain. I have to say, I didn't like his chest sounds. I'm worried about the flu or pneumonia."

Tasso went back to his desk and Annie called Fotoula Prodosiakis.

"Are you Fotoula?" Annie asked the woman who answered her call.

"Who wants to know?"

"My name is Annie Linton. I'm a nurse in the ER at the Gursky Memorial Hospital..." Fotoula gasped but didn't say anything and Annie continued, "Your father was found wandering around the Town of Mount Royal an hour ago. Is that where he lives?"

"Yes, but I don't understand. I'm at the house. He's asleep."

"Please check," Annie ordered.

Fotoula didn't say anything and Annie could hear footsteps and the sound of a door opening and closing. Toula came back on the line. "Oh my God, you're right. He's not in his bed. You said he's in the hospital?"

"Yes, the Gursky. The cops found him and brought him in."

"Oh, dear, I'll be there as fast as I can."

Annie told her where to come and Toula hung up.

"Good work," Daniella said. She was at the other computer terminal next to Annie.

"Thanks. Tasso deserves most of the credit. It was odd, though."

"How do you mean?"

"She didn't ask how her father was."

The need to triage patients overtook any possibility of further conversation between Annie and Daniella.

An hour later, while both Annie and Daniella were busy with patients, a woman knocked on the glass that separated the triage area from the waiting room. Annie looked up and saw a tall woman, beautiful, with shoulder-length hair as black and shiny as a tuxedo button. A man, a little shorter, with black hair combed back from his forehead, stood beside her.

Annie pressed the button that activated the microphone and said, "I'm with a patient. Please wait."

The woman ignored Annie's request and said, "I'm Fotoula. Toula Prodosiakis. Someone called me about my father."

"I'll see you as soon as I've finished with my patient." Annie removed her finger from the microphone button and twisted the flexible arm of the mic up to indicate conversation was over. She returned to her patient and gave her a thorough workup. Toula continued to talk for a moment or two but neither Annie nor Daniella could hear her. She finally gave up but didn't move from where she was standing next to the window.

Toula didn't wait for Annie to invite her into the triage booth. When the patient opened the door to return to the waiting room, Toula entered and the man with her followed. They were both dressed for the weather. She in a black raincoat, he in a tan trench coat. They were carrying umbrellas, which dripped water onto the floor of the triage area.

Toula sat down in the patient's chair next to Annie's desk. "I'm Toula," she repeated. "This is my brother, Iannis." Iannis smiled and extended his hand to Annie. "Are you the one who called me?" Toula continued.

"I am. Your father is here. I told you he was found on the street. Lost and confused."

"Thank you. Can we take him home now?"

"I don't advise it," Annie said. "I'm concerned that your father may have developed a chest cold or worse. He was practically hypothermic when he came in."

Toula and her brother had a conversation in Greek. They spoke quickly and Annie gathered from their tones of voice that they disagreed on how best to proceed. Annie picked up the one English word Iannis used—Hingston—preceded by *giatrós*, the word Annie recognized as the Greek word for doctor.

Annie interrupted. "Do I understand that your father had been treated by a doctor named Hingston?"

Iannis was about to answer her but his sister spoke before he had the opportunity. "No, you misunderstood us. Do you speak Greek?" She didn't wait for Annie to answer and continued a one-sided conversation with her brother.

Annie didn't believe the woman. Suspicion that something was very, very wrong caused the skin on her arms to tingle and she felt her breathing quicken.

She waited for Toula and Iannis to finish talking and said, "Did you understand what I told you? Your father is at a very high risk for pulmonary complications and possibly heart issues."

Iannis said, "Yes. Absolutely. I agree with you. He should be kept to be certain that he's okay. My sister disagrees. Can we see him?"

"Yes, I'll show you." There was something about Toula Prodosiakis that Annie didn't trust, and she wanted to keep an eye on her.

Daniella said, "I'll cover."

Annie led the Prodosiakises down the corridor to their father's room. While they walked brother and sister had another conversation in Greek. There was one English word that Annie recognized, however. Iannis said something about Hingston.

Annie stood in front of the door to George Prodosiakis's room and asked Iannis, "Did you say Hingston? Doctor Hingston?" She hoped Toula would not hear her.

"Yes, I did. He came to see us a couple of months ago. He wanted to talk about..."

Toula interrupted her brother in rapid-fire Greek, obviously telling him to shut up. Annie ignored Toula and asked, "Did he give your father any medication?"

"He did." Iannis was about to say something else. His sister pushed her way past Annie into her father's room. She pulled her brother behind her. The door slid closed.

Annie walked around to the medical area. The patients' rooms had large windows so the doctors and nurses could monitor them. She told the unit agent to keep an eye on the Prodosiakis family. She indicated the room they were in and added that the patient was not to leave, and to find an excuse to get the visitors out in ten or so minutes. The unit agent agreed.

Annie returned to the triage area. Barely five minutes later she saw Toula and Iannis Prodosiakis walk out of the hospital. They stopped in the vestibule before venturing out in the rain. Iannis waited while his sister walked a couple of paces away from him and made a short call on her cellphone.

"You can't beat those two for rude," Daniella commented when they had a minute to talk privately.

"Yeah, especially the daughter. But there is something weird. The son, Iannis, said something about Dr. Hingston seeing their father and his sister shut him down. One way or another I'm going to find Hingston and find out what the hell he's up to."

Chapter 5

The next morning Annie came in a couple of hours before the start of her shift and found an unused computer in the office tucked behind the triage area, next to Registration. She checked the staff databases for every department in the hospital. She gave up after forty-five minutes. There was no record of anyone by the name of Hingston.

Jean-Guy St-Onge came into the triage area in the middle of the afternoon, at a point when Annie was not busy with a patient. "I thought you would want to know," he said, "I just brought your patient, the Greek man, up to the Cardiac Care Unit."

"Damn, I was worried about that. Thanks for telling me."

Annie typed her patient's name into her computer and brought up the notes in his chart. It was worse than she thought. George Prodosiakis was in serious distress with heart problems and pneumonia. She couldn't understand how he could have managed to leave his house with both his children there. Something didn't make sense. Annie was determined to find out how an elderly man suffering from dementia managed to end up on the street and was now near death.

Just before she left for the weekend Annie called the CCU to check on her patient. She gasped and put her free hand to her chest; he had died an hour previously from heart failure, probably because of the pneumonia. "That's awful," Annie said to the nurse in CCU.

"Yeah, but he never regained consciousness, so I guess he didn't suffer too much," she replied.

"Has the family been informed?"

"The doctor is on the phone with the daughter now."

Annie could only imagine how that conversation was going.

Depressed, Annie left for the weekend. She hoped that dinner with her daughter and her weekend plans with Gilles would revive her spirits.

Chapter 6

When Annie arrived home on Friday evening, her daughter Pamela could see that her mother was concerned about something. Pamela, who was in medical school, felt her mother worried too much about her patients. But Annie's empathy was what made her such a good nurse.

Pamela was taller than her mother. Her height and skin colour were inheritances from her Ugandan father, as was her thick curly black hair. She owed her fine facial features to her mother's Irish heritage. The combination made Pamela a beautiful young woman. She got up from the dining room table where she had been studying and gave Annie a hug. "How was your day, Mum?"

Annie told her daughter about George Prodosiakis and his children. "That's awful, Mum, but you did your best. How about a drink to help you relax?"

"If you join me," Annie said.

Annie and Pamela spent a quiet evening over dinner, managed to kill the bottle of wine, and, after watching a movie, had an early night.

⊙

The stars that govern the relationships with daughters must have been in perfect alignment that night because Gilles' daughter Émilie was also, uncharacteristically, home for dinner. Émilie was enrolled in the drama program at the Université du Québec à Montréal. She had been an indifferent student until she discovered her passion for everything dramatic. She'd excelled in the drama program at her CEGEP, part of Québec's system of junior colleges, and was now in her first year of university. She had moved in with her father while attending CEGEP.

Gilles hadn't prepared anything for dinner and Émilie was not interested in left-overs, so they ordered Thai food. During their dinner Émilie received half a dozen text messages. "C'est assez, Lapin," Gilles said, and Émilie turned her phone face down on the table. After dinner she went off to meet her friends. Gilles washed the few dishes they had used and watched a little TV.

◉

On Saturday afternoon when Gilles called to arrange to pick Annie up for their date, she suggested that they have dinner at her place. She was still a little depressed at the death of George Prodosiakis and wanted to be fussing in the kitchen preparing a meal to help her take her mind off it. Gilles agreed. "I feel that there's something that's upsetting you," he said. "We'll talk about it over dinner. You know if there's anything I can do to help, I'll do it."

"A sympathetic ear is all I'll need. Well, a sympathetic ear and a bottle of white wine."

"I'll provide both," Gilles said.

Over dinner Annie told Gilles about George Prodosiakis and his children and the mysterious Dr. Hingston, a doctor whose name didn't appear in any of the hospital databases.

"I don't know if he's a murderer," Annie concluded. "In fact, I don't even know if he's a real doctor or an imposter. I do know that he's done something which is at the very least unethical and irresponsible. Can you investigate? Is there enough evidence for it to be considered a crime?"

Gilles's eyes focused on a point just above Annie's head. He pushed his lips in and out for a moment then said, "You know, I think you're right. I told you I would help if I could and it looks to me as if someone is presenting themselves as a doctor and giving the patient some kind of medication that ends up killing them. Maybe that wasn't the intent but it was the result. Were there any other similar cases?"

Annie smiled at Gilles. His support helped to alleviate the sadness and aloneness she was feeling. "Yeah, there was at least one other case." Annie told him about the Gluck family. "That was the first time I heard the name Dr. Hingston."

"I'm going to pay the Prodosiakis family a visit on Monday and see what I can unearth. I'll have to figure out a way of getting my boss's approval, but one way or another I'll do it."

◉

Toula arrived fifteen minutes late for her dinner with Marcus Tiddley at the Restaurant L'Express on that Saturday evening. One of the perks of being beautiful is that you can walk into a restaurant just late enough so that your dinner companion will have secured the table, and avoid waiting in line. All heads, especially those attached to men, turned to watch Toula walk to her table. She sat down and ordered a drink from the waiter who had followed her. After taking a sip of her martini she said, "You fucked up. My father died in the hospital."

"I'm very sorry. You and your brother must be devastated."

"You have no idea." Toula picked up her menu. Marcus had no choice but to do the same. They barely made small talk while they waited for their food to be brought to their table.

Marcus broke the silence. "Listen, I'm very sorry for your loss. Really. Is there anything I can do?"

Toula smiled, put her cutlery down on the table, and said, "You can hope that my brother doesn't say anything that will call attention to what you've done."

"Has he said something?"

"Yes, but I shut him up."

The colour returned to Marcus's face. "As I said: is there anything I can do?"

Toula picked up her fork and speared a couple of frites. "We can enjoy our dinner and let past events die." She put the frites in her mouth and chewed.

"Sounds like a plan. What would you like to talk about?"

Toula was silent for a moment while she swallowed her frites. She smiled and said, "Why don't you tell me about your research?"

She wasn't all that interested in what Tiddley did in his lab, but she knew he would enjoy talking about his research and she could think about other things, interjecting a "that's fascinating" or "how interesting" from time to time.

Chapter 7

Réal Fournier was walking home in the suburb of Laval on a cold, damp night. He had to wait for the traffic to pass on de la Concorde Boulevard before he could cross and walk the rest of the short distance from the Montmorency metro station to his home on Brien. The attacker came up behind him, looped a rope around his neck, and pulled tight. Surprised, Réal tried to yell and grab at the garrotte. No sound came from his collapsing windpipe and he couldn't get a grip on the rope to save himself. Traffic moves fast on de la Concorde Boulevard and none of the drivers speeding past him noticed the distress of the man standing on the sidewalk. The murderer pulled the lifeless body back from the edge of the sidewalk and deposited it in the deserted parking area next to the metro station. The murderer was on the metro back to Montreal before the body of the victim cooled in the frigid winter temperature.

The Laval police could find no clues other than the ligature marks on Réal Fournier's neck. Fournier was a sixty-five-year-old man who had recently retired from his job as a salesman for a furniture retailer. He would not have been on the sidewalk on de la Concorde at all if his car had not been in the shop for repair and if he had not had dinner with his sister at her home near the Jean-Talon Market.

The police could find no motive for the murder. Réal Fournier was well liked, happily married, and very close to his sister, his only sibling. They had been close as children and the death of their mother twenty-five years earlier had brought them even closer. Their father never fully got over the loss of his wife and Réal and his sister did what they could to bring comfort to him until he too passed away—prematurely, Réal and his sister felt—five years later.

The police chalked the murder up to a crime of opportunity committed by a sicko.

Chapter 8

Gilles made it into the office early on Monday morning and spent a couple of minutes rehearsing his pitch to his boss, Captain Lacroix, the head of the Major Crimes Division. The division occupied the third floor of a shopping centre, Place Versailles, which was located at the eastern end of the city. The shopping centre had been expanded over the years and was made up of an incongruous combination of architectural styles. There was, however, a lot of parking, and easy access to coffee in the shopping mall, so it wasn't a total disaster as far as the cops who worked there were concerned.

Gilles brought his usual bribe, a cappuccino, when he went into Captain Lacroix's office. "Oui, Gilles," Lacroix said, accepting the cappuccino as a sign that Gilles wanted something.

"Il y a quelque chose de suspect à l'hôpital où Annie travaille."

Everyone who knew Annie liked her and Captain Lacroix was no exception. She had been instrumental in helping to solve a couple of murder cases and Lacroix took her suspicions seriously.

"Really? You'd think that there would be any number of suspicious events in an Emergency Department. What's special about this one?" Captain Lacroix asked.

Gilles moved some files from a chair, sat down and explained what Annie had told him about Dr. Hingston and the Prodosiakis family. He emphasized that the doctor, whoever he was, might possibly be guilty of murder and the situation was worth looking into before there were more deaths.

"D'accord, Gilles. So long as there's nothing else that requires your immediate attention."

Gilles went to his desk and called Annie to get the address of the Prodosiakises. It was possible that Toula and Iannis would be out, perhaps making arrangements at the funeral home, but Gilles decided it was worth the risk.

Gilles had trouble finding the house. It was situated on Lazard Avenue, about a block from Kindersley Park in the Town of Mont Royal, one of Montreal's wealthier suburbs. The town was built as a planned city at the beginning of the twentieth century based on the combined ideas of the Garden City and City Beautiful movements. It was built on an X-shaped grid in order to make it hard for non-residents to find their way around and to ensure that traffic did not clog its residential streets. In 1960, when the town fathers discovered that people from the less affluent neighbouring area, Park Extension, were straying into the Town, they had a fence built on de l'Acadie Boulevard, the eastern boundary, to keep them out.

Gilles finally found the Prodosiakis house, a large brick split-level.

A maid answered the door and wordlessly led Gilles to a large parlor furnished with heavy furniture upholstered in dark shades of olive green and maroon. There were end tables with little dishes full of small pastel-coloured mints and a coffee table in front of one of the sofas. Gilles chose not to sit down, for fear of putting an ass print in the carefully fluffed sofa cushion, but stood next to the mantle of a decorative fireplace facing the arched entrance from the hall.

He had only to wait a couple of minutes for Iannis Prodosiakis to come into the room. His red-rimmed eyes made it look like he hadn't slept for a long time. His clothing was disheveled, as if he had been wearing these clothes during sleepless nights. Gilles introduced himself and extended his hand, which Iannis took in a weak handshake.

"What is it you want?" Iannis sat down on the sofa closest to the window.

"I'm very sorry about your loss," Gilles said. "But it's come to our attention that there may be some irregularities surrounding your father's death."

"How do you figure?"

"It appears that he had been given some medication by a Dr. Hingston. We can't find any evidence that such a man exists, so your father may have been the victim of medical malpractice. Not malpractice," Gilles corrected himself, "mispractice."

"Ridiculous," Iannis said. "My father got out of the house and caught pneumonia."

Gilles heard the front door open and a woman's voice call out, "Iannis, where are you?"

"We're in the living room," he called back.

"We?" Toula walked to the living room but stopped in the archway and took in the scene of her brother sitting with a stranger. "Who are you?"

Gilles got to his feet, introduced himself and extended a hand to Toula. She looked at it for a moment before she shook it and introduced herself. "Why are the police here?" Toula was nicely dressed, her black hair neatly brushed and her make-up expertly applied.

"He thinks there may be something about Dad, about Dr. Hingston," Iannis said.

"What about him?"

"Maybe he gave Dad something that made him sick."

"*To pio asteío prágma pou ákousa poté.* The stupidest thing I ever heard," Toula said.

"Not necessarily," Gilles said. "I'd like to understand how your father got out of the house. You were both home, right?"

Toula stepped into the room, flashed a smile and said, "Yes, but we weren't together. My brother was in his room, which is downstairs. I was in the study, which is upstairs at the back, and my...our...father was asleep."

"I'd appreciate it if you could show me around the house. I'd like to see where everyone was."

Toula gave her brother a look, sighed and said, "I hardly see the point in this."

"It won't take long and I'll be on my way," Gilles said.

Toula turned and led her brother and Gilles out of the living room and down the hall to a door near the back of the house. Gilles could see a large kitchen at the end of the hallway. The trio descended a carpeted stairway to a finished basement. It was a large room with a pool table in the centre and comfortable chairs and a loveseat around the edges. There was a big screen TV on the back wall.

Iannis stepped ahead of his sister, opened a door and said, "My room." He stood aside so that Gilles could enter. Toula remained at her brother's side at the door frame.

Gilles looked around a good-sized, sparsely furnished bedroom. It had a double bed, a dresser and an easy chair. The bed was unmade and there were clothes strewn about. There was a window high on one of the walls, below which there was a desk with a computer on it. Other than a mirror above the dresser, the ochre-coloured walls were bare.

Gilles wondered why Iannis was exiled to the basement. It was almost like he wasn't part of the household. It was a large house and there must have been any number of bedrooms on the upper floors that Iannis could have used.

"Thank you," Gilles said. "Now the study and your father's bedroom, if you don't mind."

With Toula in the lead the trio then went up to the second floor. "My father's bedroom is right here." She pointed to a door at the top of the stairs. Gilles opened the bedroom door and saw a well-furnished master bedroom. In addition to the king-size bed there were a chaise lounge, a couple of chairs, and paintings of landscapes on the walls.

"I'm upstairs," Toula said and Gilles and Iannis followed her. Her bedroom was at the front of the house and the study at the rear. There were other doors, closed, on both floors, probably closets and additional bedrooms.

They returned to the living room. Iannis flopped into a chair but Toula remained standing. She didn't invite Gilles to sit down. "Will there be anything else?"

"Yes. Did you have any idea what kind of medication Dr. Hingston prescribed, gave you actually, to give your father?"

"You mean the name of it? No. He probably told us but I don't remember it," Toula said.

"How about the bottles it came in? Do you have any of them?"

"No. What possible difference could it make? Our father died from pneumonia."

"Yes, that's true," Gilles said. "But there may have been something in the medication that made your father's dementia worse, which led in turn to his wandering off." Toula was about to say something but changed her mind. Gilles continued, "Most importantly, we, that is to say the hospital, can't find any trace of a Dr. Hingston on staff."

"That's ridiculous. Doctors don't just pop up out of thin air. He knew about our father's condition and the only way he could have known that was from hospital records. Now are you done?" Toula asked.

"Yes. Thank you for your co-operation." As they walked to the front door Gilles asked, "Only the three of you live here?"

"Yeah," Iannis said. "The maid comes in but she doesn't live here."

"And your mother…?"

"Our mother died twenty-five years ago," Toula said, her hand on the handle to the front door.

"Your father never remarried?"

Toula muttered something to her brother in Greek and said, "He did, but our stepmom died a couple of years ago. Cancer."

"To be clear," Gilles said. "Neither of you heard your father leave the house."

Toula spoke for both of them. "I, we, can't police our father every second of every day. He has a tendency to wander but he usually paces around the house. Sometimes we find him in the back garden. It's fenced in so he can't leave the property."

Toula double-twisted the spindle that operated the deadbolt and used her other hand to depress the thumb piece in the handle and pull the door open. Gilles had no option but to leave the house. He noticed that unless the spindle was in the horizontal position the door was unlocked. Gilles wondered if George Prodosiakis, in his condition, had the dexterity to open the front door had it been locked.

Gilles returned to his car and considered what he had learned. It was clear from the layout of the house that if Toula and her brother were telling the truth about their whereabouts, neither of them would have heard their father leave.

Annie was assigned to Resus on Monday. She'd only been at work for an hour or so when a patient, Frida Meyerson, arrived by ambulance suffering from Sick Sinus Syndrome, an issue with her heart, not with her nasal passages as the name might suggest. If undiagnosed, SSS could be fatal. It was usually treated with blood thinners and Annie was surprised that the patient had not been prescribed any of them. The patient's daughters arrived and found their way to their mother's room. Annie asked them about their mother's heart condition.

"She doesn't have a heart condition," Gloria, the older of the two daughters, said.

"She suffers from Alzheimer's," added her sister Susan.

Annie's quick diagnostic brain jumped to an unpleasant conclusion and she took a moment to consider it. "By any chance," she asked, "did a Dr. Hingston prescribe something?"

"How could you know that?" Susan asked.

"It must be in her file," Gloria said.

"No, it's not. When and where did your mother see Dr. Hingston?"

"Three months ago," Gloria said. "She tripped and we brought her to the ER. We thought she broke something."

"But she was okay," Susan put in. "Dr. Hingston called a couple of days after that and came to the house. He explained that he had some medications that might help with our mother's Alzheimer's."

"He left them with us and she took them, but I don't think they helped much," Gloria said.

Annie flipped through the chart. There was nothing about a Dr. Hingston. Annie knew patients taking medications for dementia were at risk for SSS and she suspected that whatever it was that Dr. Hingston doled out had caused it. "Do you have any of the medication left?"

"No, he only gave us a month's supply. He said he would call after that to see how things had gone," Susan said.

"And did he?"

"Yeah, he called and we told him that we didn't notice any change. He said he would get back to us for a follow-up visit," Gloria said.

"But he never did," her sister said. "Can we stay with our mother?"

"For the moment you'll be better off in the waiting room," Annie said. "As you can see, she is being treated. Jean-Guy," she paused to indicate the orderly who standing nearby, "will show you to the waiting room. Come back when you've done," Annie added. St-Onge nodded and led the sisters to the waiting room.

When he returned, he found Annie in the patient's room working with Dr. Rosen. She motioned for St-Onge to join them. She indicated one of the monitors and said, "Listen, Jean-Guy, keep an eye on the monitor. It will trigger a Code Blue if things take a bad turn. But I want you to watch it and get me or the doctor before it gets to that point." She indicated what St-Onge was to look for that would indicate that the patient was in decline. "Page me if you have to but I want to get to the patient before she codes. Got it?"

St-Onge nodded and returned to the work area. He had a clear view of the monitors and would be able to do as Annie asked so long as he wasn't called away for some reason.

◉

The software that Marcus Tiddley had programmed into his computer beeped. He was absent from work that day and the message on his computer went unnoticed.

◉

Gilles drove back to the Major Crimes Division. As he drove, he called Annie to tell her that he had seen the Prodosiakises and had the feeling that they were keeping something from him—especially Toula. He planned to interview them separately. Annie told him that another patient who had been visited by Dr. Hingston had been brought into the ER suffering from a heart condition.

"That's three that I've cared for," Annie said. "There may be more. In any case there's a clear pattern. Something the mysterious Dr. Hingston is doing is causing patients who are suffering from dementia to develop heart problems."

Gilles was about to say something when Annie spoke again, "Oh, fuck, I've got to run. My patient is in distress." The call ended.

When Gilles got to the office, he took the time to write up his notes regarding his interview with Toula and Iannis Prodosiakis and then went to his captain's office to report.

"You think there's something to investigate, Gilles?" Captain Lacroix asked when Gilles finished his summary of his morning's activities.

"Je pense que oui," Gilles said. "Another patient just ended up in the ER at the Gursky suffering dementia and a heart condition who was paid a visit by the mysterious Dr. Hingston. So that's three that Annie treated. There may be more. Secondly, I'm convinced that one of the Prodosiakises was withholding information."

"About what? They didn't do anything other than follow a doctor's orders. Not a crime."

"I think there's more there. Let's suppose for a moment that for one reason or another they wanted their father out of the way. It's possible that they knew something about the drugs that Hingston gave them. Maybe they discovered that mixed with something else their father was taking, the

Hingston meds would prove fatal. They couldn't have known that their father would wander off and get some unanticipated medical attention. All I can say is that I'm suspicious."

Captain Lacroix had been rocking back in his desk chair as he listened to Gilles. He snapped forward and looked Gilles directly in the eyes. "Tabernac, Gilles, tout ce que tu as est une possibilité. Crisse. You don't have a motive and you don't even know if they wanted to get rid of their father. Do you know the cause of death?"

"Oui. Pneumonia. The old guy was found wandering the streets in his pyjamas."

"So, even it there was something in the medications, they didn't cause death," Captain Lacroix said.

"D'accord. But something doesn't sit right. That's why I want to continue my investigation of Toula Prodosiakis and her brother. And I want to try to find the mysterious Dr. Hingston."

"You can have the rest of the day. But if you don't find anything, then that's it."

Gilles went to his desk and looked up the Collège des médecins du Québec. He checked their website for a Dr. Hingston and came up empty. He called the Collège to see if there were databases that someone there could check. A very helpful young woman did a search and reported that there was no Dr. Hingston registered in Quebec. She suggested that Gilles try the professional associations of the other provinces and added that osteopaths and some holistic healers used the term doctor. Many of them had no right to do so, but, "Well you know, it's difficult for us to police," she concluded.

Gilles expanded his search to include all of Canada and came up with a few names but none in the province of Quebec, much less in Montreal. He followed up with the

Doctors Hingston he found in other provinces, but none of them could be the person he was looking for.

Jean-Guy St-Onge motioned to Annie while she was on the phone with Gilles. She ended the call and rushed to her patient. Frida Meyerson was in distress. Annie started chest compressions and told St-Onge to get Dr. Rosen. He appeared a minute or two later. He took over doing chest compressions while Annie prepared the defibrillator and wheeled it to him. Dr. Rosen grabbed the paddles. Annie pulled the patient's gown down. "Clear!" Rosen called and shocked the patient. She bounced once but her heart didn't restart. Rosen tried again and again with increasing amounts of voltage.

"I'm going to..." he began.

"No, you're not, not until you try again at max."

"Clear!" he shouted again. "If it was anyone else but you, Annie, I would have called it. You just won't give up, will you?" The heart monitor emitted a long beep and showed a flat line.

"Only if I have no other choice."

"I think we're there," Rosen said softly.

"Yeah. I just don't get it."

"People die," Rosen said.

"That's not what I mean." Annie explained that Frida Meyerson was the third patient who had died who had been given medication by Dr. Hingston.

"Doctor who?" Rosen asked.

"Exactly. There is no Dr. Hingston."

Chapter 9

The morning after his fruitless search for Dr. Hingston, Captain Lacroix came out of his office. Gilles was the first person he saw. "A dead body." He handed Gilles a slip of paper with the address and said, "Check it out. The preliminary report from the cops at the scene is that there are no signs of violence. Identification judiciaire is on its way to process the crime scene."

Gilles looked at the slip and saw an address in Notre-Dame-de-Grâce, in the city's west end, better known to residents as NDG. "Oui, Chef," he said and turned to leave.

"Giroux," Lacroix called. "You're with Bellechasse." Stéphanie Giroux caught up with Gilles and they drove to the scene. Identification judiciaire, the forensics division of the Montreal police, had already arrived. One of its trucks was parked in front and the forensics technicians were pulling on their white coveralls—"bunny suits" in cop parlance. Gilles and Stéphanie helped themselves to a pair each.

The house was stone from the foundation to just below the first-floor windows. It was yellow brick construction above that. The house had a pitched roof and was probably built during or just after the Second World War when land was inexpensive but building materials were hard to get. The cottage was on a large lot but smaller than many of the neighbouring houses, which were built in the more affluent fifties and sixties. The path to the front door was off the driveway. The front door opened from a small porch with bay windows on either side of it. The two uniformed cops who were first on the scene were standing on the lawn, leaning against the base of the small porch. "Give me an overview," Gilles said.

"We got a 911. A delivery guy. He's in his car." The cop indicated a white car with Intelcom decaled on the door. He's in a rush to leave."

Gilles and the cop walked over to the car and rapped on the driver's window. The window rolled down. "You called the cops?" Gilles asked.

"Yeah. I had a delivery. I rang the doorbell. There was no answer so I went around back. The guy asked me to leave packages in the back when he's not home. People steal from the front porch. I looked in the window to see if there was someone there and I saw the body."

When did he tell you to leave packages in the back?"

A while ago. I don't remember. Look, I've got other deliveries to make. I'm on the Amazon clock. I've gotta go."

Gilles turned to the uniformed cop and asked, "Did you get his name and address?"

The cop nodded and Gilles told the delivery guy he could go.

"What did you do when you arrived on the scene?" Gilles asked the cop. "We went around to the back and looked in the window and saw the body. Just like the guy said."

"How'd you get in?" Gilles asked.

"Broke a window. We couldn't take the chance that the vic was still alive. There were no obvious signs of a struggle. Maybe we could provide first aid. But no, he was dead. We called it in."

"And here we are," Gilles ended the report for the patrol cop. "Good job."

Gilles and Stéphanie put on their bunny suits and then the blue booties over their shoes and entered the house. They were in a small foyer which opened to a hallway that ran the length of the house with a stairway to the upper floor on the left.

They made their way to the back of the house and found the victim lying on the floor. Gilles and Stéphanie asked the forensics techs who had followed them in to wait a minute before they started their work so they could give the body a close examination. There was no blood anywhere, nor were there ligature marks on the body. There were no signs of a struggle. The kitchen was tidy, table and chairs in place, the counters clean. The only thing that suggested murder was the rictus of pain on the victim's face, indicating that whatever it was that killed him was excruciating.

Gilles gave the body a careful look. He'd never seen one this free of signs of violence accompanied by a look of such distress on his face. "Putain," Gilles exclaimed.

"Vraiment, Gilles. Putain?"

"Oui. I've been watching a lot of cop shows from France. I guess their cursing is contagious. Do we have an ID?"

The cop at the door had given Stéphanie a copy of the 911 communication that had generated the visit. "Tiddley," she read aloud. "Marcus Tiddley. He's a doctor. Nom drôle, n'est-ce pas?"

"Did you say he's a doctor?" Gilles asked.

"Yes, why?"

"Because I've been looking for a Doctor Hingston and couldn't find such a person."

"Well, you've found Dr. Tiddley on Hingston Avenue."

"Exactly," Gilles said.

"Let's look around while they deal with the body." The two detectives gave the first floor a cursory search. The living room was furnished with a couch and easy chair with a large screen TV on the far wall, adjacent to the bay window.

The dining room held a polished dark wood table and six chairs. It did not look as if it had been used recently. Both rooms were as tidy as the kitchen. They mounted the stairs to the second floor where there were two rooms; one was a bedroom with a messy bed. "Looks like the vic was in bed, felt sick, and went downstairs for some reason," Gilles said. "Maybe to get some medicine. Anyway, he vomited in the sink and fell over dead."

The other room on the second floor was a large study. There was a window opposite the door and facing it was a desk with a comfortable desk chair. Floor-to-ceiling bookshelves covered the two other walls. An upholstered straight-back chair was placed in front of each of the bookshelves. There were files and loose papers on the desk as was Tiddley's laptop. Gilles lifted the lid and pressed the start button with his gloved finger. The laptop came to life and the password screen appeared. "A job for tech services," he said and turned off the computer. There was a small Moleskine notebook lying on the desk next to the telephone. Gilles picked it up with a gloved hand. He found names and phone numbers along with notations that looked like the names of medications. He flipped through the book and was surprised when he came across the name Prodosiakis along with some dates and medical information.

"Putain," he exclaimed again and showed Stéphanie the note book. "I was right. We did find the missing Dr. Hingston." He slid the note book into an evidence bag and placed it back on the desk. He and Stéphanie went back to the kitchen. Gilles told the technicians that the note book he'd found was a priority. He wanted it dusted for prints and then given to him.

Standing on the front stoop, he called Annie. "I found him," Gilles said.

"Who?"

"Dr. Hingston."

"Gilles, that's fantastic. Where is he? I really want to talk to him. Is he under arrest or something?"

"He's dead."

"What? Dead? How did he die?"

"We don't know yet. There are no signs of violence or a struggle. We'll know more after the forensics people finish and when we get a medical report. But I found a notebook with the names of what I take to be patients and medications or something. I'm going to bring it to you as soon as they take prints for processing at the lab."

"Call me when you're on your way and I'll arrange for a break to look it over. No interruptions."

The medical examiner, Dr. Lapointe, arrived moments later. Gilles brought the doctor into the kitchen. He asked the leader of the forensics team if they had found anything that might have contained a poison. Two members of the team were extracting evidence from the kitchen garbage can. The team leader showed Gilles and Dr. Lapointe what they had found: takeout containers from an Indian restaurant and an empty jar that had held Patak's Sweet Mango Chutney.

"The victim wouldn't have noticed poison had it been in either spicy food or the chutney that he consumed with it," Dr. Lapointe said. "I'll know more when I get the lab results and autopsy the victim."

The forensics team had moved on. Dr. Lapointe gave the body a cursory examination and mumbled something to himself.

"Any ideas?" Gilles asked.

"No, of course not. Other than the fact that whatever it was that killed him was very painful. Woke him up. Why he was in the kitchen we can't know. Can't even be sure if he was murdered or died of natural causes. What do you know about him?"

"He's a doctor, doing some kind of research, I think."

"Why do you say that?"

"Because he was giving medication to people—elderly people—and not using his own name. He called himself Dr. Hingston."

"How on earth can you possibly…?" Dr. Lapointe stopped himself in mid-question. "Wait a minute. The nurse…" He thought for a minute. "Annie, Annie Linton. She knows something about this, doesn't she?"

"Absolutely," Gilles said. Dr. Lapointe had met Annie during the course of previous murder investigations. Like everyone else who met her he was impressed by her intelligence, her quick wit, and ready smile.

A forensics technician came into the room with the notebook in its evidence bag and handed it to Gilles. "Fini." The tech held up two evidence bags, one containing several long blonde hairs. The other held black hairs. "We also found these. Clearly not the victim's. His hair is brown."

"Probably from two women. Is there enough for DNA?"

"We'll let you know if we find a match."

Gilles removed the notebook from the bag and showed some of the entries to Dr. Lapointe. "Do these mean anything to you?"

He studied the medical information on several pages and replied, "No, not really. Other than the fact that all the patients were suffering from some form of dementia."

"I'm going to show this to Annie and see what she comes up with. Three of her patients were given medication of some sort by this guy and they all died."

"Can I take him now?" Lapointe asked.

"Yeah, we're done," Stéphanie said. She went to the front door to signal the two men from the medical examiner's office to come in with their gurney.

The medical team left. Gilles turned to Stéphanie and said, "There's nothing more we can do here. I'm going to the hospital to see what Annie can tell me about the medical information in this." He held up the notebook. "You with me?"

"You bet. Always nice to see Annie."

Gilles and Stéphanie told the patrol cops that they were leaving and reminded them to secure the house after the forensics team left.

Gilles parked next to the entrance to the Emergency Department of the Gursky Memorial Hospital and flashed his badge at the security guard who came to shoo him away. Annie was waiting for him and Stéphanie in the information booth. Gilles waved a hello at Tasso and greeted Annie with a kiss when she joined them. "We can find a quiet corner here or go to the Second Cup for a coffee," she said.

"Coffee."

The trio walked to the café, which was on the floor above. Once settled at a table Gilles produced the Moleskine notebook and handed it to Annie. Before she opened it, he gave her a brief summary of what they had found. Annie flipped through the notebook looking for information on the three patients she had cared for. There were entries for each of them along with chemical information that made no sense to Gilles but which Annie understood. Gilles started to ask a question but Annie stopped him. "Give me a minute to take a closer look at this," she said. Gilles and Stéphanie chatted softly to each other and let Annie concentrate on the contents of the Moleskine notebook. After ten minutes she put the notebook down on the table and said, "Okay, I found references to the three patients I treated, plus many more. If they were or are patients at the Gursky that's going to be a problem for us. They'll all have to be contacted. I took a careful look at the meds he was prescribing to my patients. Basically, they were acetylcholinesterase inhibitors with other elements that Hingston, or I should say, Tiddley, added.

"My guess is that he was trying to find an effective cure for neurodegenerative diseases. He was making his own meds and giving them to patients. My suspicion is that they had no idea what they were taking. It's beyond unethical; it's criminal."

"And these meds caused the patients' deaths?" Gilles asked.

"It's a complicated question, but the short answer is yes. At least there's no question that they played a role in the cause of death."

"Because these drugs are experimental?" Stéphanie asked.

"Yeah, and because heart problems of various sorts are known side effects of acetylcholinesterase inhibitors. When you juice them up the way Tiddley was you're creating drugs without knowing the potential side effects."

Gilles and Stéphanie were silent as they processed what they had been told. It looked like Marcus Tiddley was experimenting on living people without regard for the consequences of his actions.

"Do you know where Tiddley worked?" Stéphanie asked.

"No, but he won't be hard to find now that we know his real name. I'll check the hospital database. And I'd like to keep the notebook."

"I need to keep it. It's evidence," Gilles said. "But you can make a copy."

They headed back to the ER. Annie looked up Dr. Marcus Tiddley and told Gilles and Stéphanie where his lab was located. They waited while Annie made a photocopy of Tiddley's notebook.

"What next?" Stéphanie asked.

"We're going to pay a visit to the lab where Tiddley worked. It's just down the street. And then we're going to pay another visit to the Prodosiakis family. There's something they're not telling me."

Gilles and Stéphanie walked the long block to the nondescript concrete building with non-opening windows that held most of the research labs associated with the Gursky Memorial Hospital. The Dementia and Alzheimer's Research Group, DARG, occupied a large part of the fourth floor. The door opened from the hallway to the lab itself; there was no reception area. Gilles expected to find a laboratory like those he saw in movies, long tables with white-coated scientists watching test tubes and flasks bubbling with chemicals. This lab had about twenty scientists wearing white coats but there were almost no test tubes or Erlenmeyer flasks. Each of the work stations had an electronic microscope, centrifuges, a computer and an array of electronic equipment. There were cages ranged along the inside wall that contained rats and other rodents for the purposes of experimentation. Gilles approached the man closest to the door, identified himself, consulted his copy of the report that generated the call to Tiddley's house, and asked to see Robyn Phillips. "People to see you, Rob," he called.

A woman, about five and a half feet tall, wearing a clean white lab coat, got up from her spot at the far end of the front bench. She pushed her glasses onto her head where they nested in her blond hair, which she wore in a ponytail. "Yes?"

Gilles introduced himself and Stéphanie and they showed their IDs. "You're the one who made the 911 call?" Stéphanie asked.

"Yes. Is everything okay?"

"Is there somewhere we can talk?" Gilles asked.

"There's a meeting room at the back of the lab." Robyn led the two cops to the room at the rear of the lab. It was empty and Gilles and Stéphanie chose a table in the back corner. The room had a window running the length of the wall that looked into the laboratory. Gilles could see the heads of the scientists in the lab turn and follow them as they entered the meeting room, closed the door and sat down. Even those working close to the staff room couldn't hear the conversation.

"I'm afraid we have some bad news," Gilles said. "Marcus Tiddley is dead. We're sorry."

"Oh, oh no," Robyn said and her eyes filled with tears. "What happened? I had a feeling something was off when he didn't show up two mornings in a row."

"Did you call him?" Stéphanie asked.

"Yeah, but there was no answer. It was rare for Marcus to miss one day of work, much less two. He was usually the first person in. I planned to drive over to his house after work to see if there was anything wrong."

Gilles and Stéphanie learned that Dr. Marcus Tiddley was well liked by the scientists who worked in the DARG lab. He was intelligent and motivated to find a cure for neurodegenerative disease. Robyn didn't know much about his personal life. He didn't socialize with those who worked in the lab, other than at their Christmas party and a staff event in the summer Tiddley hosted at his house.

"Were you aware that he was experimenting with patients who were suffering from dementia?" Gilles asked.

Robyn eyes widened in shock. It took a moment before she could speak. "Absolutely not. That is strictly forbidden. Some of our meds are not even ready for use in animals. My God, that's impossible."

"Unfortunately, that's what he was doing." Gilles showed Robyn Tiddley's notebook. She flipped through it. She looked horrified as she examined the chemical information contained in it. "Does the hospital know?" she asked.

"It does now," Stéphanie said.

"They're going to have to close us down. There'll be a full investigation. We've made some promising progress here. It'll all be for nothing," Robyn said. She was sick at the thought of having all her work and the work of her colleagues going to waste.

Gilles and Stéphanie didn't say anything but they knew she was right. "We'll need to see his office," Gilles said.

Robyn led Gilles and Stéphanie to Tiddley's office. The door wasn't locked and they entered. Stéphanie slipped a glove onto her right hand and tapped the button to launch the desktop computer. She got the same password screen that had appeared on the laptop. "Pas de surprise mais ça vaut le coup," she said. Gilles was on his cellphone to Identification judiciaire to come in and do a thorough search of Tiddley's office and get the computer to tech services.

Robyn overheard Gilles's conversation with the forensics people and said, "I don't mean to be callous, but how much time have we got?" She stammered as she spoke and fidgeted with a button on her lab coat.

"That's a hospital decision, not ours," Gilles said. "But we would like to talk to someone who can tell us something about the research you're doing here. Are you the best person for that?"

Gilles ushered Robyn out of the office. Stéphanie followed and pulled the door closed behind her. She found a pad of paper on the table in front of the door. She wrote a note stating that the office was not to be entered by order of the SPVM and taped it to the door. "Me and William," Robyn said. She pointed to a young man working at the far end of the lab table.

Before Gilles could say anything, a man carrying a walkie-talkie strode into the lab. He was a little shorter than Gilles with a shaved head. He wore slacks and a blue blazer that was a bit too small for his girth. He pointed the walkie-talkie at Gilles and asked, "You the cop?"

"Detective Gilles Bellechasse. Major Crimes. And you are?"

"I'm Peter Hillerman, the head of security. We have to close the lab. Have the staff been informed of the...well, you know?"

"I was just about to do that," Gilles said. "Please ensure, though, that everyone stays put until we can get their contact information." He turned away from Hillerman to address the scientists. "My name is Detective Sergeant Gilles Bellechasse. I'm afraid I have some bad news," he said. "Dr. Tiddley was found dead in his home earlier today."

Gasps of shock followed Gilles's announcement, along with a jumble of questions. The scientists looked shaken by the news.

"All I can tell you is that the investigation is ongoing and I can't give you any additional information. Mr. Hillerman has an announcement."

Gilles stood aside. He noticed that, including Robyn, about a third of the women and one or two of the men had blonde hair of a length sufficient to be a match for those found at the crime scene. A few of them had black hair. The rest were various shades of brown. He whispered something to Robyn and she motioned to William to join them. With his hands thrust in his lab coat pockets he came over to where Robyn and the cops were standing. Like Robyn, he was in his late twenties. He was a shade under six feet tall, with a mass of curly black hair, and he wore glasses.

“What...?” he asked.

Gilles suggested that they return to the meeting room to talk.

A dozen sets of eyes followed them to the room at the back of the laboratory. Those seated at the ends of the work tables closest to the aisle whispered questions but didn’t get much by way of response. The worried looks on Robyn’s and William’s faces told them that the situation was serious.

Hillerman waited for the quartet to get settled in the meeting room before he spoke. “In light of the unfortunate events, I’m sorry to have to tell you that the lab will be closed until further notice. Detective Bellechasse,” Hillerman pointed at the window to the meeting room with his walkie-talkie, “has requested that you remain until he’s had a chance to get your contact information.” The scientists talked among themselves in low tones, trying to guess what had happened to their boss. Hillerman leaned against one of the lab tables and watched the cops, Robyn, and William through the window.

“What can you tell us about your work?” Gilles asked.

William and Robyn looked at one another. “Robyn is the senior scientist in this lab, so she is best suited to answer your question. I can fill in the blanks if necessary.”

They turned to Robyn, who was seated adjacent to Gilles at the head of the table. She inhaled through her nose, exhaled and said, “Simply put, we’re trying to find a cure for neurodegenerative ailments such as Alzheimer’s and, of course, other forms of dementia. In order to do that we have to understand the causes, the parts of the brain affected, transmitters, a host of physiological issues really.”

“Do you do any human testing? Any at all?” Gilles asked.

"I told you," Robyn said, "absolutely not. We're years away from that. We do some animal testing but we're still at the early stages of our understanding of how neurodegenerative diseases work."

"Are you saying that you had no idea that Dr. Tiddley was doing human testing?"

"Robyn made it clear. The answer is no," William said.

"And if you had known?" Stéphanie asked.

"I can safely say that every one of us would have walked out and reported it. It would have ended Tiddley's career. Plus our own research, our jobs, our post-docs would be over in this lab. We would be disappointed, sure, but we'd find places somewhere else," William said.

"But..." Robyn said.

"But what?" Stéphanie asked.

"Human testing was wrong, totally beyond the scope of our research." Robyn spoke slowly, making certain that she chose the correct words to express her thoughts. "But...as wrong as it was, if what you say is true, I think Marcus was motivated by impatience, not something criminal. There are over three-quarters of a million people suffering from Alzheimer's in Canada and the number is going to explode as more baby boomers hit old age. Marcus was desperate to find a cure and end the suffering of those afflicted with the condition and their families."

"His motives aren't important to our investigation. His actions caused death," Gilles said.

"What do we do now?" Robyn said. Her voice had an angry edge to it and the look of horror mixed with sadness indicated how she felt about a man she had respected.

"You heard the head of security. The hospital will determine the fate of the lab, but as far as we're concerned the lab and office are relevant to a murder investigation. One of us will tell the scientists to gather their personal—and only their personal—belongings, provide us with contact information, and leave the lab," Gilles said.

"I'll do it," Robyn said. She left the room and informed the staff what they had to do. They lined up in front of the meeting room and, one by one, provided Gilles and Stéphanie with their contact information, then left the lab, congregating in the corridor. The forensics team arrived as Gilles and Stéphanie finished with the last of the scientists.

"William and I will take care of reporting to the director of research at the hospital," Robyn said. She and William gathered their belongings and left. Gilles and Stéphanie turned the lab over to Identification judiciaire and left.

They retrieved Gilles's car and drove to the Prodosiakis house.

Chapter 10

"Pas mal comme maison," Stéphanie commented as she and Gilles approached the front door of the Prodosiakis house. Gilles rang the doorbell. When no one answered the door after a couple of minutes, he rang again. Stéphanie tried banging on the door with her fist. They were about to leave when Iannis finally opened the door.

"What the fu…oh, it's you again," he said. "What do you want?"

Stéphanie parked her foot on the doorsill.

"We have some questions for you and your sister," Gilles said. "May we come in?"

Without replying, Iannis turned and led the cops into the house. He was wearing a nylon track suit and rubber shower sandals, so it was obvious to Gilles that they hadn't interrupted him doing something important. Iannis led them to the kitchen. He sat down at the kitchen table and asked Gilles and Stéphanie if they would like a coffee, but he made no move to make it, and they declined his offer. He had a glass of juice in front of him as well as an empty plate, the crumbs on it indicating that it had held toast.

"Is your sister at home? Gilles asked.

"She's at work," Iannis said and drank the rest of his juice.

"Where would that be?" Stéphanie asked. She and Gilles opened their pads on the table.

"Our family business." Gilles motioned that Iannis was to continue. "We own a dry-cleaning business, Nettoyeurs Kathari, if you want the full name."

Gilles was impressed. Nettoyeurs Kathari had franchisees all over the city along with company-owned kiosks. "Where's the office?"

"We have a plant and office on Ferrier. That's where she is."

"You don't work there?" Gilles asked.

"Yeah, I work there, sort of."

"What does 'sort of' mean?"

"I drive one of the trucks. Pickups from our large corporate clients, hotels, that kind of thing. And I make deliveries. I also service our residential clients. Toula runs the business. Especially since our father...well, you know...since he couldn't." Iannis gave them the address.

"We have some questions about your father and Dr. Hingston, whose real name was Tiddley," Gilles said.

Iannis didn't seem surprised at that news. Stéphanie shot her partner a knowing look and said, "Do you remember when the doctor first saw your father?"

"I don't remember the exact date, but it was a couple of months ago. My father had been to the hospital and Tid... Hingston called a couple of days after that. He spoke to Toula and arranged to come to the house to see him."

"What happened as a result of the visit?"

"Like I said, he dealt with Toula. But he left us some pills that he said would help our father with his dementia. But that's not what he called it. He had a longer name for it."

"Neurodegenerative disease," Gilles said.

"Yeah, that's it. He said he would check in again after our father finished the pills but we could call him if we noticed any strange side effects."

"Did you have any reason to call him? Did your father have any side effects?" Gilles wished that he had accepted Iannis's offer of a coffee. He fiddled with his pen.

Iannis rolled his empty juice glass around in his hands and said, "Me, no. I didn't notice any side effects."

"What about your sister? Did she have any contact with the doctor?"

Iannis was silent. He looked at his feet.

"I'll take that as a yes," Gilles said. "Tell me about it."

"There's nothing to tell, really." Iannis kept his eyes downcast. "Either Toula called him or he called her, because he came over a couple of times. And he didn't spend much time with my father."

"You're saying he had an interest in your sister," Stéphanie said.

"Typical of most guys who cross her path," Iannis said.

"You didn't seem surprised to learn that his name was Tiddley, not Hingston. When did he tell you his real name?"

"When he started hanging out with my sister. He explained that he had to use a fake name to protect the highly—he had a funny way of saying it—'sub rosa' nature of his research. Who talks that way?"

"Yeah," Gilles said. He got to his feet. "We're done here." He looked down at Iannis. "I'm afraid I have some bad news for you. Dr. Tiddley was found dead at his home earlier today."

Iannis looked up at Gilles, his eyes wide. "What? Dead? He was a doctor," he exclaimed, as if being a doctor exempted him from dying. "How did he die?"

"That's what we're looking into. We'll be on our way. I'm sure you have to get to work."

"Maybe later." Iannis got to his feet, as did Stéphanie. They walked toward the front door. "You can show yourselves out," Iannis said. He stopped at the top of the stairs to the basement in order to watch Gilles and Stéphanie leave.

Gilles had one more question, "Do you remember who the last person was who came into the house the night your father went missing?"

"Toula, I guess. When she came home from work."

"Neither of you left after that?"

"Not really. I may have gone out to see some of the guys. Who remembers?"

The two cops left the house and Iannis pulled the door to the stairs closed behind him.

"Strange kid," Stéphanie said as she and Gilles descended the front stairs.

"Yeah, no kidding."

"We're going to see the sister, right?" Stéphanie said as they got into the car.

"You bet."

They drove to the address on Ferrier, a street of squat buildings, mostly branch offices and warehouses, in the northwest end of the city. The buildings on the street were constructed purely for function without any thought to style. They were either square boxes with concrete curtain walls or low-rise buildings built to hold low-cost offices of companies that had no need to impress their customers with well-designed, esthetically pleasing workspaces. The building that housed Kathari cleaners was a new construction, less than ten years old. It had cement walls with large windows on the front face and red brick on the other three sides. There was a dry-cleaning counter inside the front entrance. Gilles parked and he and Stéphanie went in and asked for Toula Prodosiakis.

The woman at the counter looked at their cop IDs and used a telephone on the counter to call Toula. She whispered that there were two cops to see her and hung up. A moment or two later Toula appeared. She flashed a smile at Gilles and glanced at Stéphanie. Toula's smile was warm but the warmth did not extend to her eyes, which were cool and suspicious.

"How can I help you?" she asked.

"We have a few questions," Gilles said.

"My brother called me," Toula said. "He told me that Dr. Tiddley died. He didn't say how. That's really bad news. We had had hopes that he could help our father. What happened?"

"Can we talk somewhere privately?" Gilles asked.

"Come with me," Toula said and she led the two cops through the large dry-cleaning plant. The temperature in the room was such that Gilles felt he was walking into a sauna. The sweat dripped from his underarms down his sides, an unpleasant sensation. The place smelled of chemicals. Toula led them past enormous washing machines, past women ironing shirts, and barrels with stickers indicating that they contained hazardous waste. There was a name stencilled on the barrels in large letters: Disposition Chimie-Vert, Inc.

"What are those?" Gilles asked as they walked past the barrels to the stairs that led up to a second floor.

"Perc. The chemical we use in dry cleaning. It's disposed of as hazardous waste."

Gilles made a note of the name of the company.

Toula's office was large and comfortably furnished. There were a desk, a couple of visitors' chairs, a sofa with a coffee table in front of it and a round table with three chairs around it. The walls were almost completely bare. The only decoration was a large painting of what Gilles took to be a Greek village on the Mediterranean. Toula invited Gilles and Stéphanie to join her at the round table. She offered coffee, which the cops accepted. Gilles felt better now that he was out of the hot dry-cleaning plant. Stéphanie seemed unbothered by the heat.

Toula used her desk phone to ask her secretary to bring coffee to her office and returned to the table. "Now, what can you tell me about Dr. Tiddley?" she asked.

Gilles ignored the question and asked one of his own. "How did you know that his name was Tiddley? He presented himself as Dr. Hingston."

Toula's secretary placed three mugs of coffee on the table along with a small carton of milk and some sugar packets. Toula stroked the handle of her coffee mug and said, "Yes, he did. But we went out for dinner after one of his visits and he had made the reservation under his real name, so he was busted, I guess you would say."

"It didn't bother you that a doctor who was prescribing medications for your father was using a false name?" Gilles asked.

"It bothered me a lot," Toula said.

"How did you figure it out?"

Toula smiled fleetingly and said, "He made the dinner reservation in his real name. He spent most of that first dinner answering my questions."

"What did you uncover?"

"He told me that he used a false name to make the first approach because he didn't want the families of the patients to know that they were going to be part of his research. The way he put it, he wanted the patients and their families to be 'as is.' He believed that if they knew about his research right away they would be hesitant to try the meds or they would not report accurately on the drugs' effects and so on."

"This didn't concern you?" Stéphanie asked. Gilles was taking notes. He looked up and nodded. He wanted Toula's answer.

"Of course it concerned me. But I understood his motives and I wanted help for my father. I didn't care that he was part of a research project. Better that than the life he was leading. A confused and often angry shell of what he once was."

Gilles knew that Tiddley didn't tell other patients and their families about his real identity and motives. He made a note to figure out why Toula was so sanguine about such an important breach of medical ethics.

"How many times did you have dinner with him?" Stéphanie asked.

"Well, I've only known him for a couple of months, so I'd say four, maybe five."

"Have you ever been to his house?" Gilles asked.

"On a couple of occasions."

"When was the last time?"

"Saturday night. We went to his place for a nightcap after dinner."

Gilles sipped at his coffee. He was puzzled by Toula. Most people lied about the last time they had seen a murder victim. They didn't want to appear to be the last person to see them alive. Toula demonstrated no such fear. Gilles was certain that she was holding information back. She admitted to being at Tiddley's house because she probably knew that her fingerprints and God knew what else were all over the place.

"When did you leave?"

"I'm not one hundred percent sure but it was after eleven. I was home by midnight."

"You didn't stay the night?" Stéphanie asked. Toula didn't reply.

Gilles pushed for more information. "You had drinks at his place and made it home by midnight. That leaves several hours when the two of you were together. What did you do? Did you talk about your father's situation?"

Toula stared at Gilles. He stared back at her cold black eyes and didn't blink. Finally, Toula treated the two cops to a half smile and said, "What do you think we did? Do I have to spell it out for you, for Christ's sake?" Her eyes flicked away from Gilles' for a second.

Gilles continued to gaze suspiciously at her. "Did you talk about your father's condition? His meds?"

"Hardly the kind of conversation one has over dinner and drinks and..." Toula didn't finish the sentence.

Gilles had placed his notepad on the table and he made a few notes in it. It was clear to Gilles that she had plenty of opportunity to slip a poison into Tiddley's drink and it was also possible that she remained until she was certain that it had taken effect. He wrote the word "motive" with a question mark and said, "What about Sunday? Did you happen to see Tiddley on Sunday?"

Instead of answering Gilles's question Toula drew little circles on the table with her index finger and stared at him.

Sometimes silence and a nervous gesture were suggestive, Gilles thought. He changed the subject. "Did you observe any beneficial effects from the medications Dr. Tiddley gave your father?"

"Not really. Maybe a flash of comprehension here and there but no, no permanent effects."

"Did your father continue to come to the office?"

Toula drank some coffee. "Hardly. It's been a couple of years since he's been active in the business. If not for me there'd be no business."

"I see," Gilles said. "Is this your father's old office?"

"No, it's mine. His is next door. I've been running things for a very long time."

"He must have appreciated it," Stéphanie said.

"You'd think. But that wasn't his way. He expected hard work from me."

"What about your brother?" Gilles asked.

"Yeah, what about him?"

"What does he do?"

"Other than drive a truck and hang out and play video games, not a helluva lot."

"What happens to the business now?"

"My brother and I inherit. What else could it be? We're Greek, things stay in the family."

"I see. I have a question about the night that your father went missing. Do you remember who was the last one into the house on that day?"

"Who knows? If I had to guess, I would say it was me when I came home from work. But it just as easily could have been Iannis if he went out. Now that I think about it, I think it was Iannis. I was working upstairs and he went out for a while. Met his friends, I guess."

Gilles got to his feet and Stéphanie did the same. "We're done for the moment. I'll be in touch if I need more information from you."

As they walked out of the office Gilles asked, "Had your father ever wandered off before the time he ended up in the hospital?"

"Yeah, I guess. During the summer a couple of times. We got him home before he got too far," Toula said.

She led the cops down the stairs and out of the building.

Once they were back in the car Stéphanie asked, "What're you thinking, Gilles?"

Gilles put the car in gear and started driving back to their Division. "I think she's lying, or rather not telling us the whole truth about her relationship with Tiddley. I also think that Toula had access to poison. Did you see those drums of hazardous waste?"

"Why would she kill him?"

“Why does anyone kill anyone? Anger, revenge, or to cover something up. I can’t see anger or revenge playing a role here, so I think she knew something about the meds Tiddley administered. None of the other patients’ families knew who Hingston was. They took him at his word that he was a doctor at the Gursky. Toula was suspicious of him for some reason, and made it her business to find out more. Maybe the meds made the old man more disoriented. Which would explain why he wandered off. That alone makes me suspicious.”

“You think she allowed her father to leave the house?”

“It’s a working hypothesis. It can’t have been easy for her to run the business and take care of her father and deal with her brother who doesn’t seem to have been much help. Maybe she left the door unlatched, knowing the old man might wander off. He could have been killed in a traffic accident or succumbed to pneumonia or something.”

“So, unlucky her that the cops found him,” Stéphanie said.

“Yeah, but in the long run it didn’t make any difference. He still died. I’m going to call Lapointe when we get back to the office and suggest he look for perc in Tiddley’s blood. And I’d like to get a look at the will while I’m at it.”

“You also think she killed Tiddley? Why?”

“Because he would know just how demented Mr. Prodosiakis was, if he was likely to just walk out of his house?”

“That’s cold, really cold,” Stéphanie said.

“Which, frankly, is my opinion of her.”

For the rest of the drive back to the Division office in Place Versailles they talked about their children, not the case. Both Stéphanie and Gilles were single parents and faced problems typical of those with children making the transition from being teenagers to being young adults. Stéphanie had two children, both in university; one in law school and the other an undergraduate trying to figure out what she wanted to do.

As for Gilles' theatre-student daughter Émilie, he was greatly relieved that she had pulled her life together.

Back at the office Gilles called Dr. Lapointe only to find that he had left for the day. He left a message and joined Stéphanie in the boss's office to report on their day's activities. That done, the three of them prepared to go home. Before meeting Lacroix and Stéphanie at the elevator Gilles called Annie to see if she was free for dinner.

Annie was waiting for Gilles when he pulled up at the door of the Emergency Department. They decided to try a new Thai restaurant that had opened on Côte-des-Neiges, not far from the Gursky.

After they had ordered their meals and had two beers sitting in front of them, Gilles asked what had happened as a result of closing Tiddley's lab.

"From what I heard, all hell broke loose," Annie said. "The powers that be called meetings with everyone from the board of directors down to the people who wash the floors. Total panic."

"I gather you're only exaggerating a little."

"Yeah, the floor washers are pretty much off the hook. The hospital has to work out how Tiddley found the patients he approached. Obviously, it had something to do with the ER. The patients I saw were all ER patients before he called on them. He had access to the hospital's database and must have used it to find patients who had a certain medical profile."

Annie paused to savour the chicken pad thai she had ordered and to take a sip of beer. "Any number of administrators, IT people and doctors from Emerg, Gerontology and God knows where else were all over the ER asking questions about the patients whose names they'd culled from Tiddley's notebook. All of them will have to be contacted and given full workups, and any meds they had from Tiddley confiscated and analyzed."

Gilles ate while he listened. He realized that the problem was close to being overwhelming. All the patients that had had contact with Tiddley would have to be closely followed in order to be checked for side effects. This would tax the already overburdened hospital.

"And," Annie concluded, "There is a strong possibility of lawsuits. I expect the hospital will be full of lawyers tomorrow. There hasn't been a scandal of this nature at the Gursky for twenty-five years."

"What happened twenty-five years ago?"

"There was an orderly who was killing patients he considered to be terminal and in pain. At his trial he claimed he was helping them."

Gilles couldn't fathom killing people as somehow helping them. "Do you know what happened to him?"

"Well, all this happened just before I started in the ER. He went to prison, obviously. I think he was murdered in prison."

Gilles drained the last of his beer and asked, "Is there some way you can figure out what was in the drugs Tiddley was feeding the patients? To Mr. Prodosiakis, for example? What the side effects would be?"

"No, not specifically, not without more information. I can tell you that if he had been messing with acetylcholinesterase inhibitors, he was also increasing the likelihood of side effects. Everything from anorexia to heart problems."

"Could he have made the dementia worse?"

"Possibly," Annie said. "I would have to know more about the biochemistry of the meds and the patients. Why?"

"Right now, my thinking is that there is more to the death of Mr. Prodosiakis than his taking the pills Tiddley gave him.

It's possible that his daughter knew that the drugs Tiddley was feeding him could be fatal. She spent more time with Tiddley than any of the other patients' family members. She was at his house the night before he died."

"You think she killed Tiddley to get rid of an accomplice?"

"Yes. It's a distinct possibility," Gilles said.

Annie and Gilles had finished their meal and decided to have a coffee at one of the cafés in the neighbourhood. They walked a block or so to the closest café and made themselves comfortable. Annie sipped at her coffee and nibbled at the slice of carrot cake they had decided to share. Annie was obviously lost in thought.

"You know," she said after a while, "there's another possibility."

"Really? What's that?" Gilles asked.

"It's possible that the daughter noticed that whatever it was that Tiddley was giving her father had an interaction with other meds, and that caused some kind of side effect."

"Would the combination have killed him or hastened his death?"

"In and of itself, not necessarily. Depending on the dosage it's possible that he would have had a negative reaction and that would have given her the hint that the combination was dangerous. If she had monkeyed with the dosages, she could have discovered the fatal combination."

"That would mean," Gilles said, "Tiddley figured out what she had done or what she was attempting to do, and was going to do something to stop her. There's no question he was acting unethically, but I don't think he set out to kill anyone. If that's right then Toula had an even stronger motive for getting rid of Tiddley, her unwilling accomplice."

"Right. He may not have intended to kill anyone but that was the result of his unethical behaviour. Morally there's no difference between that and premeditated murder in my opinion. Now that I think about it, it's worse. It's careless disregard for human life. A total violation of the Hippocratic Oath."

"Dear God, I never considered that possibility," Gilles said.

"Enough of this," Annie said. The conversation turned to much more pleasant topics, their kids and the plan to spend a long weekend in New York as soon as they both had enough time off. Annie smiled at her boyfriend and said, "So what's it to be? My place or yours?"

Gilles returned her smile and said, "You don't have your car, so yours. Do you have an early day tomorrow?"

"Yeah." They left the café holding hands, eager to get to Annie's place.

Chapter 11

It was a short walk from the Longueuil metro station to where Nancy Tessier lived on rue de la Barre. She was returning home after her shift on the tech support desk at Chipsolutions, a company that supplied software to communications businesses. The clients of Chipsolutions worked long hours, so the company kept its tech support service open until midnight every weekday. Nancy was listening to music on her cellphone as she walked past the park next to her apartment building. Suddenly she felt the loop around her neck. In a panic, she instinctively tried to turn her head while pulling at the rope that was choking her. She struggled to escape, hoping to run the last block to safety. But her attacker had the advantage of surprise. Nancy was dead within three minutes, and her body was left partially hidden behind one of the cement bollards that lined the street side of the park.

Several hours later Paul Lefebvre was walking north on Papineau in front of the new CBC building. The block between Notre Dame and René-Lévesque Boulevard was deserted at that time of night. Paul had walked that block countless times on his way home from his job as a security guard at the Molson building. The rope was around Lefebvre's neck just as he reached the edge of the parking area in front of the CBC building. He got no further. His killer left the body in the parking area and walked up Papineau to the nearest metro station.

The police might not have connected the deaths of three people—one in Laval, one on Montreal's South Shore, and one in Montreal itself, as they took place in different jurisdictions, if not for Dieudonné Yves-Pierre, a journalist with the *Journal de Montréal*. He was on the scene at the CBC building when his office called, telling him about another body found on the South Shore. Dieudonné lived in Laval and was aware of the murder by strangulation that had occurred there a week or so earlier. In his article on the murders, he tied the three of them together and gave the murderer the sobriquet, "L'Étrangleur".

The name stuck and journalists for the other news outlets, TV, radio, online and print, adopted it.

Chapter 12

Gilles stopped for a coffee on his way to his desk in the Major Crimes Division. He got settled in his cubicle and called Dr. Lapointe on his cell.

"Bonjour, Gilles. I hope you haven't called to nag me for results."

"No, not yet," Gilles said. "But I may get back to you on that. I have some information that may be helpful to you."

"Ah. I see."

"A possible name of the poison that killed Tiddley."

"And what would that be?"

"Perc," Gilles said.

"Percocet? Essentially it's tetrachloroethylene. What makes you think that was the poison used?"

"One of the prime suspects owns a dry-cleaning company and there are barrels of the stuff in the plant where the work is done."

"And how do you think your suspect got the poison into the vic? It's not exactly a taste treat."

"Spicy food. Remember, we found takeout containers from an Indian restaurant in the garbage." Gilles was pleased that he'd bested Dr. Lapointe. It was rare that the medical examiner didn't have the last word. "Or possibly a drink. Scotch maybe?"

"Hmph," Dr. Lapointe said, "a drink is unlikely unless the drinker was really drunk. We'll see. I'll let you know when I know." He ended the call before Gilles could say anything more. Gilles looked at his phone and muttered something about Lapointe's bedside manner. Cop-side manner, really.

Just as Gilles hung up, Captain Lacroix came out of his office holding a copy of *Le Journal de Montréal*. He called a meeting in the squad room. His stare silenced everyone. He held up the front page of the tabloid and said, "We've got a serial killer on our hands." He slowly moved the *Journal* in an arc so all those assembled could see it. "Unless I say otherwise, you're all on this. If you have another case put it on the back burner. If you can't do that then work this every chance you get. Gaston Lemieux is in charge. He'll make the assignments and report to me. Any questions?"

Lacroix didn't wait to see if any of his squad had questions. It wouldn't have made a difference. Other than three corpses, all strangled, there was no useful information in the newspaper. Lacroix returned to his office and Detective Sergeant Lemieux took charge of the meeting.

Gilles followed the captain into his office and asked, "Do you want me to suspend my investigation into the murder of Marcus Tiddley?"

Captain stood behind his desk and sighed. "It's always something with you, eh Gilles? How close are you to clearing it?"

"I've got a suspect. I'm waiting to hear from Lapointe about the poison used. I found a couple of hairs at the scene, not the victim's, and I'm waiting for forensics to give me a DNA match if there is one."

"And if there isn't?" At this point in the investigation Toula Prodosiakis was Gilles' main suspect and it was very unlikely that her DNA profile was in a police database. Gilles would have to contrive a way of getting a sample from her.

"Next on my list. Get one," Gilles replied. "I'll be ready when the forensics comes in."

"Okay, Gilles. But you're on your own. Stéphanie is on the L'Étrangleur task force."

Gilles left his boss's office and the building before Lacroix could change his mind. As he walked to his car, he thought it would be a good idea to get a DNA sample from Iannis Prodosiakis as well and decided to try him first.

While he drove, his fingers tapping to the blues on the car's sound system, Gilles thought about the best way to approach Iannis in order to get a DNA sample. He had no legal right to compel the young man to give one. It took Gilles almost as long to navigate the crazy-quilt layout of streets in the Town of Mont Royal as it had to get to the suburb itself, which gave him plenty of time to think. His plan involved a convoluted medical theory that he hoped would be convincing to someone who knew less about science than he did.

He rang the doorbell at the Prodosiakis house and waited. It was barely ten in the morning and he figured that Toula would be at work and Iannis probably at home. Gilles waited for five minutes and tried the bell again. It occurred to him that Iannis was asleep in his basement room and couldn't hear the doorbell. He tried banging on the door with his fist. No answer. Gilles gave up and returned to his car. He noticed that there was a large olive-green garbage pail in the driveway next to the house. It had the house address in large numbers on it. Gilles flipped the lid and saw that it was full. He pulled a latex glove onto his right hand and fished around looking for something that was likely to contain Iannis's DNA. He found a Red Bull can and a ramen noodle container, both empty, both well known to be foods of choice for gamers. He slipped each of the containers into an evidence bag. He wasn't certain that the evidence, if indeed that's what it turned out to be, would stand up in court, but it would certainly help in his investigation.

He poked around looking for something that bore traces of use by Toula but didn't find anything, and he didn't want to attract attention to himself picking through the garbage in the upscale neighbourhood.

He drove off, intending to try his luck in getting a DNA sample from Toula. His phone rang just before he arrived at the office and plant of Kathari dry cleaners. Dr. Lapointe was on the line. "I hope you have good news for me," Gilles said.

"I have preliminary results for you and I ran a quick check of the victim's blood for tetrachloroethylene."

"And?"

"Not present," Dr. Lapointe said. "I can't say that I'm surprised. It would be very difficult to disguise the taste, no matter how spicy the food. However..."

"However what?" Gilles said. "I think you did find something."

"Yes, we did. There was nothing in the food containers but there were traces of poison in the chutney jar. More tests will tell us more about it."

"Tiddley could have started feeling ill after he went to bed and gone down to the kitchen to investigate the food he'd had."

"A distinct possibility. I'll know more after the autopsy," Dr. Lapointe said.

"When will that be?" Gilles asked.

"A day or two. We're only slightly backed up here."

Gilles thanked the medical examiner. He had to accept the possibility that his suspicion of Toula Prodosiakis might not be well-founded. He headed to the Gursky to see if Annie could help him get more of the information he needed.

Thirty minutes later he parked in front of the entrance to the Emergency Department and found Annie in Triage. She was chatting with the other nurse; the ER was uncharacteristically quiet. After a greeting embrace and a hello to Daniella, Gilles sat in the patients' chair. "I need your help," he said.

"Not a problem. How about I take your blood pressure?" she reached for the cuff and smiled.

"It'll be high. I've run into a dead end. I need to know something about the chemicals, poisons especially, that are likely to be found in a research lab such as Tiddley's. Is there someone I can talk to?"

"I don't know who's in charge of research. I suggest you start with Dr. Hirsch."

"What's his job?" Gilles asked.

"Head of medicine. He took over when Kavanaugh was arrested." Gilles had, with Annie's help, arrested the former head of medicine, for multiple homicides.

"Oh, Christ," Gilles said. "Is he gonna hate me?"

"Hardly. No one liked Kavanaugh. And now the hospital is going to have to deal with the fallout from whatever problems Tiddley caused."

"What can you tell me about him?"

"I've been here a long time, so I got to know him before he became head of medicine. He's not an ER doctor, but when we referred patients to his service, he always followed up with us," Annie said.

"He's a hands-on kind of doc," Daniella added. "He comes around every once in a while, to see how things are going and to see if there's anything we need. Anytime anyone asks him for something he delivers."

"He's very well thought of and very popular. He's the opposite of Kavanaugh. Not an arrogant bone in his body."

"Is his office in the same place as Kavanaugh's was?" Gilles asked.

"Yeah, Pavilion A," Annie said.

Gilles got to his feet. "I'm going to take a chance that he's in." He followed the labyrinth of corridors to Dr. Hirsch's office and asked the secretary if he was available. Gilles showed his badge.

He only had to wait a minute or two before Dr. Hirsch came to the door of his office and invited Gilles in. Gilles remembered the office of the chief of medicine as being expensively furnished. Dr. Hirsch had gotten rid of the expensive furniture and replaced it with functional office furniture, which included a round table for meetings and bookshelves loaded with reference books and professional journals. One corner of the office was screened off; it was where Dr. Hirsch saw patients.

"I'm Frank Hirsch," he said and extended a hand to Gilles. Dr. Hirsch was tall and slim, the same height as Gilles. He was somewhat older and his dark hair had begun to recede, leaving a widow's peak in the middle. He wore a white lab coat over his checked shirt and Dockers. He was tieless. "How can I help you?" Dr. Hirsch indicated that they should sit at the round table. He was the kind of doctor everyone wished they had, Gilles thought, unpretentious and knowledgeable.

Gilles introduced himself and explained that he was investigating Dr. Tiddley's murder.

"It's a nightmare," Dr. Hirsch said. "We have to follow up with every patient he saw and hope that he hasn't harmed them."

"I imagine that's a big job," Gilles said.

"You have no idea. I'm going to create a team of doctors, nurses, and social workers who will become the primary resources for anyone Tiddley had contact with. But that's not why you're here, is it?"

"No. I need to know something about Tiddley's lab."

"I'll give you the name of the head of all research, Dr. Marilyn Russell." Dr. Hirsch took a notepad and pen from his lab coat pocket and wrote the doctor's name, office location, and telephone number on it.

Gilles asked, "Generally speaking, are there poisons amongst the chemicals in the research labs?"

"Yes. Absolutely. And they have to be handled very carefully. Obviously. But you have to understand even benign chemicals when mixed with others can become poisonous. Research scientists are careful with everything they use."

Gilles got to his feet and asked, "Do you know if Dr. Russell is in her office? I'd like to see her now if at all possible."

Dr. Hirsch went to his desk and called Dr. Russell's extension and explained that the detective investigating Tiddley's death wanted to speak to her. Gilles couldn't hear what Dr. Russell was saying, but he heard Dr. Hirsch tell her, "Good point. I'll bring him over." There was a pause and Dr. Hirsch continued, "Okay, I'll pick a couple up. Be there in five."

Dr. Hirsch led Gilles out of the office and explained as they walked. "Marilyn suggested that I attend your meeting with her. She'd have to report it to me anyway. I'm going to pick up a couple of coffees on the way. Would you like one?"

They stopped at the Second Cup Café in the lobby of the Gursky. Dr. Russell's office was down a corridor and on the right of the neighbouring pavilion. Like most hospitals in Quebec with their many pavilions built at different times, the Gursky was a rabbit warren. Gilles was sure he'd not have found the office on his own.

"She's not in the building with the labs?"

"Her lab was in this building before the new one was built and she wanted to stay. That's about to change."

They walked into a small outer office. A secretary was on the phone. She motioned for Dr. Hirsch and Gilles to enter Dr. Russell's office. Before they went in Dr. Hirsch placed a coffee on the secretary's desk and she gave him a smile of gratitude. The door to Dr. Russell's office was open and Dr. Hirsch poked his head in to ensure that she was not busy. "Come in, come in," she said. Dr. Russell had straight grey hair and an aquiline nose. She cleared a place on her desk for the coffees.

"How can I help?" she asked, taking a sip.

"I need to know what kind of poisons are likely to be found in the research labs," Gilles explained.

"You name it, one of our labs has it. Everything from arsenic to, well, to zed. Why? Surely you don't think Tiddley killed himself?"

"No. But someone killed him, and I have to examine all options. To get back to the poison in your labs. How is it accounted for and how is it disposed of?"

"By accounted for do you mean is there some sort of log of who uses what?" Dr. Hirsch asked.

"Yes, exactly, and if there is residue or unused quantities what happens to them?"

Dr. Hirsch cleared his throat and crossed his legs. He looked straight at Gilles and said, "All labs have sign-up sheets. We're super rigid about narcotics. We worry about theft and dealing and so on. They're under lock and key and very few people have access to them. Our controls are audited and we always get top marks for our security. But poisons and other chemicals are another story, I'm afraid. The researchers are supposed to record chemicals that they use. But I doubt that it's accurate. People are in a rush or just plain careless from time to time. I can say that our purchasing hasn't changed all that much over the years. So that suggests that theft is not a problem."

"You mean you're purchasing the same amount of chemicals now that you did, say, ten years ago?"

“No, not the same gross amounts,” Dr. Russell said. “The ratios haven’t changed. The amounts we purchase for the labs are pretty constant on a per researcher basis.”

Gilles thought for a moment and asked, “How is any surplus disposed of?”

“We have a service. We treat all the chemicals as hazardous materials and a company, Disposition Chimie-Vert, picks them up,” Dr. Hirsch said.

“I see. Where do you keep the disposal vat?” “Vats,” Dr. Russell said. “We don’t mix the chemicals willy-nilly. There are rules, strict ones. We don’t want to blow something up or cause contamination, both of which would be deadly.”

“Sorry,” Gilles said. “Then vats. Where are they stored for pickup?”

“There are locked pickup areas in the alleys behind some of the buildings,” Dr. Hirsch explained.

“I’d like to see them, if I may,” Gilles said.

Dr. Russell got to her feet and said, “Not a problem. We’ll do it now.”

Gilles and Dr. Hirsch also stood. “I’ll take care of it, Marilyn. I have the codes and I’m responsible if anything has gone wrong.”

Gilles and Dr. Hirsch left Marilyn Russell’s office and Gilles was treated to a walk through the basement of the Gursky. The walls of the basement corridors of the Gursky were painted concrete. Some of the walls were an institutional drab olive green and others were covered with bright primary colours. There were junctions with other corridors that led off in different directions. For Gilles, without landmarks of some kind, it was impossible to know the direction they were taking.

They exited to the alley that gave access to the loading dock and other service areas. Dr. Hirsch used his code book to work the locks on a series of heavy metal doors. Each cement room held one or two disposal vats with instructions stencilled on them indicating which chemicals could be placed in them. The last place they checked was the alley behind the pavilion that held the labs. The storage room was much larger than the others and held half dozen disposal vats. Like the others, instructions were stencilled on them indicating which chemicals they contained. Gilles was impressed with the security of the system, but as good as it was that didn't mean that someone couldn't have snuck some poisons out of one of the labs in small quantities. Over time that could result in a large stash.

On their way back to Dr. Hirsch's office they cut through the ER. Dr. Hirsch greeted all the staff members they encountered, many of them by name. While they were waiting for the elevator Dr. Rosen came up to them and said, "Frank, I heard you were slumming down here." The two men shook hands. "If you've got a minute, I'd like your opinion on one of my patients."

"Absolutely, Alex." Dr. Hirsch turned to Gilles and said, "Are we done? Or do you want to wait for me?"

"I have one more question, so I'll be in the waiting room."

Dr. Hirsch smiled and said, "Say, hi to Annie for me." He walked off with his colleague.

Gilles returned to the Triage area and saw that Annie was busy with a patient. He waved a hello and found a place to sit down. He made some notes in his notebook regarding all that he had learned so far.

When there was a break in the flow of patients Annie came over to where Gilles was sitting. He got to his feet. "Busy day?"

"Normal. You?"

Normal for Annie meant that over the course of twenty-four hours three shifts of nurses would triage three hundred or more patients. “Interesting,” Gilles replied. “I’ve had a tour of the basement of the hospital and met the head of research.”

“Along with the amazing Dr. Hirsch,” Annie said.

Gilles smiled and said, “Yeah. He says hello.”

Annie laughed loudly. “I’ve known Frank Hirsch for a very long time. In some ways he’s been like a father to me. When he took over and heard about us and how I’d helped you and so on, he said that cop or no cop, you’d be in trouble if he didn’t approve.”

“Crisse, he waited two years?”

“That’s Frank Hirsch. He never forgets.”

At that point Dr. Hirsch returned to the waiting room and joined Gilles and Annie. “Surely there’s a law against harassing nurses. Do I have to call a cop?”

“Frank,” Annie said, smiling. She gave his hand a squeeze.

He returned the hand squeeze and the smile and said to Gilles, “You had another question for me? We can talk while we head back to my office.” Annie returned to work and Gilles and Dr. Hirsch walked back to his office. On the way Gilles said, “I’d like, if possible, to have a meeting with the staff from Dr. Tiddley’s lab. Can that be arranged?”

“Yes, of course, if you feel it’s absolutely necessary. Let’s go back to Marilyn Russell’s office. She’ll have to make the arrangements.”

Dr. Hirsch explained what Gilles wanted and Dr. Russell agreed to set something up for the next day. “Let’s do it in the afternoon,” she said. “It’ll give me time to get in touch with everyone.”

Gilles gave Dr. Russell one of his cards and asked her to call him on his cellphone when the arrangements had been confirmed.

Dr. Hirsch went back to his office and Gilles to the Emergency Department. Annie was again with a patient and Gilles waited until she was free to say goodbye. She suggested that he come to her house for dinner and he gratefully accepted. “Bring Émilie,” Annie suggested. “I haven’t seen her in what seems like forever.”

“I’d love to, but she’s having a late dinner with her mother. She doesn’t have a class tomorrow morning so she can sleep over. Next time.”

Chapter 13

Gilles next planned to visit the chemical disposal company that, by coincidence, served both the hospital and Nettoyeurs Kathari, to see what he could learn about how someone—one of the lab scientists who worked with Tiddley, or Toula Prodosiakis (still his favourite candidate for murderer)—might be able to gain access to poison.

The company was located in a triangle of land in Lachine, bordering on Dorval, just north of Highway 20, the expressway that connected the east end of the city with the West Island suburbs. The area was home to a variety of warehouses, shipping terminals, and other storage facilities. Thirty minutes after leaving the Gursky, Gilles was in the ground floor reception area of the three-story building that housed Disposition Chimie-Vert. He presented his badge to the receptionist and asked to see the CEO. The receptionist looked at Gilles's badge but didn't get up from her desk behind the counter. She gave him a fleeting smile and said, "I take it you don't have an appointment. May I tell Mr. Chenier what it's about?"

Gilles was a little surprised. His badge usually got receptionists to their feet and then they rushed to find the person he wanted to see. This woman, pretty with dark hair, in her mid-forties, was no more impressed than she would have been had Gilles been a UPS driver making a delivery.

Gilles gave the receptionist his best green-eyed stare and said, "I'm investigating a murder and I need to ask him some questions."

"Oh my," the receptionist said. "I hope it's no one we know. I'll ring Mr. Chenier and ask if he can see you. Why not have a seat?" She pointed to a seating area on her right. Gilles walked over to it but didn't sit down. He gazed out the window and saw that there was a massive warehouse, the equivalent of two football fields, that ran from the rear of the office building. It was not fully visible from the front of the building.

He didn't have to wait long before a man dressed in business attire came down the stairs located to the left of the receptionist. He walked to Gilles with his right hand extended. "Bonjour, je suis Jacques Chenier, le directeur général. Comment puis-je vous aider?"

Gilles took the offered hand and introduced himself. Jacques Chenier was a tall slim man in his mid-fifties with grey hair. He had a welcoming smile. "I'm investigating a murder and I'd like to ask you a few questions, if you don't mind. Is there some place we can talk?" Gilles asked.

"No one I know has died recently, much less been murdered, so I can't imagine how I can be of any help, but we can talk in my office."

Chenier's office was furnished with a large desk and comfortable-looking black leather desk chair, an expensive ergonomic design. There was the usual collection of additional furniture: a table and chairs for meetings and two visitor chairs in front of the desk. The office window looked out over the warehouse roof.

"Can I offer you something to drink?" Jacques Chenier asked. "Coffee? Water?"

"Non, merci."

Chenier shrugged and said, "So to business. How can I help you? Who exactly was it that was murdered?"

Gilles gave Chenier a brief rundown of the murder of Dr. Marcus Tiddley and said that someone who knew the victim, one of the last people to see him alive, owned a dry-cleaning business which was one of Disposition Chimie-Vert's clients. Gilles added that Chenier's company also picked up the hazardous waste from the Gursky Memorial Hospital where the victim worked.

"My questions," Gilles concluded, "are what happens to the chemicals when you get them to your facility? Is it possible for someone to get their hands on lethal amounts of something? And finally, do you know Toula Prodosiakis and has she ever been here?"

"To answer your last question first: yes, I know Miss Prodosiakis. My business specializes in hazardous waste from hospitals, universities, pharmaceutical companies, those kinds of operations. I've not done much with the dry-cleaning industry. Their quantities are massive and I don't think I can handle them."

"But," Gilles prompted.

"Miss Prodosiakis can be very persuasive. She found out about Chimie-Vert somehow and came to see me. She wanted me to take over the management of her waste chemicals, perc."

"Why?"

"She was concerned that the company she had been dealing with was not sufficiently careful and that they were disposing of the perc in an unacceptable fashion. Even though we would be more expensive she wanted the satisfaction of knowing things were handled properly."

"She visited your facility?"

"Absolutely. She insisted on a complete tour. Which I gave her."

"Please tell me what transpired between you."

Jacques Chenier inhaled, exhaled, and rocked back in his chair. He rocked forward and placed his elbows on his desk.

He stared at Gilles for a moment. "I can't see the connection between Miss Prodosiakis and the murder of a doctor, but okay. She had a lot of questions about how we deal with the hazardous waste we pick up. Most of the stuff is recycled or otherwise disposed of according to governmental policy. But, in a nutshell, what makes us different from our competitors is that we're actively trying to find ways to re-engineer the poisons to turn them into a benign product. I'm a chemical engineer and the second floor of this building is a research facility where we're trying to solve that problem."

Gilles was impressed by the notion that hazardous waste could by some alchemy be turned into a benign product. "Have you had any success?" he asked. "Did you show Miss Prodosiakis the laboratories?"

"So far, limited but hopeful, and yes. I suppose you'd like to see them as well?"

"Very much."

Jacques Chenier got to his feet and led Gilles to the second floor. They had to pass through a security door that Chenier opened by typing a four-digit code into a number pad. Gilles had no problem seeing the numbers he entered: 5-7-2-4.

Gilles and Chenier were in a clean room. It had a large window that covered half of the wall opposite the security door and afforded a view of the laboratory. There were hazmat suits hanging from hooks on the two adjacent walls. Chenier removed his suit jacket, took one of the hazmat suits and put it on. Gilles did the same. Once both men were covered from head to toe, with masks and gloves, they went into the laboratory.

It was a large, brightly lit room with a dozen research benches. At the rear of the lab there was a large glassed-in room and Gilles could see that scientists were working on projects in a glove box. He marvelled at the control it took to work with their hands in thick rubber gloves which were held by cables to rings attached to a bar on the ceiling of the glove box. As the scientists moved their gloved hands the rings slid along the bars allowing the workers to pick up and mix chemicals without risk. Gilles looked around and noticed that the scientists worked in groups of two or three people, discussing procedures and results as they worked. All in all, it was an impressive display of inquiry.

"There must be a lot of money in waste management to cover the cost of all this research," Gilles said.

Gilles could see from Chenier's eyes that he was smiling. "We're not in the waste management business. We're in the research business. The world is overwhelmed with all kinds of garbage, some hazardous in the short term, all of it a problem in the long term. Whoever can figure out how to turn this stuff into something useful will make a fortune. I'm talking about billions, many billions, of dollars."

Gilles took a moment to digest what Chenier had said. "Wow," seemed like the only appropriate comment. "Where do you store your laboratory supplies?"

Chenier led Gilles down the aisle that ran along the inside wall of the lab. Just before they got to the enclosed area there was a door on the left. Chenier opened it and showed Gilles a storage room with shelves of glass flasks, each labeled with a skull and crossbones along with the name and chemical composition of its contents.

"Got it," Gilles said and gave Chenier a thumbs-up sign. "I have an additional question or two."

"Let's go back to my office."

Back in Chenier's office the two men sat at the meeting table. Jacques Chenier again offered Gilles a coffee. This time he accepted. Chenier got up and went to a closet behind his desk. It contained a Nespresso machine and a small refrigerator. Chenier made two coffees and brought them to the table.

"You told me that when Toula Prodosiakis came to your office, you gave her a tour of the lab," Gilles said.

"Yes, she was very interested in our research. In fact, she told me that the main reason she wanted to sign with us was because we were trying to do something positive with the materials we pick up. She asked for a prospectus so she could invest in the company."

"She saw the storage room, the clean room, and everything else?"

"Absolutely. And the warehouse where we store the vats as they come in." Chenier indicated the large facility at the rear of the office building.

"One last question. Was she ever alone in the lab? Or the warehouse?"

"I was with her during the time of her visit. But now that you mention it, she politely refused my offer to show her out. She was alone, I guess you could say, from the time she let my office until she left the building."

Gilles got to his feet and thanked Jacques Chenier for his time. The men shook hands. "Can you see yourself out?" Chenier asked.

"Yes, thank you," Gilles said. On his way down the stairs, he paused for a moment on the laboratory floor. He looked around and realized that anyone who knew the code to the security door could gain access to the lab. When wearing a hazmat suit, the person would be indistinguishable from one of the scientists working in the lab. It had been easy enough to get the code by watching Chenier type it in.

Gilles was very pleased with the results of his visit to Chimie-Vert. Not only was Toula Prodosiakis still on his list of possible suspects, it was nice to know that someone was working on a way to save the planet from being overrun with garbage.

On his way to Annie's house he stopped at a liquor store and a florist.

⊙

Gilles didn't talk about the Tiddley case over dinner. He and Annie chatted about her day in the ER. She brought Gilles up-to-date on hospital gossip as it concerned the people they knew in common. Over the years that he and Annie had been in a serious relationship he had formed the opinion that her friends in the medical professions led unusually complicated lives. Most of the nurses were divorced and had to juggle shift work with single parenthood. He was also of the opinion that nurses were special people who couldn't stop working in the caring profession even if doing so would make their lives easier. They were finishing the last of the wine when Pamela, Annie's daughter, came home.

"Are you hungry?" Annie asked. Pamela came into the dining room and kissed her mother and she and Gilles exchanged kisses on both cheeks, Quebec-style. "Sort of," she answered. "Are there leftovers?"

"Not leftovers, we saved you a plate. Sit down. I'll bring it."

Pamela sat down and talked about her life as a medical student between bites of her dinner. When she finished eating, Gilles carried her empty plate into the kitchen and did the dishes while she and her mother talked.

Annie and Gilles were searching for something to watch on Netflix when Gilles's phone rang. It was Émilie, his daughter. "Allô, Lapin," he said.

Before he could say anything more Émilie, sounding panicked, yelled, "Quelque chose est arrivé à Maman!"

"What, what happened?"

"Someone attacked her. I just got here and I found her sitting on the floor. She's bleeding." Émilie started to cry.

"Get out of the house immediately and take your mother with you. The attacker might still be there."

"Non, Pa. He's not. Maman told me it's someone she knows and not to call you."

"You did the right thing. I'm going to put Annie on the phone. I'm on my way. After you speak to Annie call the Longueuil police and try to get them to wait for me. But if your mother has to go to the hospital, I'll meet you there. Got it? Just text me."

"Oui, Pa."

Gilles handed Annie his cellphone and gave her a brief rundown on what Émilie had told him. Annie, speaking in a relaxed way that helped Émilie calm down, gave her a series of instructions, telling her to check for bleeding, open wounds, and so on.

"Does your mother seem confused?" she asked.

"Not confused. Upset. She doesn't want to talk."

"Okay. Do your best to make her comfortable. The police will probably want to photograph any injuries. If she's bleeding from a facial cut try to staunch it by covering the wound with a clean cloth. Be gentle. I'm coming with your father. You're terrific, Émilie."

Annie handed the phone to Gilles. "We're on our way. There's no traffic so we should be there in about forty-five minutes. Call if you need me."

Gilles drove as fast as traffic would allow. Since his ex-wife lived on the South Shore it meant taking the Jacques Cartier bridge across the St. Lawrence River. They made the trip in just under forty-five minutes. There were a cop car and ambulance parked on the street in front of the house. He and Annie found Émilie and her mother, Yvonne, at the kitchen table. There were two cops and two EMTs, with them. One of the EMTs was putting a bandage on a cut just above Yvonne's left eyebrow. Gilles identified himself to the cops and asked if they knew what had transpired.

Annie asked the EMT caring for Yvonne to let her give her a preliminary examination, explaining that she was an ER nurse. While Annie examined Yvonne, Gilles identified himself and moved into the living room to talk with the two Longueuil cops. "Madame doesn't want to give us any details. She said it was an accident. Mais nous savons que ce n'est pas la vérité."

"Yes, absolutely," Gilles agreed. "Let me try." He and the uniformed cops returned to the kitchen. Annie was sitting at the table holding Yvonne's hand. She was speaking to her in a soft voice. She looked up when the cops entered and said, "So far as I can tell Yvonne's condition is not too serious. I don't think there's a concussion but I recommend a visit to the hospital to be certain. They'll probably want to keep her overnight."

"Je ne veux pas," Yvonne whispered.

"It's for the best," Annie said. "I'll come with you if you like, but I'm sure you would prefer Émilie."

Yvonne started to cry and said, barely audibly, "Oui."

"Tell me what happened Yve?" Gilles asked.

Yvonne stared at him. Émilie answered in her mother's place. "From what I could get out of her, I think it was Michel."

"Who's Michel?"

"Michel Genest. They've been going out, I guess you could say."

One of the Longueuil cops asked, "You know this person?"

"Yeah, he's the neighbour. Michel Genest. A dentist. I'll pay him a visit," Gilles said.

"Let us take care of it," the cop said.

Annie walked Yvonne, Émilie, and the EMTs to the ambulance. Gilles and the two cops joined her on the front lawn. "I'm not going to hurt him," Gilles said and headed to the house next to Yvonne's. He used his fist to bang on the door. Michel Genest, much to everyone's surprise, answered. He was not a large man, an inch or two shorter than six feet, thin with a pot belly. He squinted at Gilles through his glasses. He was about to say something when Gilles grabbed one then the other of his hands and examined his knuckles and palms. There was a cut on Genest's right hand where it had come into contact with Yvonne's earring.

Gilles grabbed Genest by the shirt and said in a quiet but menacing voice, "If you ever go near Yvonne again, you're going away. Get it? You'll spend time inside." He gave Genest a hard shove. The Longueuil cops, who had followed Gilles to the door, intervened. One of them said, "We'll take it from here." They went into the Genest house and led Michel to the kitchen. The second cop told Gilles to let them handle things and promised to call and tell him what transpired.

"At the very least, arrest the fucker," Gilles said.

"You can depend on that," the cop said and closed the door.

Annie and Gilles walked back to his car and leaned against it. Annie hugged Gilles and stroked his hair. Gilles put his arms around her and held her close. His breathing slowly returned to normal.

"Do you want to go to the hospital?" she asked.

"Yes, but I think Yvonne would rather we didn't."

They got into the car and Annie said, "We'll go. I'll talk to the doctor just to be sure that she's alright. You can talk to Émilie, make certain she's okay."

Gilles drove to the Charles-Le Moyne Hospital, a major teaching hospital for the South Shore region, and parked in front of the Emergency entrance. Annie found the nurse who triaged Yvonne and the doctor who was about to see her. Gilles and Émilie sat in the waiting room. He hugged his daughter and told her, "You were wonderful, Lapin. Your mother is lucky that you came when you did. Do you want to stay with her for a while or do you want to come back to Montreal with us?"

"Je resterai."

"D'accord. Keep in touch. I spoke to Genest. He won't be bothering your mother again."

Gilles kept his arm around his daughter's shoulder while they talked. Annie joined them and explained that Yvonne didn't seem to have anything seriously wrong with her physically but she would be staying overnight to be certain. Émilie hugged Annie and thanked her. Émilie went in search of Yvonne and Gilles and Annie returned to Montreal.

Chapter 14

Tony Zacardi left his hardware store later than usual, much later. He'd stayed to do the job that he had been putting off for most of the month, the job his wife Claudia used to do—bringing the store's accounts up to date. Claudia was pregnant with their third child and found working at an old desk and chair in the cramped office space to be uncomfortable. Tony called his wife to say he was on his way and expected to be home in thirty minutes. He took a shortcut through the deserted Jean-Talon Market to his car. With his hand on the door handle of his Civic he felt a rope on his neck. He gasped and reached for it as it was tightened. Tony was a natural fighter and did his best to get his fingers under the rope and loosen its grip around his neck. His struggle made things worse as he expended valuable breath trying to save himself. With one last burst of energy, he rocked forward, hoping to pull his assailant over and thus loosen his deadly hold. Anticipating the move, L'Étrangleur pulled back just as Tony rocked forward. Tony breathed his last breath lying on the hood of his car, "Claudia" dying on his lips.

Claudia became increasingly nervous as the half hour passed and Tony didn't arrive home. After an hour's wait, she called the police. She was concerned that Tony had been in an accident. She was told that there were no accidents reported in the area of Tony's store and that her husband was just late. She begged them to check the area where she knew Tony parked, in case he had had an accident of some sort as he walked to his car. She knew something was wrong.

A patrol car found Tony's body. An hour later, Dieudonné Yves-Pierre managed to get his article into the next day's *Journal de Montréal.*

Chapter 15

Gilles got to the office late on Thursday morning, at half past ten. He'd had difficulty falling asleep the previous night. He worried about what could have happened had Genest attacked his ex-wife while Émilie was at her mother's house. It would have made a very bad situation very much worse. Gilles felt guilty as well as powerless, not being able to defend them. He finally fell into an uneasy sleep at about four in the morning. He awoke at nine and quietly moved through his morning routine, making certain not to wake Annie. He looked in on her before he left and saw that she was sleeping soundly.

As he walked through the Place Versailles with a coffee and a muffin on the way to the elevators that would take him to the Major Crimes Division offices on the second floor, he noticed the headline on the front page of the *Journal de Montréal* in 30-point type: L'Étrangleur – 4, Police – 0.

Gilles cursed Dieudonné Yves-Pierre for making what was bound to be a very tough investigation much more difficult. Gilles guessed that the division phone was ringing off the hook with false leads and insults.

When he got to the office, he found most of the squad at a meeting led by Gaston Lemieux. He was standing at a whiteboard with the names of the victims on it. Gilles slipped into the room and found a place at the rear. "Ah, Gilles, bon matin," said Captain Lacroix, also seated at the back of the room.

"J'explique plus tard," Gilles whispered and turned his attention to Detective Sergeant Lemieux.

"Donc," Gaston Lemieux said, "we have another victim." He tapped the whiteboard next to Tony's name. "And so far no connection between any of them. Have any of you found anything that links any of them? Giroux?"

Stéphanie Giroux was seated directly opposite Lemieux. She got to her feet. "We've checked everything we can and we'll do more, but so far we've looked at telephone records to see if there was any contact amongst the victims. We'll add Zacardi to our list and start again. We've done web searches on the names and other than finding all kinds of people with the same names, so far nothing else. We've canvassed the neighbourhoods where the victims lived and no one heard anything. None of the vics were angels but none of them had any enemies either."

"In other words, nothing," Gaston said.

"Sadly, yes. We'll retrace our steps with Zacardi. We're going to add another element to our investigation. According to early reports, Zacardi owned a hardware store. We're going to add the shopping habits of the vics to our inquiries." Stéphanie walked across the room looking at each of the detectives and continued, "Look for store receipts and get permission to examine credit card statements. We're going to cross-reference shopping habits in the hope of finding a connection."

Stéphanie sat down and Gaston said, "You heard her. Detective Giroux has your assignments. See her and get to work."

The cops gathered around Stéphanie. They talked about the work ahead and dispersed. When the room was empty, with the exception of Gilles, Gaston, and Captain Lacroix, the captain said, "My office. Please join us, Gaston."

The trio went into the captain's office and sat down. "You first, Gilles," the captain said. Gilles explained the reason for his tardiness. Neither Lacroix nor Lemieux asked for further explanation or made a comment. "How are things going on the Tiddley investigation?"

Gilles brought his boss and Gaston Lemieux up to date and told them about his meeting with the scientists from Tiddley's lab, scheduled for later that day.

"Good," Gaston said. "Then you can help with L'Étrangleur until your meeting."

"Glad to," Gilles said. "Anything on the weapon?"

"Nothing. In all cases it's yellow polypropylene rope available at any hardware store including Home Depot and, I assume, Zacardi's. Giroux knows to look for a connection. There's no DNA on the rope, which indicates that the perp was wearing gloves, because we can tell from the marks on the rope that it was wrapped around his or her hands. There would be DNA if they were bare-handed."

"I have to be at the Gursky in a couple of hours but I'm going to try a more detailed search. We're assuming that the victims were randomly selected, like most multiple murders of this type. I'll check criminal and legal records to see if there was some kind of connection. Maybe an inheritance or a business deal gone bad."

"Like a tontine?" Gaston asked.

"A what?" Gilles said.

Gaston explained the nature of a tontine, a bizarre scheme in which a group of people pay into a fund and the proceeds go to the person left alive after all the others have died. Gilles shrugged and said, "It seems farfetched, but something like that. You never know."

"Give it a try. If only to eliminate the possibility," Gaston agreed.

Captain Lacroix got up from behind his desk just as Gilles got to the door of the office. "How's Yvonne?"

"And how's Émilie?" Gaston asked.

"As well as you would expect. The Longueuil police will keep an eye on Yvonne *and* Genest. I think he'll move. Merci."

Gilles went to his cubicle and started to do searches in databases available only to those who worked in the justice system. He started with Zacardi. He checked each Tony and Anthony and Antony Zacardi along with every other variation of Tony that he could think of, looking for anything that mentioned any of the other victims. Gilles was surprised by the large number of people with the family name Zacardi and a given name that was Tony or one of its variants. There were a couple of instances where the name Zacardi and the family name of one of the other victims popped up, and Gilles made note of them and went on to the next victim.

After looking at half a dozen results for Nancy Tessier, Gilles noticed it was time to leave for his appointment with the scientists at the Gursky.

Chapter 16

Gilles was pleased to find Dr. Russell waiting for him in the main lobby of the Gursky. She wore a white lab coat over her street clothes, a grey skirt that came to just below her knees and a blue shirt. The only jewelry she wore was a silver chain necklace. "It's a bit of a labyrinth around here so I thought it would be best if I met you and brought you to the amphitheatre," she said while shaking Gilles's hand.

"Oui, merci, I appreciate it. I have the room number but you're right. There are a lot of corridors to go down."

On the walk to the amphitheatre Dr. Russell explained that all the researchers in Tiddley's lab were there, but there was a risk that they would not be forthcoming with information. There was a hospital investigation going on and they were afraid of losing their grants, or not being reassigned to other labs. "Your first step will be to put their minds at ease," Dr. Russell concluded just as they arrived at the door to the room where the scientists awaited.

Gilles and Dr. Russell entered and Gilles found himself in the well of a room with fifteen rows of desks banking up. There was a blackboard behind him, covering the entire back wall of the amphitheatre. There was no podium but there was a long counter, very much like the research benches in Tiddley's lab, about three feet from the blackboard. Dr. Russell directed Gilles's attention to two clip-on microphones lying on the counter. They each put one on and Dr. Russell introduced Gilles to the scientists. That done she took her place at one of the empty desks in the first row.

Gilles walked around to the front of the counter and leaned against it at its centre point. He said, "Some of you may remember me from my visit to your lab on the day that Dr. Tiddley's body was discovered. At that time, we didn't know much about what had happened, other than it was most likely murder, murder by poison. Frankly, I don't know that much more at the moment, which is why I would like your help." Gilles paused and cast his eyes from left to right to see if he was having an effect on his audience. They were looking straight at him but he didn't detect a willingness to help.

"I want you to know four things at the outset. The first is that any information that you can provide, no matter how seemingly inconsequential, will be helpful. The second is that I'm aware that the hospital will be undertaking its own investigation owing to the...the curious way in which Dr. Tiddley did some of his experiments. My investigation has to do with the murder. It is very unlikely that the police will be participating in the hospital's investigation, but it's just as certain that the paths of the two investigations will cross. Third, I expect that the person who leads the investigation for the hospital will share information with me if, and only if, it is related to the murder investigation. Finally, if any of you are uncomfortable answering questions in a public forum such as this you can get in touch with me and I'll arrange for a private meeting with you."

Gilles walked to the blackboard and printed his name and his cellphone number in large letters. None of the scientists occupied the first three rows of desks. Gilles went to the person sitting on the far left on the third row and handed her a pad he brought from the office. "I would like each of you to write your name and phone number on the pad so we'll know if anyone who was at the lab on Monday is not here today." Gilles heard grumbling as he returned to the blackboard. Dr. Russell got to her feet, turned to face the researchers and said, "Please do as Detective Bellechasse asks. Thank you." She sat back down.

Gilles gave the scientists a moment to settle down. "How many of you knew that Dr. Tiddley was performing drug tests on patients?"

The scientists chatted amongst themselves. Gilles did nothing to prompt an answer to his question, hoping that his silence would encourage someone to say something. After five minutes of nervous chatter Robyn Phillips got to her feet, cleared her throat and said, "Some of us knew he was up to something, but we didn't know what it was."

"Well, what made you suspicious about your boss?"

"Well, he was totally committed to finding a cure for degenerative diseases like Alzheimer's. His heart was in his work. But at times he would receive some kind of text message or email on his cellphone, check his computer, and then disappear for a while. At those times he suddenly became sort of distracted. His mood would change."

"And what made you think that this had something to do with his research or testing methods?"

Dr. Phillips was quiet. She looked nervously around the room but said nothing. Another of the researchers sitting a couple of places away from Robyn got to her feet. She was just under five and a half feet tall, dressed in jeans and pullover and wearing a lab coat. She had black hair, cut short, and was very pretty.

"It's okay, Rob," she said. "I think we can tell him what we did."

Robyn nodded.

"You are?" Gilles asked.

"Jacqui Di Camera. Like Robyn said, we suspected he was up to something that he didn't want to share with us. One day when he left the lab in the middle of the afternoon, I sort of followed him. I gave him a couple of minutes to get out of the building and I caught up with him on the sidewalk. I saw he was heading east, toward the main building, so I walked with him, pretending that I was heading to the main building as well. Pure coincidence. We went in through the Emergency entrance and he headed into the ER proper where the patients are. I slipped into the ER using a different entrance and spotted him going into a patient's room from the hallway. I returned to the lab."

"Jacqui told me what she discovered," Robyn said. "And I... we formed the opinion that Marcus had some way of knowing when a patient exhibiting certain kinds of symptoms was admitted to the ER. He was trolling for test subjects."

"Guinea pigs, you mean," came a male voice from the back of the room.

Gilles ignored the comment and asked, "Were you able to confirm your suspicions?"

"No. We tried, but no."

"How did you try?"

Robyn, who was clearly in charge of the team, looked up at those assembled. She focused her attention on one of the men. He got to his feet and Jacqui Di Camera sat down. "I'm David Fogelman," he said. He too was wearing a lab coat over jeans and a plaid shirt. "Robyn asked me to check Tiddley's computer to see if I could find anything like a message from the ER. It occurred to her that he had a contact there feeding him information."

"What did you find?" Gilles asked.

"Nothing. His computer was password-protected and I couldn't log in."

"Why did Robyn ask you to check?"

Fogelman smiled. "Because I have very good computer skills." There was a spurt of laughter from the scientists.

"A final question," Gilles said. "Do you remember how long Tiddley was away from the lab?"

"I would say somewhere between fifteen minutes and half an hour," Robyn replied.

"I want to end where I started," Gilles said. "You have my phone number so you can call me if you can think of anything to add to what I've learned today, no matter how small and unimportant it may seem. If it has something to do with any of Dr. Tiddley's behaviour that was unusual I would like to know about it."

Gilles walked up the stairs to the last person on the right, the desk that held the sign-up sheet. Gilles picked it up and returned to the front of the class. "I know how to get in touch with each of you should that be necessary. Thank you all very much for your time and your help. Unless you have any questions, I'll be on my way." Gilles nodded in the direction of Dr. Russell and added, "I also want to express my appreciation to Dr. Russell for her help."

The scientists got to their feet as Gilles left the room. He heard her say, "Please don't leave. I want to discuss how the hospital's investigation of Dr. Tiddley will proceed." The scientists returned to their seats.

Gilles decided to pay a visit to the Emergency Department to talk to the doctor in charge to see what, if anything, he knew about Tiddley's visits. He decided to walk to the ER via the street rather than snake through the hospital. As he walked, he called his daughter. "Allô, Lapin. How are you feeling? Did you have class today?"

"Awful, Pa. I'm worried about Maman. She's home now but frightened. There was a cop car parked in front of the house but it left. One passes by a couple of times an hour. But she's still scared."

"I understand, Lapin. It's only to be expected. She had a serious scare. It would have been a lot worse if you had not shown up when you did. Do you know if she has a friend who can stay with her?"

"She must have. I'll make sure she arranges it."

"I'll be home for supper. Do you want me to pick something up or should I cook something for you?"

"I think I'll I stay with Mom and make certain that she finds a friend to stay with her. She's feeling vulnerable."

"You're right, Lapin. I'm sure she'll feel more comfortable if you stay with her. I'm very proud of you," Gilles said.

"I love you, Pa."

"And I love you, Lapin." Gilles turned into the ER.

Annie was at her preferred post, working in Triage. She was with a patient but returned Gilles's smile. Gilles approached the Information booth and spoke to the woman on duty.

"I need to see Dr. Rosen. I have some questions I need help with. Can you put out a page?"

"Absolutely."

About five minutes after the page went out over the PA system Dr. Alex Rosen came into the registration booth.

"What can I do for you, Gilles?" The two men shook hands.

"I need to check some information about Dr. Tiddley. His visits to the ER. That kind of thing. Is there somewhere we can talk?"

"My office is best." Dr. Rosen used his security card to open the sliding doors and led Gilles down a couple of corridors to his office. Gilles had to slow his pace so as not to get ahead of Dr. Rosen, who was a head shorter than Gilles and a little overweight. The office was small, with just room for a desk and chair and one visitor's chair. The desk was strewn with papers and the shelving unit on the wall behind the visitor's chair held files, journals, and medical reference books.

"How can I help?" Dr. Rosen asked.

"Did you know that Dr. Tiddley made visits to the ER and why?"

"I saw him here once. The only reason I knew he was on staff was because he had a hospital ID on a lanyard." Dr. Rosen held up his ID to show Gilles what he meant. "I had no idea who he was. He really had no business here so I asked him if he was here as a patient or to visit one."

"What did he say?"

"Not much. He mumbled something about a friend of his and left. Why do you ask?"

"I have reason to believe that he had some kind of program or app or something that told him when a patient with certain symptoms was brought into the ER. Would he have access to all the departmental computers?"

"Yeah, I guess so. He was on staff, a senior staff member with his own lab. We all have access to patient information. But if I understand what you're saying we have a major problem. Bigger and worse than I thought."

"To be clear," Gilles said, "there's no hospital software that alerts a doctor when a patient with certain symptoms presents?"

"Absolutely not." Dr. Rosen half rose from his chair, then collapsed back into it, red-faced, the left jugular vein in his neck visibly throbbing. "It would be a total violation of policy, professional ethics, probably the law, you name it. Tell me what you think happened."

Gilles understood Dr. Rosen's anger. "The underlying question is: do all the staff at the Gursky have access to the hospital database of patients?"

"Not *all* the staff, no, but all the medical staff have unrestricted access once they sign in." A thin line of sweat appeared at Dr. Rosen's hairline.

"I think Tiddley wrote a piece of software," Gilles said, "that alerted him when a patient with some kind of dementia showed up. He would meet the patient or the family, arrange for a home visit, and give the patient one of the drugs he was working on."

"Dear God, no." Alex Rosen placed his elbows on his desk and his face in his hands. He slowly shook his head a couple of times. From behind his hands he asked, "Does Dr. Hirsch know...yet?"

"I just figured this out, so I haven't told him. I was in a meeting with the lab personnel. Dr. Russell was there so she knows, of course."

Dr. Rosen placed his hands on the armrests of his chair and looked straight at Gilles. "She's probably told Dr. Hirsch but I'll make certain he knows. I knew the hospital would have to investigate Tiddley but I didn't realize that the ED was involved."

Gilles thought for a minute and said, "You know, I might be able to help you there."

"Really? How?"

"His laptop and cellphone are both at the Computer Crimes Division. If we, the technicians there, can get into Tiddley's computer, they'll know when he got the message to look for a patient in the ER. Maybe even the name of the patient. But even if not, you'll know the date and time so you'll be able to cross-check that with patients admitted with dementia at around the same time. My guess is that Tiddley was looking for patients that had dementia but were here for some other reason."

Dr. Rosen got up from his desk and took a couple of paces to where Gilles was sitting. Gilles got to his feet. Dr. Rosen shook Gilles's hand and held his elbow with the other. "You're a lifesaver. Really. Things are bad enough for the hospital, but if we can say the risk was isolated to a specific number of patients the situation will only be very, very bad, not a total disaster. When can we expect to get the results you mentioned?"

"I don't know," Gilles said. "I'll call computer crimes and see where they are and let you know."

Dr. Rosen wrote his cellphone number on the back of one of his business cards and handed it to Gilles. "Call me as soon as you know something."

Back at Triage, Annie mouthed the word "wait" when she saw Gilles and held up a finger. When she was done with her patient, she joined Gilles in the waiting room. "How's Émilie?" Annie asked. "I was going to call her."

"Still a little shaken. She's worried about her mother."

"Poor child. I'll talk to her as soon as I get a break."

"I have a better idea," Gilles said. "Have supper with me. I ordered a lasagna from Tavolino Guido—too much for one person. Émilie's staying with her mother. We can call her together."

"I get off at five."

"I have to get back to the office. Do you mind driving over?"

"No, no, that's fine. I'll be there by six at the latest."

"You're the best," Gilles said and he bent down to kiss Annie. An announcement came over the PA system in Tasso's voice, "There's to be no kissing in the Emergency Department." Annie and Gilles turned and looked into the Registration booth and saw Tasso and a couple of other staff members waving at them.

"You guys," Annie said.

Chapter 17

Back at the office Gilles wrote up his notes with the information he'd gleaned from his meetings with the scientists from Tiddley's lab and Dr. Rosen. He was about to call Suzanne Rigaud in the Computer Crimes Division when his phone rang. It was a cop from Identification judiciaire ready to report on the evidence from the crime scene at Dr. Tiddley's house and the garbage Gilles had retrieved from the Prodosiakis bin.

"Qu'est-ce que tu as pour moi?" Gilles asked.

"Je vais commencer par les ordures. You'll see why when I give you everything I've got. I found DNA residue in the ramen container and the drink can that matched. Both from the same person, male. This is where it gets interesting. These two samples are from a first-degree relation to one of the samples we found at the crime scene, the black hairs."

"First degree relation means sibling or parent, right?" Gilles asked.

"Absolument."

Gilles smiled, pleased that he now had proof that Toula Prodosiakis was still his prime suspect.

"What about the blonde hairs?"

"They weren't human hairs. They were synthetic, from a blonde wig."

"Hmmm," Gilles said, more to himself than to the technician. The blonde hairs might mean that there was a second suspect, or possibly Toula wore a wig for some reason. "Is there any way to know how long each of the hairs was at the scene?"

"No, not really. My guess is that they're both current, let's say since the last time the house was cleaned. And that assumes that whoever cleaned house did a thorough job of it."

"What else have you got?" Gilles asked.

"Fingerprints. Not a crazy number, which makes the job of matching difficult, but enough to indicate that there were more than three people at the house at one time or another. Again, check to see when the place was last cleaned. My guess is that, based on shape, two of the sets belonged to females or males with delicate hands."

Gilles added the information to his case notes. The fact that the blonde hairs found at the scene were from a wig was a problem. It expanded the list of people he had to question, and the list of possible suspects, to anyone who might have a blonde wig. A large number of people, obviously. He had to find a way to narrow down this list of possibles to a manageable list of probables.

He called Suzanne Rigaud to see if she had been able to find a way around the passwords and get into Tiddley's computers.

"Ah, Gilles," Suzanne Rigaud said when she answered his call. "Always by telephone and never in person. I'm beginning to think you're avoiding me."

"Pas du tout, Suzanne. But I'm never in Ville St. Laurent—not your part of it, at any rate. Perhaps if you killed someone I might be put on the case."

"I'll give it some thought," Suzanne replied. "What can I do for you, as if I didn't know?"

"The Tiddley computers. Were you able to get access?"

"Of course. It's a rare person who can keep secrets from me. There was all sorts of complicated stuff on the laptop that referred to experiments, chemistry and the like. There were also case notes about the people who took certain drugs and their reactions."

Gilles looked around for someone with whom he could share a high five.

"Was there anything else? Something like a link to a network?"

"Funny you should ask. There was an app, I guess you'd call it, that connected to a network that was a Citrix-based program. The app was written especially for that software, not something commercially available. Here's the strange thing, though: the app was written for a much older version of Citrix than is on the market today."

"What's Citrix?" Gilles asked.

"It's network management software. A pretty good one, if you ask me. But it's old. The first version was written in the eighties. I don't understand why your vic would link to an older version. They update regularly. Do you know who, or actually which company, uses it?"

"I'm guessing it's the software that the Gursky uses to manage its network so that the medical staff has access to patient records."

"Yeah, that makes sense," Suzanne agreed.

"Can you send me a pdf of the patient files, the ones with information on the drugs they were given? All of them, regardless of the details."

"Sure thing. It will be a pretty thick file if you print it. Give me a couple of hours. Anything else?"

"Yes, please make sure the computer is no longer password protected. I may need access again and I'm pretty certain the hospital will need to pull more information." Gilles gave Suzanne a brief rundown on what it appeared that Tiddley was up to.

"Not surprised that someone killed him. I would have been tempted if he had used someone in my family as a guinea pig."

"Then I'd have to arrest you," Gilles said with a chuckle.

"Yeah, so you said."

Gilles was pleased with what he had learned and added Rigaud's information to the case file. He planned to pay Toula Prodosiakis another visit the following morning and hopefully wrap up the case.

He checked the list of names of the victims of L'Étrangleur and went back to researching them. He hadn't gotten very far when he noticed that it was just after five, which meant that he would have to rush to get to Tavolino Guido and home by six.

He took the list with him, planning to do some research from home after dinner. He made a marginal note to remind himself to ask Annie if the hospital ran Citrix software.

After dinner Gilles called his daughter and put his phone on speaker so Annie could participate in the conversation. Gilles asked Émilie if she was certain she wanted to stay with her mother. She told him that she did and Annie added her support for the idea. "It will help to restore her sense of safety," she said.

After dinner, Annie kept Gilles company while he cleaned up after the meal. Seated at the counter that separated the kitchen from the dining room, she sipped at a glass of wine while they chatted. Annie, as always, was amused by Gilles's almost obsessive sense of order, cleanliness, and tidiness. "You know," she said, "If you ever get tired of the police business, I can get you a job preparing the OR for surgery."

"Très drôle," Gilles said.

"Or better yet, a job as a scrub nurse."

Once the dishes were done and the kitchen was spotless, they settled in the living room to watch TV. Annie found a food show on Netflix that she liked. After a couple of minutes Gilles said, "I've got some work to do. I hope you don't mind." Annie didn't take her eyes off the TV but nodded, signalling her agreement. She curled her legs under her and got comfortable on the sofa. Gilles opened his laptop on the dining room table. He decided to try Google searches on the names of the victims. He did an exhaustive search on Zacardi's name and moved on to Tessier. Tessier is a common name in Quebec and Gilles was determined to take a look at all the entries for Nancy Tessier no matter how remote the likelihood of finding one that referred to the victim.

After thirty minutes and many Google pages he looked up at the ceiling and rubbed his eyes. Annie paused the television and asked, "What exactly are you doing?"

Gilles gave her a brief explanation and she came over to where he was working to get a better look. She gave him a playful nudge and parked herself on the chair next to him. She looked at the page numbers at the bottom of the screen and said, "Boy, you are looking for a needle in a haystack."

"There are times I think I'm looking for the haystack itself." He moved the cursor to the next entry for a Nancy Tessier. Annie's eyes widened when she noticed an entry lower on the screen.

"Wait, wait a minute." She pointed. "Go to this one."

Gilles moved the cursor to where Annie was pointing and saw the highlighted entry referred to a Gazette article about someone named Tessier who had testified at the sentencing hearing after a murder trial. The date was 1995.

"Are you serious?" Gilles asked, "This is a twenty-five-year-old entry."

"Read it," she commanded.

The story was concerned with the sentencing of Ian Chambers for murder. One of the victims who spoke at the sentencing hearing was a woman by the name of Nancy Tessier, who told of the tragedy of losing her mother while the elderly woman had been hospitalized.

"Is it possible that the Nancy Tessier could be that woman?"

"Well, the ages make sense. If she had been between thirty-five or forty in '95 she would be the age of the victim. What made you notice this entry in particular?"

"The trial. The guilty person is Ian Chambers. He was an orderly at the Gursky. He killed patients he thought were suffering at the end of their lives. He considered himself a hero. The court said he was a murderer."

"You knew him?"

"No. I started at the hospital just after the trial. But everyone was still talking about it and trying to deal with the aftermath of his murders. All kinds of procedures were instituted to make certain nothing like that ever happened again."

Gilles clicked on the article and he and Annie read it. The story, written by Gazette reporter Linda Gyulai, told of the moving testimony of two witnesses. The case may have been twenty-five years old, but Gilles was moved almost to tears by Tessier's account of what had happened to her mother. He was about to close the article when he noticed the name of another witness who testified at the sentencing hearing: a woman by the name of Rose Tiddley.

"Tabernac," Gilles shouted and shifted his weight on the chair, almost knocking Annie off it. She got to her feet.

"What, what is it?"

Gilles pointed to the name. Annie leaned on the table and bent over to see where Gilles was pointing.

"Read the rest of the article."

Annie sat on Gilles's lap and they read that Rose Tiddley recounted that the death of her husband left her to care for her son on her own. “The worst part,” Gyulai quoted Rose Tiddley as having said, “is that Marc, my son, didn’t have the opportunity to see his dad in his last hours. Maybe he would have died anyway. No one knows. But one thing is for certain: my son and I would have had the chance to spend some time with my husband. He loved his son and the feeling was mutual.” According to the article, Rose Tiddley broke into tears at that point and couldn’t continue her testimony.

“That’s a connection I didn’t expect to find,” Gilles said. “What happened to Chambers?”

“Life in prison, no parole. A public flogging would have been too good for him.”

“Is he still in prison?” It occurred to Gilles that if Chambers was connected to two murders, he would be worth an interview even in prison.

“No. According to the hospital grape vine he was killed in prison a couple of years ago,” said Annie.

“Oh,” Gilles said. He was silent for a moment or two. He shifted in his chair.

“Am I too heavy?” Annie asked.

“Hardly.” He put his arms around her and pulled her close. “I don’t know if I would have noticed the connection between Tessier and Chambers and Tiddley. You’re the best.” He kissed Annie.

She had her arms around his neck and rested her head on his shoulder. “What’s your next step?”

“Tomorrow morning I’m going to get the full transcript of the trial and the sentencing and see if any of the other strangling victims are connected with the Chambers case.”

Gilles closed his laptop. He and Annie watched a little more television and headed to bed.

Chapter 18

One of the other members of the book club gave Ruth Ettinger a ride home to NDG. Ruth didn't want her friend to drive a city block out of her way so she got out of the car on the corner of her street and de Maisonneuve Boulevard. It was a half a block to her house. She walked up Park Row West on the side of the street that bordered Trenholme Park. She neither heard nor saw her assailant slip out of the park and fall in behind her. A shriek of surprise started in her throat but was cut short when L'Étrangleur pulled the yellow rope tight around her neck. Ruth, terrified, grabbed at the rope, trying to get her fingers between it and her neck. L'Étrangleur forced Ruth to her knees and continued to pull the ends of the rope in opposite directions until Ruth went limp.

Annie's daughter, Pamela, was walking down Park Row West, having got off the 24 bus at the corner. Just before she got to her house, she noticed someone on their knees farther down the street. Pam's first thought was that someone had slipped on the icy sidewalk. She was approaching to offer help when she recognized her neighbour and saw that she was being strangled. "Hey, hey, fuck off!" she shouted and rushed to Ruth's aid. As L'Étrangleur let go of the rope and ran through the park, Ruth fell over. Pam got to Ruth's side, knelt beside her, loosened the rope and carefully rolled her over. She checked to ensure that her airway was clear and applied CPR.

Ruth coughed and almost simultaneously croaked, "Get off me."

"I'm trying to help you," Pam said. "Don't move. I'm going to call for an ambulance."

Pam pulled out her cellphone, called 911 and gave her location. She told the operator she would remain with the victim. She then called her mother.

Annie and Gilles were lying naked in Gilles's bed in the twilight between wakefulness and sleep when her cellphone rang. Annie intended to ignore the call but looked at the screen anyway. When she saw it was from her daughter, she answered. "What is it, darling?"

"Someone tried to strangle Mrs. Ettinger! Pam shouted.

Instantly awake, Annie sat up in bed. "What is it? Are you okay? Were you attacked?"

"Not me, Mum, Mrs. Ettinger from down the block. I called 911. They're on their way. Are you home?"

Pamela was speaking loudly enough so that Gilles could hear her. He got out of bed and pulled on a pair of jeans and a sweatshirt. "No, honey," Annie said. "I'm at Gilles's. Where are you?" Annie was out of bed, trying to get dressed with one hand while holding the cellphone in the other.

Pam gave her mother her location. Gilles said, "Tell her we're on our way."

Annie repeated Gilles's message and added, "If the ambulance gets there before we do, insist that they take you to the Gursky. I'll call and we'll meet you there. If they give you any trouble call and Gilles and I will straighten them out."

Chapter 19

Gilles and Annie drove at cop-car speed to Park Row West, some fourteen kilometers away. While en route Gilles had Annie call police dispatch. He told the operator where he was headed and instructed them to get forensics and a patrol car to the scene.

Gilles and Annie arrived at the scene just as the ambulance was pulling away. They followed it to the Gursky. Gilles called police dispatch back and told the operator that the squad car was to secure the crime scene and he would return as soon as he could. The ambulance pulled into the bay and Gilles parked in a corner of the driveway at the entrance. Annie ran to the ambulance bay and caught up with Pamela and the EMTs as they were wheeling Ruth Ettinger into Triage.

Annie hugged her daughter. "Are you alright?"

"I'm fine, Mum. Mrs. Ettinger is the patient." In spite of Pamela's brave words Annie was worried about her. Pamela returned the hug and said, "Really, I'm fine. Why don't you see to Mrs. Ettinger?"

"I'd like to ask Pam some questions," Gilles said.

Annie released her daughter and went to the triage area; Gilles and Pamela found a couple of empty chairs in the waiting room. "Are you okay to answer some questions?"

"Of course I am. I want to help."

"Tell me, in as much detail as you can remember, exactly what you witnessed."

"I was walking home from the bus stop and I saw what looked like someone who had slipped and fallen. It was dark and I couldn't see more than that but as I got closer, I realized that someone was being attacked, so I ran to see what was going on."

"You ran toward the trouble?" Gilles asked. "You weren't fearful?"

"I really didn't think about it. Someone was in trouble. I got close enough to see it was Mrs. Ettinger. She was on her knees and someone behind her had a rope around her neck. The street is not all that well lit but I could see that the rope was yellow. I screamed and ran to Mrs. Ettinger. That scared the assailant off."

"Was Mrs. Ettinger conscious?" Gilles asked.

"No, she fell over when the strangler released his grip. I did chest compressions and called 911. You know the rest."

"You're very brave," Gilles said. "I can't say I'm surprised, though. You're your mother's daughter."

Annie heard the last part of Gilles's comment as she approached them. "She sure is," she said.

Gilles got to his feet so Annie could sit next to her daughter. "How well do you know Mrs. Ettinger?"

Pamela and Annie started to speak at the same time. "Not well," Annie said. "She's been a neighbour for a long time but I only know her to say hello and have a short chat when we meet on the street. I think she's a widow."

"Yeah, she's lived on the street as far back as I can remember," Pamela added. "How is she?"

"She seems fine. A little shaken up and in shock. There are some bruises on her neck but she's otherwise okay. She'll spend the night in the Emergency Department but I'm sure she'll be released tomorrow morning. I'm on early so I'll make certain to see her before she's discharged."

"If we're done here, I'll drive you home. The forensics people will probably be at the scene and I want to see them before they leave."

"Oh, shit," Annie said during the drive to Park Row West.

"What is it?" Gilles asked.

"My car's at your place."

Annie wanted to spend the night at her place with Pam but didn't want to wake up early to be driven to pick up her car. Pam convinced her mother to return to Gilles's and spend the night, or what was left of it. "I'll be fine. I wasn't the one who was attacked," she pointed out. "But if it will make you happy, I'll double-lock the door and put a chair against it."

Pamela was only half serious but Annie was not mollified. "No. If I'm not going to be at home, you'll spend the night with my sister. No arguments."

Annie's sister lived next door to them and would have no objection to having Pamela spend the night. Pam was about to say something but changed her mind. It was easier to humour her mother than to argue.

Gilles parked in front of Annie's house and while Annie got Pamela settled at her sister's, Gilles spoke to the forensics people, who were just about ready to leave.

"Est-ce que vous avez trouvé quelque chose?" Gilles asked.

"Pas beaucoup. There are all sorts of footprints in the snow coming from the park." The technician motioned to the park and Gilles could see that there were prints indicating someone coming out of the park and ending where Ruth Ettinger had been attacked. The snow was a mess of swirls, showing patches of earth in some places indicating a struggle. But the sidewalk was icy and the faint prints became a dusting of snow when whoever left the footprints got to the sidewalk. "We'll take impressions and photos," the technician said. "But there's no way of knowing when the prints were made. If you find a pair of matching boots, well, then you'll have confirmation that the person was here."

The technician showed Gilles an evidence bag that contained the yellow polypropylene rope that had been used to try to strangle Ruth Ettinger. It was the same type of rope that had been used on the other strangling victims. It was obvious that all the crimes were connected.

"Maybe we'll get some DNA from this one," Gilles said.

"Only if the perpetrator wasn't wearing gloves," the technician replied. Gilles gave the crime scene his own inspection before he let the Identification judiciaire crew leave. As they pulled away, Gilles was approached by Dieudonné Yves-Pierre, who had been lurking in the shadows. He identified himself as a journalist working for *Le Journal de Montréal* and asked Gilles, "Do you have any comment about a serial killer on the loose?" The reporter was an inch or so shorter than Gilles, thin, wiry and fearless. He stood close to Gilles and held his cell phone in front of his face, recording their conversation.

Gilles ignored the question and asked one of his own. "How the fuck did you get here so fast?"

"Police scanner. Can you answer my question...please?" Yves-Pierre took a selfie of himself and Gilles.

"No comment," Gilles said. "Call the communications department."

Chapter 20

Gilles and Annie were up early, having had barely four hours of sleep. Annie left for the hospital and Gilles for the Major Crimes Division office at the same time, neither of them taking the time for breakfast.

On his way up to his office Gilles purchased a copy of *Le Journal de Montréal.* The photo on the front page was the one the reporter had taken the previous night. In the photograph Gilles had an angry look on his face—much the same as he'd had when he spotted the photograph on the newsstand. The headline read: L'Étrangleur - 5, Police - 0.

Once ensconced at his desk on the second floor of the Place Versailles shopping centre, a coffee and muffin in front of him, Gilles wrote up his report of the events of the previous night. He called the office of the crown prosecutor, Manon Tremblay, and left a message saying that he needed the transcript of a trial from twenty-five years ago and to please call him as soon as she got in.

He read the article by Yves-Pierre and was pleased that there was nothing in it to embarrass him personally. Gaston Lemieux arrived before the captain, so Gilles told him what he had discovered the previous evening, that Tiddley's father was a victim of Ian Chambers, as was at least one of the other victims of L'Étrangleur. He finished his report by saying, "J'attends un rappel de Manon. I want to get the transcript of the trial to see if all the victims are connected to it."

Gaston had pulled a chair into Gilles's cubicle. He rocked back slightly as he considered what Gilles had just told him. "Your murder and my serial killer are connected. The question is how and why."

"I think Toula Prodosiakis murdered Tiddley," Gilles said.

"What possible motive would she have?" Gaston asked

"My suspicion is that she left the front door to the house unlocked knowing that her father was likely to wander off and die of exposure. If this was true she would appear to be innocent. Tiddley knew what kinds of meds the old man was on and the likelihood that they could worsen Prodosiakis's dementia. If he suspected Toula and said something then she would have motive." Gilles said

"It's a bit of a stretch but I see your point," Gaston said. "How does that tie in with Tiddley's connection to the strangling victims?"

"That's my problem. I see a connection between the murders of Dr. Tiddley and George Prodosiakis, and there may be a connection to the stranglings and the murder of Dr. Tiddley in spite of the different methods. But there is no connection between the crimes of L'Étrangleur and the murder of Prodosiakis. There's something about the way his daughter acts that makes me very suspicious about her possible role in Tiddley's murder. That plus the evidence that she was the last or one of the last people to see him alive. She was up to something."

Gaston smiled and said, "Well, Gilles, you have a perfect conundrum. The proof of one disproves the other. If Toula Prodosiakis killed Tiddley to cover up her role in the death of her father then his death had nothing to do with L'Étrangleur. On the other hand, if the Tiddley murder had something to do with L'Étrangleur then Toula is off the hook, right?"

"Oui, exactement. That is until I question Toula Prodosiakis again and get some clarification. At the very least I think she's in some way implicated in the death of her father."

Captain Henri Lacroix arrived at the office just as Gilles and Gaston were finishing their conversation. Lacroix's demeanor was like that of an army officer. He was tall and stood ramrod straight. Gilles could picture him in a khaki uniform with battle ribbons on his chest. Lacroix was, as usual, dressed in a three-piece grey suit. He stopped to chat with Gilles and Gaston. This was unusual. Lacroix was not a chatty kind of boss. He had an old-school formality and kept a distance between himself and the people under his command. The only member of the team with whom he had a remotely friendly relationship was Gaston.

"Bonjour, Captain," Gaston said and got to his feet. Gilles got to his feet and echoed Gaston's greeting.

"Asseyez-vous," Lacroix said and patted the air down with his free hand—the other held a coffee. "What have you got?"

Gilles gave his boss a summary of what he and Gaston had been talking about. Lacroix kept his eyes on Gaston, expecting him to say something. Gilles finished his report by saying, "I'm going to bring Toula Prodosiakis in for questioning and maybe arrest her."

"Let me know when Manon gets you the information on the connection with L'Étrangleur. That was good police work. Lucky for you that your girlfriend was looking over your shoulder. And her daughter saved a woman's life. I should bring them both onto the force," Lacroix said.

Gilles thought that comment had ended their meeting, but Captain Lacroix remained leaning against the partition of Gilles's cubicle. He didn't say anything for an uncomfortable moment or two. Finally, he cleared his throat and said, "There are changes on their way, Gaston."

"Vraiment?" Gaston replied. "How do you mean?"

"Well, my time is up at the end of the month. I can retire at full pension."

"That will be too bad," Gaston said. "Do we know who'll be coming in?"

"No. They asked for my recommendation and I proposed you."

"I appreciate that," Gaston said. "But I think you know my feelings."

"Oui, that's what they said at HQ. They knew you weren't interested. That's what I mean by changes. HQ want diversity." Lacroix shrugged as if he was unclear on the meaning of the term. "The mayor, you know."

"Diversity isn't a bad thing, Captain," Gaston said.

"Yeah, I suppose. I think they're going to offer the job to Stéphanie."

"Giroux?" Gilles said. "Stéphanie Giroux?" She had joined Major Crimes shortly after Gilles and showed herself to be a hard worker, a team player, and an overall good investigator.

"Are you surprised?" Lacroix asked.

"At first, yeah," Gilles said. "But when you think about it, she's a good choice. She's taking night courses toward an MBA at the HEC. She likes organizational stuff."

"And the brass like her," Lacroix said. He went to his office.

"How do you feel?" Gaston asked Gilles. "You have a bit of seniority."

"Not a job for me no matter what. I like working cases too much. I don't think the brass know I'm alive."

"Not an altogether bad thing," Gaston said.

Gilles was about to say something when his desk phone rang. He looked at the display and said, "Manon," before he picked up the receiver. "Salut, Manon." Gilles explained what he needed. She told him that she would send him an email with the link to the transcript and a password so he could peruse it on line.

"It will be a couple of thousand pages," Manon explained. "Do you plan to read it all?"

"I know what I'm looking for, names of witnesses and victims, that kind of thing, so I'll be able to word-search most of it with the names of the victims. Thanks, Manon."

Gaston Lemieux had left Gilles's cubicle while he was on the phone with Manon Tremblay. Gilles went in search of him and told him that he would dig into the transcript of the Ian Chambers trial as soon as he could; in the meantime he planned to ask Annie what she knew about the case. "But first things first," Gilles said. "I'm on my way to see Toula Prodosiakis."

On his way out of the office Gilles ran into Stéphanie Giroux, who was arriving for work. He gave her a warm greeting which included a hug. "Qu'est-ce qu'il y a, Gilles?"

He didn't say anything.

Chapter 21

Gilles noticed that there were no customers in the store part of the Kathari dry-cleaning plant and there were only a couple of cars, one of them a Mercedes, in the parking lot. Gilles assumed that the Mercedes belonged to Toula. At the counter he asked for her by name. The employee made a call, said a couple of words in Greek and then spoke to Gilles. "Ms. Prodosiakis is not available. You'll have to make an appointment and come back."

Gilles smiled and shook his head slowly. In his experience it was an indication of guilt when someone he wanted to question tried to avoid him. He took the handcuffs from his belt and dangled them in front of the employee. "Call her back and tell her I'm here to arrest her and if she doesn't come to me then I'll go to her."

It was a bluff, of course, but the worried look on the employee's face told Gilles that it was a successful one. She had barely ended the call when Toula appeared behind the counter. She gave Gilles a hostile stare and said, "Arrested for what?"

"Why don't we talk in your office?" Gilles said.

Once settled in the office, Toula stared at Gilles, her black eyes unwavering, unblinking. Gilles responded to her stare with one of his own. After almost a minute of this Toula got to her feet and said, "If you have nothing to ask, the meeting is over. I'll show you out."

Gilles didn't move. "Sit down," he said. "I have some questions for you."

Toula made a dismissive noise and sat back down and resumed staring at Gilles.

"How well did you know Marcus Tiddley?" he asked.

Toula looked down at her desk and rearranged some of the things on it before she answered. More accurately, she asked a question of her own. "What makes you think I know him 'well'? Other than as a doctor, of course."

Gilles crossed his legs and leaned back in his chair. "What makes me think you knew him is the fact that you already told me that you had dinner with him on at least one occasion and we found some of your hair at his house, the scene of his murder. That's how."

Toula smiled. It had slipped her mind that Gilles knew about her dinner with Tiddley. "Funny, I don't remember giving you a DNA sample. So I can't imagine how you could possibly know if the hair samples you discovered were mine or not mine."

In spite of the fact that Toula was avoiding answering his questions, Gilles was enjoying the interrogation. She was a challenge and that would put a high value on any information he managed to get out of her. She preferred to evade rather than lie. He smiled. "I'll tell you how I know. I found some things with your brother's DNA in the garbage and the hair samples we found are those of a first-degree relative. The only one currently alive is you. But you make a good point. I'd like to take a sample to confirm or deny our conclusion." He reached into his pocket and pulled out an envelope containing a DNA testing swab in a tube. He held it up for Toula to see.

"Unless you've got a warrant in there you can put the thing back in your pocket."

Gilles waved the envelope gently back and forth a couple of times. "If you have nothing to hide this will help you."

"I'd very much like to meet a person who has nothing to hide. Including cops."

Gilles returned the test kit to his jacket pocket. "You already told me how you met Dr. Tiddley. I'd like to know more about your relationship with him."

"You assume a lot. But I'll tell you what I already told you. I met him at the hospital, in the ER, when I took my father in with some kind of flu."

"I see," Gilles said. "How long did your father stay in the hospital?"

"Just overnight."

"And when did you meet Tiddley?"

"In the morning, just before we left. He came to my father's room and told me that he had read his chart and wanted to talk to us about medications that might help with his dementia." Toula spoke calmly, as if she were recounting an event to a friend.

"And did he give you medications for your father?"

"Not then. He told me that he wanted to come to the house and give my father a thorough examination before prescribing anything. We made an appointment for the next day."

"It didn't strike you as odd that he was a doctor who made house calls?"

"I didn't really think about it. I made it clear that I wasn't going to drive my father back and forth to the hospital for something that 'might' help. He came over. Spent some time with my dad. Asked him a lot of questions and gave me some pills to give him. He also asked me to make notes about any changes in my father's behaviour."

"He came alone?"

"Yes."

Toula was silent.

"Dr. Tiddley—you still thought his name was Hingston at this point, right?—was at your house and gave you medications to give your father. Did he give you a prescription for more? How did that work? How many times a day was your father supposed to take them?"

"Yeah, Hingston. He told me to call him when I ran out. As I remember it my father was to take two pills a day. One in the morning and again in the evening. With meals both times."

"Dr. Tiddley came back to your house to check your father and gave you more drugs. Is that correct?"

"Yeah, that's it."

Gilles tried another approach. "I take it that following one of those visits he invited you out to dinner..." he paused until Toula was about to answer and then continued, "...to discuss your father's case."

Gilles expected Toula to blush. She didn't. She did however smile and say, "Yeah, that's right. I already told you. We went out to dinner." Toula flipped her hair. Gilles understood that a woman as beautiful as Toula probably had a large number of dinner invitations.

"More than once, I'm thinking."

Toula sighed, resigned to providing Gilles with the information he sought but determined to make him work for it. "Yeah, more than once." She emphasized her answer with another hair flip.

"At some point he invited you to his house, didn't he... for dinner?"

"Yes."

"Were you at his house on Sunday or Monday night for dinner, Indian food?"

"No. Not to my taste. We had a late brunch Sunday morning and I left."

"When was that?"

"I'm not certain. Some time between one and two," Toula said.

Gilles tapped his notebook against his thumbnail. "You know Jacques Chenier, right?"

Toula's eyes widened. She was surprised by the question. "Jacques Chenier. Yeah, he picks up the chemicals, his company does."

"You've visited his plant?"

"Yes. How is that important?"

Gilles narrowed his eyes and looked directly into Toula's eyes. "I'll tell you why it's important. Dr. Tiddley was poisoned and the poison may have come from ChimieVert."

"And you think that Jacques Chenier was handing out samples of poisons to all those who came to his office? Like free samples of perfume at a department store? That's nuts."

Toula was right, but Gilles chose not to tell her that he knew that she had been on her own during her visit and had plenty of opportunity to steal whatever chemicals she wanted. Gilles made another choice that turned out to be more consequential. His original plan had been to ask Toula a few preliminary questions and then bring her in to the division office for more formal questioning—with or without a lawyer—that would have been Toula's choice. His intent was to make her understand she was what the police called "a person of interest," or, more accurately, a suspect.

But now Gilles thought it better to keep his suspicions to himself and continue to question Toula in her office. There was the possibility that in a relaxed atmosphere, where she felt comfortable, she might let slip a useful piece of information. Toula's last comment was not exactly a denial.

"Nuts? I don't think so. All I meant was that you had access to poisons, not that Chenier was handing them out. But I want to get back to your relationship with Marcus Tiddley. How many times would you say you saw him socially?"

Toula gave Gilles a fleeting half-smile. "I can't say for certain. Maybe a dozen times. Maybe fewer. Certainly no more."

"These dates, did they take place at your house or his?"

"You're assuming a lot, Mr. Detective. Mostly they took place in restaurants. We went out to dinner. Sometimes we went out for drinks."

"But you also spent time at his house, right? And the last time you saw him was at his place, correct?"

"Yes. I already told you that," Toula said.

Gilles was silent for a moment or two, hoping she would add some more information. When none was forthcoming, he asked his question: "Am I correct in thinking that there was a good possibility that following your dinners out you returned to his place and that you stayed the night?"

Toula got to her feet, placed both hands on her desk and leaned forward so that she was looking down at Gilles. "You can assume anything you like, but one thing is certain, this visit is at an end."

Gilles remained seated and said, "Not quite. I have a couple more questions. Please sit down."

Toula sighed and did as she was asked.

"Did you or any member of your family have a connection to Ian Chambers?"

"What? Who the hell is he?"

"He worked at the Gursky twenty-five years ago and was convicted of murder," Gilles said.

"*Gia ónoma tou Theoú*, I was a child. I didn't have contact with anyone at the hospital twenty-five years ago and certainly not with a murderer."

"What about adult members of your family? Did anyone die in the hospital at that time? And don't bother lying. They keep records and we can check that kind of thing."

Toula got to her feet again and walked to the office door. "I told you, no. Now this meeting is really over. If you insist on staying, I'm calling my lawyer." She held the door open for Gilles.

Gilles got to his feet and politely thanked Toula for her time. He couldn't put his finger on it but he had a strong suspicion that there was a connection between Toula's interest in Tiddley and the death of her father. As he passed the service counter on the ground floor, he heard one of the employees talking on the telephone say, "Yes. He's leaving now."

The iconic orange ball that housed the Orange Julep drive-in restaurant dominated the skyline in this part of the city. Gilles hadn't been to the place since he was in high school and newly in possession of a driver's license. He decided to treat himself to the drink for which the place was famous and a couple of hot dogs. He felt he deserved an indulgence after fencing with Toula Prodosiakis.

Gilles was pleasantly surprised that the Orange Julep had not changed the recipe for its eponymous drink or the way in which it served hot dogs in spite of modern considerations with diet. He thoroughly enjoyed his guilty pleasure and hoped his stomach would not protest his choice.

Chapter 22

Gilles listened to the blues on the drive back to the office. The combination of music and the fact that he was on mental autopilot for the drive allowed him to consider what he had learned. It neither brought him any closer to solving the mystery of Tiddley's death nor eliminated Toula as a suspect. It occurred to Gilles that Toula might be implicated in the deaths of her father and Tiddley for reasons that had nothing to do with the meds he fed the old man.

Back at the office he got settled at his computer, a coffee close at hand. He checked his emails and found one from Manon Tremblay, the crown prosecutor, with the link to the transcript of the Chambers trial. He spent the rest of the afternoon giving a fast read, focusing on the names of the victims and witnesses at the trial. At this point in his investigation, he was not all that concerned with the details of the trial itself. He learned that all the victims had a connection to the trial.

As Gilles read the testimonies of the families of Chambers' victims he thought about the final days of his parents. He recalled the difficulty of being witness to their suffering as each of them approached the end of their lives. He knew that they would not have wanted heroic measures but he also knew that he would cherish forever the final hours he had spent, first with his father, and eight years later with his mother, as they slipped away. His father slipped into a coma as his life drew to a close. One of the nurses told him that even if he gave no sign his father could hear what Gilles said to him. Gilles spent the time telling his dad how much he loved him and appreciated all that he had done for him. He repeated the practice with his mother. Neither of his parents regained consciousness in their final hours but the sound of his voice seemed to relax them.

Thinking about his parents caused him to think of his own mortality and the need for a living will so as to spare Émilie from having to make an end-of-life decision for him.

He had learned of Tiddley's connection to the Chambers trial from his web search. Thanks to Annie's quick eye he now had a clue possibly connecting Tiddley's murder to the stranglings.

After a couple of hours of skimming through the transcript and in spite of the large coffee he consumed while doing it Gilles felt sleepy. He pushed his computer keyboard aside and rubbed his eyes. He texted Annie at work and suggested that they have dinner.

She agreed with a thumbs-up emoji and the time 7 p.m. This would give her a chance to get home and changed. Gilles picked her up at the agreed-upon time and suggested that they go for burgers and beer at the Burgundy Lion.

Annie smiled and said, "We're going to what is possibly the noisiest pub in Montreal? Why do I think you want some information without being overheard?"

"Coupable," Gilles said.

Once they were settled at the last available table with their beers, their orders placed, they continued the conversation they had started on the drive to the Burgundy Lion, which had to do with their days at work. In addition to the mundane, Annie had a lot of questions about Émilie and how she was coping with the attack on her mother.

"In a way that makes me super proud of her. She normally considers her weekends sacrosanct, her time to be with her friends. She is going to spend this weekend with her mother. No prompting from either of us."

Annie leaned forward to kiss Gilles. She stroked his hand and said, "Wonderful. But I'm not surprised. She's a great kid."

Once their cheeseburgers had been placed in front of them and a few bites consumed, Annie swirled a french fry in ketchup and popped it into her mouth. "Okay, Gilles, what did you want to ask me?"

"I need to know about the Chambers case. I have the transcript but I'd like to know if there was any hospital gossip, things that might not have come up at trial."

"Well," Annie said, "the whole thing happened just before I started at the Gursky, but it kind of became a touchstone. All kinds of procedures were put in place as a result of the killings. All non-medical staff had to sign a special sheet at the back of the chart whenever they were alone with a patient."

"Is the policy still in effect?"

"More or less, I'd say. Anyone who is in a patient's room, especially in Resus, is supposed to indicate their presence on a form in the chart. Just the time, date and reason for being in the room, along with a signature. The medical staff are careful in their charting but the non-medical staff don't always provide much in the way of information. Usually, a date and time and a scrawl of a signature. And the kitchen staff don't bother at all, they're in and out so fast."

"That's not really what I mean. Is there something you can tell me about Chambers that was not part of his trial?"

"Everyone who talked about him said pretty much the same thing. They were surprised by his actions. He was considered a compassionate human being who did his best for the patients he interacted with. The feeling was that he should have been a nurse. That's why we—well, they—were so surprised that he did what he did."

"That comes out in the transcript of the trial. His lawyer tried to present him as a person who acted to spare his patients further suffering."

"It's a decision doctors and nurses have difficulty making with the families of terminal patients, so it certainly wasn't his to make."

"In the transcript he's referred to as a family man but there's nothing about his family. Did he have children?"

Annie thought for a minute. "Yeah, two young children. A son and a daughter. And a wife, of course."

"What happened to them?"

"Don't know. Whenever the Chambers thing comes up the wife and kids are only mentioned as additional victims. As far as I know they left Montreal after the trial. Can't really blame them. Life must have been hell. Their kids were very young, and I seem to remember someone saying that they ended up in foster care. But I don't know if that's true or not."

"One last question and then I'm done with work. Is there any one of your friends at the hospital who knew him, worked with him, who might be able to give me more information?"

Annie drained her beer and said, "Yeah, I think Daniella worked with him. She might know more. She's been there a little longer than me."

"Okay, I may want to talk to her next week. I'll see."

They ordered a couple more beers and conversation turned away from crime to things they wanted to do. They'd been talking about taking some trips, including a long-postponed weekend in New York with their daughters.

Chapter 23

Émilie arrived at her mother's house at six and found her and a friend, Brigitte, in the living room enjoying a glass of wine. Émilie judged that they had killed a bottle of Pinot Grigio as both women seemed to be in excellent spirits, laughing like schoolgirls at something Brigitte had said just before Émilie arrived.

Brigitte had been Yvonne's neighbour for fifteen years and had known Émilie as long. Brigitte's children had been her playmates growing up. Émilie joined the women and said, "Vous semblez toutes les deux de bonne humeur. Is there any left for me?" Émilie picked up the bottle and showed the two women that it was empty.

"You'll have to open another, sweetie," Yvonne said.

Émilie retrieved a fresh bottle and a glass from the kitchen, refilled her mother's and Brigitte's glasses, and poured a drink for herself. She sat beside her mother and held her hand. Émilie could tell her mother was still feeling stressed beneath the Pinot-induced good feelings. "Do I smell a chicken roasting?" she asked.

"Brigitte and I spent the afternoon cooking. Roast chicken in a white wine sauce."

"Wonderful. Smells great."

Émilie and the two women spent a half hour or so catching up on her life as a student in the theatre department at UQAM and with the lives of Brigitte's two children. When the oven timer rang, they adjourned to the kitchen and sat down to eat. They ate slowly and were just about finished when there was a loud bang on the door. The three women jumped in their chairs, hearts beating rapidly. Émilie ran to the door and saw through the glass that it was Michel Genest. "Call 911," she shouted to her mother. She fastened the chain on the locked door as an extra precaution and ran back to the kitchen. Her mother and Brigitte were frozen in fear, so Émilie called 911 herself. The dispatcher asked how many people were in the house and told Émilie they should lock themselves in a bathroom. The cops would be there in five minutes maximum.

Émilie quickly got her mother and Brigitte to safety and looked around the kitchen for something to use to defend herself. There was a rolling pin on the counter. She picked it up and returned to the front door. Michel was screaming threats and had managed to break the door open a crack. All that prevented him from invading the house was the chain lock and it wouldn't take long for him to smash through the door. He was pushing at it. Émilie swung the rolling pin baseball-bat style and she could hear Genest's knuckles crack. He shrieked in pain and pulled his hand away. Émilie pushed the door closed with her shoulder. She leaned against it and called her father.

Gilles and Annie were close to his condo when he answered the call, "Âllo, Lapin. What's up?"

"It's Michel. He's trying to break into the house."

Terror for his daughter and ex-wife gripped Gilles for a moment and in spite of his police training he had trouble speaking for a couple of seconds. "Call the cops. I'll be there as fast as I can." He could hear Michel screaming, "You bitch. You broke my hand. I'll kill you."

"Are you safe?" Gilles asked.

"I called 911. The cops are on their way. I hear the sirens."

"I'm almost at the bridge. I won't be long," Gilles told his daughter.

When Gilles and Annie arrived at Yvonne's house they found the Longueuil police in control of the situation. One of the cops was standing on the doorstep talking to Émilie, who still had the rolling pin in her hand. Gilles and Annie rushed up to her and enfolded her in a hug. He looked into the house and saw that Yvonne and Brigitte were standing next to one another, their arms around each other's waists, eyes wide with fear, the colour drained from their faces.

"Where is the son of a bitch?" Gilles asked the cop at the door.

"L'ambulance," he said, and indicated the ambulance parked on the street in front of the house with a nod of his head.

"What the fuck? Why isn't he in cuffs?"

"He will be, as soon as he's bandaged." Émilie held up the rolling pin and the cop explained that her fast thinking had prevented Genest from harming the women. Annie stroked Émilie's hair and whispered words of support. She noticed that Yvonne and her friend appeared to be in shock and she went into the house to see if she could help them.

Gilles strode to the ambulance and hopped into the back of it where the EMT was taping Genest's hand. Gilles flashed his badge and with a nod of his head indicated that the EMT was to leave. When he hesitated, Gilles said, "The police have a question for you."

The EMT shrugged and left the ambulance.

Gilles pulled the door shut. He grabbed Michel Genest's wounded hand and gave it a hard squeeze. Gilles was indifferent to Genest's shriek of pain and pallid colour. "What did I tell you, shithead?" Genest couldn't have spoken even if he'd wanted to. Gilles leaned in close without releasing his grip and whispered, "I can kill you and they'd never find the body. Are we clear?" Genest, eyes wide, tears running down his cheeks, nodded.

"On Monday I expect to see a for sale sign in your yard and you gone. Clear?" Genest nodded again.

Gilles released Genest's hand and left the ambulance. The EMT and two cops took charge of Genest. He was led in cuffs to a cop car. The senior officer at the scene approached Gilles and took him aside for a private conversation.

"Écoute, Bellechasse, I don't need to know what took place in the ambulance, but it would be best if nothing further happened to Genest."

Gilles nodded and said, "I think he'll be moving out of the neighbourhood very soon."

"Thanks to your daughter I think his days of being a dentist are over."

"Yeah," Gilles agreed. He returned to his daughter. He found her with her mother, Brigitte and Annie.

Annie was speaking softly to the women. She got up and went to Gilles and told him, "Yvonne and her friend were in a state of shock but are fine now. Heart rate returning to normal. I'm a little worried about Émilie."

"Her fast thinking prevented what could have been a tragedy," Gilles said.

"Right. And she's not showing much of a reaction at the moment. There will likely be a delayed reaction of some kind. I think she should be with us, not left alone with her mother and her friend."

Gilles pulled a chair up close to Yvonne, Brigitte, and Émilie. He leaned in close to them and said quietly, "Listen. I don't think you should stay here tonight." He looked at Yvonne. "Can you stay at Brigitte's? I can assure you, you won't be bothered by Genest. He'll be in jail for the weekend. I'll drive Émilie home and she'll be with us all weekend."

"Non, pa. Je resterai avec Maman," Émilie said. "If that's okay with Brigitte."

Brigitte put one arm around her friend, the other around Émilie, and said, "Don't worry, Gilles. Yvonne and Émilie can stay with us for as long as necessary."

Chapter 24

In order to show his appreciation for all that she had done for his daughter and ex-wife, Gilles did his best to pamper Annie over the weekend. This included a nice dinner and letting her sleep in on Sunday morning while he prepared breakfast. He even went so far as to help her with household chores. Pamela wasn't aware of the full extent of the events of the preceding couple of days but she guessed that something serious had occurred. She knew that Gilles hated housekeeping.

He got back to his condo on Sunday evening in time to watch *Tout le monde en parle* and have pizza with Émilie.

The last thing he did before turning in for the night was call Yvonne to ensure that the repairs had been made to her front door. The conversation did not go quite as Gilles had expected.

"Tu sais, Gilles, I feel like crap. I don't think I'll ever feel safe again. Not completely safe," Yvonne said.

"I understand. I can get you help if you like. We have a list of therapists we refer people to in cases of domestic violence."

"That's all that you have to offer? How about you fuck yourself."

Gilles was surprised that Yvonne was directing her anger at him. He was about to say something conciliatory when she continued, "I blame you. This never would have happened if you hadn't left us. And then you took Émilie and left me all alone. So, yeah, fuck you."

Gilles did his best to control his own anger. "It wasn't my idea to leave. You forget that you gave me an impossible choice. Have you forgotten that you told me, 'la force ou la maison'? What was I supposed to do?"

"Choose your family," Yvonne replied.

"Your selective amnesia isn't going to help the situation. I did choose my family, but I'm a cop. That's all I ever wanted to be and that's what I was when you married me and when Émilie was born. You knew what I was. You decided that you didn't want to be a cop's wife and you also knew that giving me an ultimatum would push me out the door."

Given Yvonne's fragile state Gilles didn't want to end the phone call on the unpleasant note of the argument that he and Yvonne had had countless times. Speaking softly, he said, "Of course this weekend has been hard for you. I understand. But Genest won't come near you again. I'm pretty certain that his house will be on the market on Monday. And Émilie and I are here for you."

"Oui, Gilles, if you say so." Yvonne ended the call.

Gilles watched a *Law and Order* rerun on Amazon Prime and sipped a gin and tonic to help him relax.

Chapter 25

Alain Patenaude's condo was located on Hutchison between Villeneuve and St. Joseph. Before it was renovated and converted to condos, the building housed inexpensive apartments that, in the 1950s and 1960s, were home to immigrants and students. The building was located a block and a half from the chic boutiques and restaurants on Laurier Avenue and a short walk to the less expensive, less fashionable shops on Park Avenue. Alain got back to his condo following his morning run on Mount Royal at about 6:30. He pulled off his gloves, his toque and runner's jacket and the other layers that had kept him warm on this cold morning. He left his runner's fuel belt, so-called because it held half a dozen small bottles of water, on the kitchen counter and headed for the shower. Warm and refreshed, dressed in his bathrobe, he made himself a healthy smoothie and looked at the headlines in *Le Devoir* while he drank it.

By eight o'clock he was on Park Avenue waiting for the number 80 bus that would take him to the law office where he worked. He looked north and saw the bus was on its way. Before the bus got to the corner of St. Joseph where Alain was in line waiting for it, he collapsed. He bumped into the woman standing next to him as he fell. The weight of his body caused her to fall as well. Alain landed on top of her. "Monsieur," she shouted but received no answer. "Aidez-moi," she shouted when she realized that Alain had fainted.

A couple of the other passengers rushed to her as the bus pulled up to the stop. Someone helped the woman to her feet and called 911. The operator asked for details and the caller could only say that a man had passed out and was in distress, coughing and drooling.

Minutes later the ambulance arrived. A police cruiser on its regular patrol on Park Avenue stopped to direct traffic. Alain was loaded into the ambulance and had an oxygen mask placed over his mouth and nose. The ambulance turned right on St. Joseph and then onto Côte-Ste-Catherine, siren blaring. The EMT beside Alain tried to get information from him as he applied the blood pressure cuff to his arm, but Alain was unconscious.

The ambulance radioed ahead to the Gursky Memorial Hospital that they were on their way with a patient in serious distress. Annie and Stavros, the orderly on duty, rushed to the ambulance as it pulled into the bay. The EMTs pulled the gurney out of the ambulance and they and Annie and Stavros took an involuntary step backward as Alain suffered an attack of diarrhea.

All four held their breath as they wheeled Alain to a triage room. "Blood pressure," Annie called to the EMT, trying not to inhale through her nose. "Eighty-eight over fifty-eight," he called back.

As they turned the corner into the triage room, Annie noticed that the patient was drooling and sweating. She felt his forehead and found his temperature was seriously elevated. Dr. Rosen rushed to assist. Annie applied chest compressions. She paused for the couple of seconds it took to attach the EKG contacts. "We're losing him," Rosen called. He grabbed the paddles of the defibrillator, called "clear" and shocked Alain's heart. The EKG beeped the monotone of a flat line. "One more time," Rosen shouted. "Increase the voltage." He shocked Alain's heart one more time. There was no response. Rosen sighed and said, "I'm calling it."

Stavros wheeled Alain to a holding area. Annie, Dr. Rosen, and the EMTs went to the small room where the EMTs wrote up their reports. "What the hell happened?" Rosen asked.

"He was on the sidewalk when we got there," one of the EMTs said. "Unresponsive, sweating and drooling. A mess."

"I've never seen this combination of symptoms," Annie said. She looked at Dr. Rosen and asked, "How about you?"

"Not in this combination. God, the stench."

"I'm calling Gilles," Annie said. "This is something more than a cardiac crisis or some other physiological event."

⊙

Gilles got to the Major Crimes Division office at a couple of minutes after eight. The squad was gathering for the regular Monday team meeting in the open area at the rear of the squad room. Gilles noticed that there was an urn of coffee and a selection of doughnuts and muffins on a long table that had been set up at the rear of the room. This was unusual and indicated that something special was about to happen. Captain Lacroix came into the room. He stood at the front of it for a moment or two, which allowed those present to finish their conversations and turn to face him. He cleared his throat and said, "I have an important announcement to make." He paused for a couple of seconds and continued, "I've put in my papers and I'll be retiring at the end of the month." Those in attendance made comments of dismay. Lacroix had been their boss for as long as any of them could remember. They liked the man and respected his leadership.

"C'est assez," he said, raising his voice above the din. "I'll be here for another month to help with the transition. My replacement has been chosen." At this point all the cops in the room turned their attention to Gaston Lemieux, the expected replacement for Henri Lacroix. Gaston betrayed no emotion. His lack of acknowledgement caused a short buzz of babble. "As I am certain you are aware," Captain Lacroix continued, "the selection of a squad commander is never easy and the brass and I made certain to choose someone who was devoted to the high standards we've established and is blue to her core. I'm pleased to announce that the new commander is Lieutenant Stéphanie Giroux. Please join me, Lieutenant Giroux." He extended an arm and Stéphanie strode to the front of the room and stood beside Captain Lacroix. The cops were silent at first. The silence was followed by surprised chatter and then applause led by Gaston Lemieux.

"Help yourselves to coffee and snacks and we'll get on with the morning briefing," Lacroix said. "As her first official act, Lieutenant Giroux will conduct it." Lacroix moved away from the podium to make space for Stéphanie.

The cops settled down with their coffees and snacks and Giroux began her briefing. She was no more than a dozen words into it when Gilles's cellphone rang. He was about to refuse the call when he noticed it was from Annie.

Giroux looked up from her notes and said, "Gilles..."

Gilles blushed, embarrassed by the interruption. He knew Annie would not call unless it was important so he walked to a corner of the room where he could take the call without disturbing the rest of the squad. A moment later he returned to his place and waited for the lieutenant to finish what she was saying. He caught her eye and nodded so she would know he had something to report. "Okay, Gilles, what've you got?"

"Something very suspicious, possible poisoning," he said and then reported what Annie had told him about the patient who had just died in Triage.

Stéphanie said, "Take the call. Someone will catch you up on the briefing when you get back." She held up her cellphone, indicating that she expected a report as soon as he had some information.

On his way to his car Gilles called dispatch to see what they had and to let them know he was on the case. He told them to have the uniformed cops who answered the call get information on and from any witnesses and to remain on the scene until he could speak to them.

He arrived at the entrance to the Emergency Department just after nine.

Annie was waiting for him. She led him to the room where the body lay on a stretcher covered with a white sheet. Gilles got two paces into the room when he hit the overpowering stench. He took three steps backward out of the room. "Christ, what happened to him?"

"I don't know, but whatever it was wasn't normal, by which I mean something physiological that would explain why he died. That's why I called. This poor guy was poisoned," Annie said.

"Okay, I get that. Are the EMTs still here? I want to talk to them before I check the victim again."

"They're in the room we have for Urgences-santé." Gilles followed her to the small room in the corridor that led to the ambulance bay. The two EMTs were completing their report. Gilles identified himself and asked, "Did the vic say anything while you had him in your truck?"

"Rien," one of the EMTs replied. "Nothing intelligible anyway. Just a lot of groaning at first. Obviously in pain and then nothing."

"We've had patients die on us," the second EMT said, "so we've seen it all, but never something like this."

"You mean the smell?"

"No, that happened here. I mean the pallor along with the sweating. You'd think someone emptied a bucket of water on him."

Gilles took the names and ID numbers of the EMTs and said, "I may want to talk to you later, and I'm sure the medical examiner will have questions. I'm going to call him now."

Gilles requested that a medical examiner be sent to the Gursky. He was told Dr. Lapointe would be there as soon as he could be located. Dr. Lapointe taught in the medical faculty at the University of Montreal and was sometimes hard to track down if he was teaching. The cop at the call centre asked where to send the forensics team. "I don't know yet. I'll call you back."

He turned to the EMTs and asked, "Did you get ID?"

"No, like I said, he was unresponsive, and we had bigger issues to deal with."

Gilles sighed and said, "Then I guess I'll have to try to find it."

One of the EMTs offered Gilles a small jar of Vicks VapoRub. Gilles smiled and pulled out his own vial of the stuff and showed it to the EMTs. "Not my first time."

Gilles applied a generous blob of the strong-smelling substance to his upper lip and handed the jar to Annie. She smiled and said, "You think? You're on your own."

Annie remained at the threshold of the room swinging the door back and forth on its hinges, hoping to create some circulation. Gilles pulled medical gloves from the dispenser next to the door, slipped them on and went in. He lifted the sheet at its mid-point and patted the victim's pockets looking for a wallet. He didn't find anything. He noticed that the victim's suit jacket had been thrown across his feet and he found a wallet in the inner breast pocket. He checked the other pockets and found a card case. He brought them out to the hallway to examine them.

Its contents were typical of a man's wallet. There were credit cards and in a see-through pocket at the bottom of the wallet the vic's driver's license. It identified him as Alain Patenaude with an address on Hutchison. The cards in the card case confirmed his identity and had the added information that he was a lawyer with the firm Sevigny, Stein LLP.

Gilles stopped what he was doing and thought for a minute. Annie recognized the look and asked, "What is it?"

Gilles showed her the driver's license in the wallet and said, "I know that name."

Annie looked at the photo and said, "Well, I can confirm that's the patient."

Gilles was lost in thought for another moment or two, his eyes closed, his lips, pursed, moving in an out. "Got it," he said and snapped his fingers. "The judge in the Chambers case was Patenaude. They could be related."

Gilles called the Major Crimes Division office and spoke to Stéphanie. He explained the situation and was about to tell her to check to see if the judge in the Chambers case was related to his victim. He caught himself and said, "Would it be possible for someone to check to see if the judge was related in some way to an Alain Patenaude?" Gilles gave the victim's age and other identifying information he found on the driver's license.

Lieutenant Giroux said she'd put someone on it and get back to him. Gilles called dispatch and told them where to send the forensics team. He was told that Dr. Lapointe was on his way. Gilles said he would meet the forensics team at Patenaude's condo. He then asked to be dispatched through to the cops at the scene, the spot where Patenaude had passed out.

The cop at the scene reported that no one knew Patenaude. He fell over and one of them called an ambulance. "We have names, addresses and phone numbers and we checked ID. You can speak to them if you need to."

"Good work. Let them go about their business and you get to the victim's condo. It can't be more than a block or two away. Identification judiciaire is on the way. Secure the place. I'll get there as soon as I can."

Annie had returned to the triage area where she gave her hands a thorough washing and was about to see a patient when Gilles came in through the back door. "Sorry, chérie. I have a few questions before Lapointe gets here."

Daniella, the other nurse on triage duty, gave Annie a thumbs-up sign and called the next patient. Annie and Gilles found a corner in the area behind Triage. "Lapointe is going to want to know how you concluded that Patenaude was murdered and not sick," he said.

Annie leaned against an empty desk and said, "It's very rare to see the combination of symptoms he showed. I think I can count on the fingers of one hand the number of times I've seen that kind of drooling and sweating on a patient. Plus the explosive diarrhea just before he died. His body was reacting to a powerful agent. He was poisoned. And not all that long before he collapsed."

"I don't suppose you can think what poison it was?"

"Hardly. We don't see all that many cases but I can tell you it's not cyanide or strychnine or one of the common ones. We know the symptoms. There's new stuff being invented every day and maybe this was one of those."

Gilles had been making notes and he slid his notebook back into his pocket. "I'll wait for Lapointe in the waiting room so you can get back to work." Annie returned to the triage desk. Gilles paced near the door to the Emergency

Department in order to catch Dr. Lapointe when he came in.

He didn't have to wait long. Dr. Lapointe was bundled into a Kanuk overcoat, the bottom of his lab coat flapping against his shins as he walked. He shook Gilles's hand and said, "You and your girlfriend are developing the bad habit of finding victims. What is it this time?"

Gilles gave Dr. Lapointe a brief rundown on what he knew so far, and led the medical examiner to the room where the corpse of Alain Patenaude lay. Gilles offered some of his Vicks VapoRub to the doctor, but Lapointe refused. "Years of practice, Gilles. I don't want to smell Vicks for the rest of the day."

Lapointe found a place to leave his overcoat, pulled a mask and gloves from the wall dispensers, and went into the room. He paused at the threshold for a second. "Mon Dieu, that's an awful stench. Worse than I expected." He gave the body a onceover and asked, "Any visible wounds or signs of violence?"

"No. I checked as best as I could," Gilles said. "And the EMTs didn't see any either."

"I need to talk to Annie, then I'll have the body moved to the lab for further examination. . . and cleaning."

Gilles and Dr. Lapointe found Annie in the triage area, just finishing typing notes into the computer. They waited for her patient to return to the waiting room. Dr. Lapointe greeted Annie warmly and asked, "Had the victim evacuated before he came in?"

"No, he waited until he was in Triage," Annie replied.

"Which means he was still..." Dr. Lapointe started to say.

"Alive. Right." Annie finished his sentence. "But just barely and not conscious."

"You diagnosed poison and not natural causes?"

"Yes," Annie said. "Low blood pressure, sweating and drooling, and then the diarrhea. I don't know which poison caused this but I'd be surprised if I was wrong."

"I agree," Dr. Lapointe said. "Well done. We'll have to run a lot of tests to determine which poison caused death, but we'll figure it out."

Dr. Lapointe turned to Gilles and asked, "Do you know anything else about the victim?"

"He's a lawyer, thirty-nine years old. Alain Patenaude."

"Really? Alain Patenaude? Do you know the name of the firm he was with? Was it Sevigny, Stein?"

"How could you know that? Did you know the victim?"

"No, I knew his mother. The original name of the firm was Patenaude, Sevigny, Stein. The name changed when Louise Patenaude was made a judge. I knew about her son but had never met him."

Gilles and Dr. Lapointe retrieved their coats and found an unoccupied corner of the waiting room. "I recognized the name and asked my boss to check to see if he was related to Judge Patenaude. There may be a connection to another case."

"What case is that?"

"There's a series of murders that is linked to a murder trial that took place twenty-five years ago. Judge Patenaude presided. It was the Chambers case. He was an orderly here who killed a number of elderly patients. He claimed it was to mercifully end their suffering."

"Oui, je me souviens. The case was famous at the time. What's the connection?"

"There's been a series of murders—well, one of them was an attempted murder—of people connected to witnesses who testified at Chambers' sentencing. They were strangled on the street, with one exception, Dr. Tiddley. He was also poisoned."

"I was at the scene on that one as well," Lapointe reminded Gilles. "You have your work cut out for you. In my experience it is rare for a murderer to change MO, to go from strangling to poison."

"I'm going to meet the forensics team at Patenaude's condo. Maybe there's something there that will shed light on the perpetrator or perpetrators."

"On espère," Dr. Lapointe said. "I'm going to have the body removed. I'll let you know when I find something."

At Patenaude's condo on Hutchison, the Identification judiciaire van was parked in front and the three technicians were having a smoke and drinking coffee from cardboard cups. It was a cold, damp and cloudy day; not good weather for standing outside. Gilles marvelled at the inconveniences smokers put up with in order to damage their lungs. The two cops were smarter; they were enjoying a coffee in the warmth of their car. They told Gilles that they had tried the obvious approach—ringing the buzzer of Patenaude's condo. There was no answer. They located the concierge and told him to be prepared to open the door when required.

"Not necessary," Gilles said. "I retrieved the keys from the victim's pocket." He signalled to the forensics team to join him in the lobby. He rang at the concierge's apartment, identified himself, and told him that they had keys for Patenaude's condo. It was now a crime scene and no one was to enter.

Gilles and the forensics crew made their way to the ground floor unit. The uniformed cops joined them, bringing yellow police tape with them in order to seal the apartment.

One of the forensics team handed Gilles a bunny suit and booties and they went into Patenaude's condo. Gilles did a walk-through to see if there were signs either of a struggle or of Patenaude having been sick, but found nothing. The apartment consisted of one bedroom, a smaller room which was used as a study, a large open living room–dining room area and a galley kitchen. He spotted the blender and glass in the sink, both filled with water, and the runner's fuel belt on the counter. He told one of the forensics people to bag and tag those items.

Gilles wandered through the condo doing his best to keep out of the way of the forensics technicians. The bedroom was at the back and overlooked an alley. The forensics people were working their way from the front to the back of the condo, so they had not yet inspected the bedroom. Gilles stood at the doorway and looked around the room. It contained a queen size bed, a long dresser with four banks of four drawers each, a dumb valet and an easy chair. The dresser was opposite the bed. Gilles opened the cupboard door next to the dresser with a gloved hand and found himself looking at a large custom-designed closet the size of a small room. Patenaude's suits were hung neatly, arranged by colour. Shirts and sweaters were stacked on shelves, the ties arranged on tie racks. Sports jackets, blazers, and slacks had their own section. A full-length mirror was attached to the door.

Gilles dressed according to the demands of his job and didn't concern himself with his wardrobe beyond that. In spite of this he was impressed by Alain Patenaude's closet. He gave the carpeted floor an examination but noticed only that it appeared to be spotless. If there were any clues in the carpet, the forensics crew would discover them.

Gilles turned his attention to the bed. It was neatly made and there were no stray hairs on either of the double pillows lying side by side. Gilles lifted the corner of the comforter on the side he concluded, from the placement of the alarm clock and a book on the bedside table, was the side Patenaude slept on. Nothing visible there. He thought for a couple of seconds and walked around to the other side of the bed. If Patenaude had company, Gilles reasoned, they would sleep on the other side of the bed. Gilles lifted the comforter. Nothing in the way of evidence was visible—not to the naked eye, at any rate. A more thorough inspection by the forensics team might yield a different result. Gilles was about to leave the bedroom when he had an idea. Holding the corner of the top pillow he carefully lifted it and was rewarded with the discovery of some blonde hairs lying on the second pillow. He moved the top pillow to the side, took a photo of the hairs and replaced the pillow. On his way out of the condo he told the leader of the forensics team about his discovery.

Chapter 26

Back at the Major Crimes Division Gilles found half a dozen of his colleagues hanging out in the break room drinking coffee. Gilles poured himself a cup of what passed for coffee in the break room. He'd forgotten to buy the good coffee on offer in the shopping centre. He was about to head to his cubby to write up his notes on the Patenaude murder when one of the cops asked him, "Vous avez travaillé avec Giroux plus que nous autres, n'est-ce pas?"

"Oui, mais. . ." Gilles said. He guessed that the cop who asked the question wanted to pump him for information about their new boss. Gilles wanted to avoid office gossip on the topic of Giroux's promotion.

"Well, tell us, how the fuck did she manage to get promoted over everybody? Gaston has been here the longest. Christ, even you've been here longer than her."

The others voiced their agreement, some being louder and more vulgar than others.

Gilles was taken aback by the vehemence of the comment—it was hardly a question. Gilles was the least senior of the group in the break room and over the three or so years since he had been promoted to the division he had tried to get along with the rest of the team. He realized that Stéphanie had made less of an effort than he had and so the guys didn't know her. "Well, you know," Gilles said, "I'm sure Captain Lacroix and the brass had their reasons."

The cops in the break room wanted to continue the conversation but Gilles didn't. "I've got a report to write," he said and went to his desk, ignoring the sound effects of kissing from behind him.

Later that evening after he and Annie had finished dinner and the washing up, they were enjoying a final glass of wine. Gilles told Annie about the conversation he had had with his fellow cops.

Annie didn't say anything for a while as she swirled the wine in her glass. Finally she looked at Gilles and said, "You know, honey, I'm a little disappointed in you."

Gilles blushed and said, "Me? What did I do? Nothing. I tried to change the subject."

"That's what I mean. You know Stéphanie better than the rest of those guys. You should have defended her. She got the job because she earned it. Maybe those other guys aren't as sharp as she is, did that ever occur to them? Or to you?"

Annie had met Stéphanie Giroux on a couple of occasions and liked her. In a way they were kindred spirits—smart and hard-working.

"Well, they had a point, sort of," Gilles said. "Lemieux has more seniority."

"Really? And does he want the job?"

"No way. He could have had it before Lacroix if he had wanted it."

"You understand that women have to work twice as hard to get half as far as men, don't you?"

"Yeah, but promoting someone because the downtown brass wants some diversity is just as wrong, no?"

"No. Look, I don't know Stéphanie as well as you do, but if she didn't think she could do the job she wouldn't have taken it. Maybe she really is the best person for the job. She's been a woman a lot longer than she's been a cop and she knows full well that if she makes mistakes she'll be blamed for them in a way that a man, Lacroix for example, wouldn't be. You can bet that she knows she's under a spotlight and I think it would be a good idea if her friends stuck up for her. Get it?"

Gilles stared at his wine glass as if he could find something to say in it. This *vino* didn't produce anything in the way of *veritas* to contradict anything Annie had said.

"Now that you point it out, it's more than likely that the brass are hiding behind the diversity thing to avoid blowback from the troops. Stéphanie is probably one of the few cops on the force that has management training. I'll do better next time. And you can be sure there'll be a next time."

Annie's smile told Gilles that she expected no less from him.

Chapter 27

Gilles got to the division office at nine Tuesday morning and if he didn't know better, he would have sworn that that same group of cops was in the break room, gossiping. The members of the group were in fact different but the gossip was the same. Gilles poured himself a coffee and joined his colleagues. One of them was complaining that Stéphanie had been unhappy with a report he had written.

"Suis-je censé être écrivain ou flic?"

Gilles was about to say something sympathetic in support of his fellow detective when he remembered his conversation with Annie. He also noticed that the complaining cop referred to Stéphanie Giroux, now Lieutenant Giroux, by her first name. The normal way of referring to the commander was "the boss" or something similar. There were times when members of the squad referred to the commander by their rank. Gilles hadn't previously realized that it was these little things that made it difficult for women, once they had achieved a measure of success, to gain the respect that went with it.

Gilles inhaled through his nose and said, "You know, I've known Giroux from our days on patrol and she's been my partner on any number of cases since we both joined the division. She's conscientious and always gives her best. And it's true she wants reports to be clear and complete. I can't tell you how many times she corrected my, well, my writing."

"And it didn't bother you?"

"Yeah, at first it did. But when I followed her advice, I realized that our reports were the better for it and the captain appreciated not having to ask a lot of questions to understand what was going on. I once overheard Lacroix tell her that if all the reports he had to read were as good as hers it would save him hours he spent getting things clarified. Probably one of the reasons she was promoted."

The complaining cop stared at Gilles and said, "Tabernac, Gilles," and made kissing sounds.

"Really?" Gilles said. "All I know is that time is too precious to waste having to do things twice."

While they were talking, Gaston Lemieux joined the group. He was the one everyone had expected to get promoted when Captain Lacroix put in his retirement papers, in spite of the fact that he had on any number of occasions made it clear that he had no interest in administration. He heard the last bit of conversation and had no trouble surmising the rest—he was a detective after all. "Is this a schoolyard or a squad room?" he asked. He didn't say anything else. He poured himself a coffee and left.

"Break room, not squad room," the complaining cop said, making a weak joke in order to save face. The cops returned to their desks.

Gilles wrote a report on the Patenaude murder and sent it to Lieutenant Giroux when it was done.

He called forensics to see if they had anything to report. "It's too soon. Give us a day or two," he was told.

"What about the hairs on the pillow?" Gilles asked. "Anything there?"

"That I can tell you. They're synthetic, from a wig. More than that, nothing. We'll call you."

His next call was to Dr. Lapointe to see if he knew what kind of poison had been administered to Patenaude.

"Patience, Gilles," Lapointe told him. "I did some research on the symptoms and it looks like it's something called VX poison. I'll know more when we do an autopsy and run some tests. It looks to me like it's the same stuff that killed Tiddley."

Gilles thanked the doctor and went to see Lieutenant Giroux to give her the updates that, he realized, should have been in his report.

"I'm reading your report," she said when Gilles appeared at the door to her office. "It's very well written." She smiled.

"I have a little more to add," Gilles said. "It's not conclusive but suggestive."

"So, not in your report?"

"Right. Forensics is pretty certain that the hairs on the pillow in Patenaude's bedroom were synthetic, from a wig."

"The same as the ones found at the Tiddley crime scene?"

"Don't know. And I won't know until they've done the full workup. I don't know if they can match synthetics. Also, Lapointe is pretty certain the poison is something called VX. He too will know more after the autopsy and more tests."

Giroux made some notes and said, "Okay, Gilles. What are your next steps?"

Gilles raised a forefinger and said, "First a visit to Patenaude's office to see if I can learn anything there." He held up the second finger. "And then a trip to Chimie-Vert to see if they have the poison in question."

"And if they do?"

"Toula Prodosiakis had been poking around there. She may have found a way to swipe some. When I talk to the people at Patenaude's firm I'll see if there's some kind of connection to her."

"Keep me posted," Giroux said and returned to reading on her computer screen.

Driving in Montreal is difficult at the best of times, requiring the skill of a slalom skier and a stock car driver to avoid the orange cones on the city's streets. Gilles parked on Drummond and walked to the forty-seven-storey high-rise where Sevigny, Stein had its offices. The building was part of the last wave of high-rise construction that added office towers, hotels, and condos to René-Lévesque Boulevard, all within a stone's throw of the Bell Centre, the home of the Montreal Canadiens. Gilles only had to leap one snowbank and two slush puddles to get from his parking spot to the front door of the building. The security guard at a desk in the lobby directed him to the twenty-ninth floor. The elevator opened to the law firm's reception area. Gilles had many years previously formed the conclusion that the size of a firm's waiting room was an indicator of the fees the firm charged its clients. The Sevigny, Stein waiting room was enormous.

The reception desk was to the right of the elevators. There was a curved staircase in the centre of the room that led to offices on the floor above. Gilles counted at least half a dozen seating areas organized for privacy, each comfortably accommodating four people on chairs and a small couch around a coffee table.

Gilles identified himself to the receptionist. She stared at his ID and looked up at him as if making certain he was the same person pictured in the photo. In a soft voice she said, "I suppose you're here about poor Alain Patenaude." She sniffled.

"Yes. Is there someone in charge I can talk to?"

"I'll call Ellen Schwartz, she's the managing partner. She's probably the best person to speak to. Why don't you sit down?"

Gilles removed his coat and made himself comfortable at the seating area closest to the receptionist, facing the staircase. He didn't have to wait more than five minutes before he heard footsteps on the stairs. He looked up and saw a woman with short blonde hair wearing a black pantsuit and white blouse descending. "Are you the detective?" she asked. Gilles got to his feet and they shook hands. "I'm Ellen Schwartz," she said. "I understand you're here about poor Alain."

"Yes. Is there somewhere we can talk?"

"There's a conference room." She turned to the receptionist and asked, "Is number one available?" The receptionist nodded and Ellen led Gilles to a small meeting room that opened onto the reception area.

"How did you find out about Patenaude's death?" Gilles asked when they were seated at the meeting room table. He threw his coat over an empty chair.

"Alain's secretary, Delphine, got the call from the hospital. She reported it. It didn't take long for the bad news to circulate."

"What were you told?"

"I heard that he had an attack of some sort while waiting for the bus? That's horrible. It makes no sense. Alain was in great shape. He ran marathons. Terrible." She paused for a moment and looked at Gilles. "If you think an investigation is warranted, you must think there's more to it than an emergency health issue?"

"Yes. We think he was poisoned. That's why I'm here."

"That makes no sense. Who would want to poison Alain? Everyone liked him." Ellen made little circles on the table with her index finger.

Gilles placed his notepad on the table and said, "That's my first question. Is there anyone who didn't get along with him?"

"No. I told you. He was well-liked."

"How about someone from one of his cases?"

"That's almost funny. Lawsuits can be contentious, but rarely spill out of the courtroom. Offhand, I can't think of any work he did that would generate that kind of feeling."

"Can you check?"

"I can check, but there's very little I can tell you about the legal work we do. You understand, don't you?"

Gilles understood perfectly. It was easier to break the seal of the confessional than to get a lawyer to betray a client's confidential information. This in spite of the fact that lawyers were among the world's worst gossips—all off the record of course. "Yes, but..." He didn't continue as another idea occurred to him. "Do you know if he had any cases dealing with anyone by the name of Prodosiakis?"

"The name doesn't ring a bell but I can check." There was a credenza with a computer on it against the back wall of the room. Ellen tapped the enter key to bring it to life and typed the name, which Gilles spelled out for her, into the computer.

"There is something from several years ago. A case involving Kathari Dry Cleaners. Does that mean anything to you? Someone by that name was the owner."

"Yes, exactly. Toula Prodosiakis, right?"

"George Prodosiakis, actually."

"What was the case about?" Gilles's eyes widened slightly and he smiled indicating he was pleased he had so quickly found a connection between Toula Prodosiakis and Alain Patenaude. He hoped Maître Schwartz did not take his reaction to be callousness.

Ellen hit the enter key and read the contents of the file. She returned to the table and said, "Under normal circumstances I couldn't discuss this, but the case was settled so long ago I don't think there'll be a problem. But Alain wasn't involved in it. Let me talk to the lawyer who was."

She used the phone next to the computer to make a call and had a whispered conversation with the person at the other end of the line. She hung up and leaned against the credenza. "Here's the thing. One of our clients brought a suit against the dry cleaner for ruining a fur coat."

"Are you serious? A firm like this handles a dry-cleaning case, like you see on Judge Judy?"

Ellen sighed. "Yeah. We have clients who pay us big retainers and in return they expect us to handle every little contretemps they get into. It's a serious waste of time and money but we have to keep the client happy."

"How was the case resolved?"

"We sent some letters threatening this and that. The dry cleaner ignored most of them. We did get one letter from them, signed by the person you mentioned, Toula Prodosiakis, telling us, in essence, to eff off. I give her points for having a sense of humour. She wrote that if we could find a judge to hear a nuisance case, she'd buy the client a new coat."

"And..."

"And, nothing. That ended it. It was all bluff on our part. The client would have done better on his own. He probably could have got some free dry cleaning. Are we done?" Ellen moved toward the door to the conference room.

Gilles remained seated and said, "Not quite. I'd like to talk to someone who worked with Maître Patenaude. I need to know if there was anyone who might want to hurt him. Maybe one of the other lawyers or his secretary. I also want to talk to whoever handled the Prodosiakis file."

Ellen gave Gilles a you-can't-be-serious look, sighed loudly to make her displeasure known, and made a few phone calls.

A couple of minutes later two women knocked and entered. Ellen introduced them as Francine and Delphine. Francine was a paralegal who worked with Patenaude, and

Delphine was his secretary. Francine was blonde and tall, Delphine had black hair and was an inch or so shorter. Both women looked as if they had been crying.

Gilles expressed his condolences and told the women that he would take as little of their time as possible. The women sat down.

"How did you hear about the death of Maître Patenaude?" he asked.

Delphine answered. "I received a call from the hospital. He must have given me as a contact at some point. He has no close family."

"It must have come as a shock."

"Absolutely. I'm, I mean we're, still in shock." Francine nodded her agreement.

"Was there anything you can think of in any of his cases that would make someone angry enough to want to hurt him?"

Delphine was about to answer but Francine put a restraining hand on her forearm. "I can answer that," she said. "The answer is no. I can't say that he didn't handle some tough cases. People on the losing end certainly weren't happy. But it's crazy to think he was murdered. No one had that kind of hatred for him. Everyone is angry at the lawyer who beats them, but none of them commit murder. Forget it."

Delphine nodded her agreement.

"What about his private life?" Gilles asked. "Girlfriends, boyfriends, that kind of thing."

Delphine said, "Oh," and covered her mouth with her hand. "J'ai complètement oublié, I completely forgot. Audrey. She must be going crazy."

"Audrey?"

"Oui, Audrey Gélinas, Alain's girlfriend. They've been seeing each other for about a year. I should have called. Oh my God."

"Does she work here?" Gilles asked.

"Work here? No, of course not. She's a social worker at a hospital. The Gursky, I think. I can find her number. I'm going to call her as soon as we're done here. The poor woman."

"It's okay. I know the hospital. I'll track her down." Gilles wrote her name in his notepad.

While they were talking a young man slipped into the room. He was tall and well dressed. He had a stylish mop of blonde hair and an unstylish English moustache with waxed tips.

Ellen introduced him as André Boisvert. "He was a paralegal who handled the Prodosiakis suit. He's a lawyer now."

"What do you remember about the case?" Gilles asked.

"It was a lot of noise for nothing," Boisvert replied. "We have a client who threatens to sue anyone who he thinks wronged him or his family, no matter how minor or innocent the mistake. He pays a large retainer so we have no choice but to get all lawyerly when he gets his boxers in a knot. It was one of these things. Something about damage to a fur coat. I remember it because it was so ridiculous."

"Did you happen to have anything to do with Toula Prodosiakis during the dispute?"

"Yeah, she was the last person I talked to. Her father offered to take a look at the damage and see if there was something he could do to correct it. Then she called and told me the case was closed." Boisvert smiled for a second or two as he recalled his conversation with Toula Prodosiakis. "Can you believe it? *She* told *me* the case was closed."

"What did you do?"

"I got all lawyerly with her. Told her I would decide when the case was closed, that we'd see her in court, that she'd end up paying court costs and so on."

"How did it end?"

Boisvert looked at Ellen and said, "It's kind of crude." She nodded and he continued, "She told me to fuck off and hung up. That ended it. I found a way of winding the client down and he found some other problem to occupy himself with."

"And you never saw or heard from Toula Prodosiakis again?"

"Never saw her at all and, yeah, never heard from her again."

Gilles flipped through his notepad. He tapped it on the table a couple of times and asked, "I have one more person to ask about. Does the name Tiddley mean anything to you? Are there any cases involving him?"

Ellen did another search and said, "No, but the name rings a bell. Didn't I see it in the newspaper?"

"Yes," Gilles said. "He was murdered, also poisoned."

"That's an awful lot of murdering. It may be all in a day's work to you but it seems horrid to me. In any event there is no connection to the firm." Gilles flipped his notepad closed and returned it to his pocket.

"If you have no more questions, I'll show you out," Ellen said and got to her feet.

Gilles slid his card to each of the people he had questioned, got to his feet and said, "Call me if you think of something you forgot to mention."

André, Francine, and Delphine filed out of the conference room.

He turned to Ellen and said, "The same for you. Please think about Patenaude's cases and let me know if there's anything out of order. In fact, I think I'll call you in a day or two to see if you've come up with anything."

Before Gilles left the building, he called the Gursky Memorial Hospital and asked to be put through to Audrey

Gélinas. He spoke to the secretary in the Social Services Department who told him that Audrey was in but unavailable to speak on the phone. Gilles identified himself and asked the secretary to tell her that he was on his way to the hospital and would appreciate a couple of minutes of her time.

Gilles called Annie and told her that he had to interview someone at the hospital and suggested that they meet for lunch.

"You bet," Annie told him. "As long as it's not in the hospital. I need a break. Who do you have to see? Anyone in my department?"

"No, a social worker, Audrey Gélinas. Do you know her?"

"The name rings a bell, but she doesn't work in one of the emergency services."

"Okay, chérie, I'll see you soon."

Gilles parked in the corner of the horseshoe driveway at the main entrance to the Gursky. He made his way to the third floor of Pavilion A. He had only to wait a couple of minutes for Audrey Gélinas to appear in the waiting room. Gilles showed her his ID and they made their way to her office. Audrey wore a lab coat over her street clothes. She was an inch or two over five and a half feet tall with thick, shoulder-length caramel-blonde hair. Her smile was warm in spite of the sadness in her brown eyes, magnified by her glasses.

The office was not large. "You're here about Alain," she said softly once they were seated.

"Yes, I'm sorry for your loss."

Audrey mumbled a thank you and nodded her head. She waited for Gilles to ask his questions. "How long have you and he been going out?" he inquired.

"Just over a year. We met at a New Year's party last year." Audrey was silent for a moment as she replayed their meeting in her mind. "I was there with a friend of the woman he was with. Odd how people meet. Our dates were just that, nothing serious. He got my number from the hostess, also a mutual friend, and called me."

Gilles was about to ask about the people with whom they attended the party to see if there was any animosity there but changed his mind. If there were any hard feelings they would have dissipated after a year. And Audrey gave the impression that there had been no recriminations from former partners.

"When was the last time you saw Alain?"

"Sunday. We spent the weekend together. At my place."

Gilles had to lean forward to hear Audrey. "Every weekend?"

"Yes, with the exceptions of the weekends when I was on rotation here."

"Did anything happen over the weekend that seemed unusual?"

"No. We went to dinner with friends at the Bistro Nolah."

Gilles thought he knew most of the "in" restaurants in Montreal but he had never heard of the Nolah. "Nola," he said. "N-O-L-A? I've never heard of it. Where is it?"

"Almost. It has an h at the end. But it stands for New Orleans, Louisiana. I don't know why the h was added. It's in the West Island."

Gilles made a note of the name of the restaurant and its location.

"Sunday, like most Sundays, we ran on the lakeshore and spent the day not doing much of anything. Reading. Hanging out."

"I take it you live on the West Island."

"Yes. I have a townhouse in Pointe-Claire."

"You didn't spend Sunday night with him?"

"No. He was not fond of the commute and never stayed over on Sunday night when we were at my place."

"Did you see one another during the week?"

"Sometimes," Audrey replied. "It depended on our schedules. Alain was a very hard worker. And I sometimes had to work an evening shift."

Gilles could see that talking about her boyfriend was upsetting for Audrey. "I only have one more question for the moment," he said. "Can you think of anything that happened or that he said that would have indicated that there was anyone who wanted to harm him?"

"No. I'm not saying he was a saint. He was a lawyer and I'm sure there all kinds of files he worked on where one or more people were not pleased with the result of whatever the case was. But to kill him? No."

He asked her for the names of the friends they saw on Saturday and left her office. She walked him to the elevator. He handed her one of his cards and asked her to call if she remembered anything that she had forgotten to tell him.

He called Annie as he walked through the hospital to see if she was ready for lunch. "Give me a couple of minutes," she said.

They agreed to meet in the main lobby of the Gursky.

There was something about Annie's compassionate personality, or maybe it was the warmth of her smile, that usually allowed her to appear stress-free no matter how many patients she had to treat. Today was different. Gilles could see immediately by the lines around her mouth that she was anxious about something.

A light snow was falling and the street was slippery but they managed the walk to the Âllo! Mon Coco restaurant on the corner of Côte-des-Neiges and Côte-Sainte-Catherine.

Once they were seated and sipping their coffees, Gilles covered Annie's hand with his and said, "You look stressed, chérie. Rough day?"

Annie gave Gilles a wan smile, nodded and said, "Yeah. It shows?"

"Is it the number of patients? Are you short-handed?" Gilles knew that the ED was chronically understaffed and the nurses were often required to work double shifts.

"Yeah. But that's normal for us. There is something going on. A new strain of the flu."

The waitress appeared to take their orders, interrupting Annie. Once they placed their orders Gilles asked, "What do you mean a new strain of the flu? It's the season, no?"

"It's not that. People who've had their flu shot are presenting with symptoms that are part of a new disease. Some of them very, very sick. We have to put them on ventilators. It's part of a new epidemic. We're calling it Covid, Covid 19. It's coming from China or Europe and it's serious. Scary serious."

"Why? Don't we have vaccines for this kind of thing?"

"Not this one. That's the problem."

They were silent as they ate their omelettes and Gilles absorbed what Annie had just told him.

"No vaccine? Won't that mean..." Gilles started to say.

"Exactly." Annie finished his sentence. "It will mean that we won't be able to stop the spread. We're already seeing it in the most vulnerable."

"How do you mean?"

"The elderly. It's spreading through seniors' residences at an alarming rate. With high mortality."

There were a number of residences for the elderly that brought the residents to the Gursky when they became ill, sick beyond the capacity of the residence to care for them. It was an open secret that most of these operations were little more than warehouses for the aged. A place to wait to die.

"Then we'd better hope that they, whoever they are, can find a cure or a preventative or something," Gilles said.

"The doctors tell me that's not happening and as soon as it gets into the general population it's going to spread like crazy. They're worried about another epidemic like the Spanish flu."

Gilles had only a vague notion of what the Spanish flu was but he did know that it was deadly and had lasted two years, killing millions around the world.

"Tabernac," he said.

"Exactly. And now you understand why we're so stressed in emerg."

Gilles did his best to change the subject and suggest things that he and Annie could do to alleviate her anxiety. He could see that she was pleased by his suggestions but they did nothing to lessen the worry she felt.

Chapter 28

Annie returned to her post in Triage so that one of the other nurses, Daniella in this case, could take her lunch break. "Take my advice," Annie told her friend, "have lunch anywhere but in the hospital. Taking a complete break from this place does wonders."

"Right," Daniella said with a smile, "especially if you have a boyfriend to have lunch with."

"Yeah, no kidding. But still..."

"Got it. I'll go to Java U."

Annie had just finished with her patient, who had complained of an unexplained rash on his stomach, when Dr. Rosen came into the triage area. Annie and Yves, the other nurse on duty, looked up. He waited until both nurses were free and said, "I would like to have an informal meeting with as many of the staff as possible, as soon as possible." He directed them to meet at the Rapid Action Zone desk, which everyone called the RAZ. It was meant to get patients registered to be treated and on their way as quickly as possible but, in practice, RAZ patient registration took place with all other patient registration and the counter in front of it had never been used for its intended purpose.

Annie and Yves were surprised by this. Meetings were usually scheduled well in advance and they never took place on the fly in a corridor of the department. Dr. Rosen replied to the unasked question. "I know. It's very unusual, but we have a crisis headed our way and I want to get planning started stat. Dr. Hirsch will be joining us."

This was a triple surprise. Dr. Hirsch was the head of medicine and almost never interfered with the operation of the Emergency Department.

"You go," Yves said. "One of us has to see patients. You'll tell me what happened." Annie headed to the corridor.

Dr. Rosen asked for quiet and said, "I'm sure you've realized by now that there is an epidemic, likely a pandemic, headed our way. It's had a couple of names but we're calling it coronavirus or, more accurately, Covid-19. It can be deadly and there's no vaccine. It's hitting the elderly particularly hard. We're going to develop more detailed protocols for dealing with it in the next few days but for the moment, and this is effective immediately, everyone wear two gowns, one tied in front and the other in back. Wear a face mask and gloves at all times. And lots of handwashing. This is the minimum. We're going to develop stricter procedures to make certain that none, and I mean none, of our people get it."

Before any of those assembled could ask questions, Dr. Hirsch spoke in his normal calm, reassuring tone of voice. "We, by which I mean everyone who works in the hospital, will be taking precautions so that everyone is safe. You are the front-line people and your safety, security, and health—and, by extension, that of your families—are of prime importance to us. I, we, don't want you taking this disease home with you. Dr. Rosen and I will make certain that you have enough protective gear so you can do your jobs without risk. You are the best and you are the best because you do your best. We'll make certain you all have whatever you need so you can continue to be the best. Finally, the security guard at the door to emerg will ensure that everyone who comes into the department will be issued a mask and will disinfect their hands. Dr. Rosen and I will try to answer any questions you have."

There weren't that many questions. The medical staff understood the problem and the need for protection. The non-medical staff knew from experience that the doctors and nurses had policies for the protection of all.

Following the meeting, Annie returned to Triage. She brought Yves up to date and they donned the protective gear that they would be wearing for the foreseeable future.

Annie noticed that the guy in charge of the security agents appeared with a box of masks about ten minutes after she returned from the meeting. She couldn't hear what he said but surmised from his gestures that he was telling the security guard what to do and to ask one of the nurses or orderlies for more masks when he ran out.

Annie and Yves triaged three or four patients each before there was a lull. Annie was pleased to see that everyone in the waiting room was wearing a blue mask. The break didn't last long. It never did.

Two ambulances pulled into the ambulance bay and Annie, Yves, and a couple of orderlies, Jean-Guy St-Onge and Suze Guimond, went to meet them with stretchers. The EMTs were also wearing masks. One of the EMTs told Annie and Yves that both ambulances were from a seniors' residence and both patients were having difficulty breathing. Annie said, "And so it begins." She and Yves gave one another knowing looks.

The patients, a man and a woman, were frail and breathing with the help of oxygen canisters. The orderlies and EMTs transferred the patients to hospital gurneys and made the change from the ambulance oxygen canisters to those belonging to the hospital. The EMTs began the process of disinfecting their trucks as the orderlies, following Annie and Yves, wheeled the patients into the Resuscitation Unit. The patients were running fevers and Annie was certain that they would have to be put on ventilators.

As she and Yves were returning to their computers to enter their diagnoses and get a doctor to see the patients, she heard Jean-Guy say to Suze, "These poor souls are practically dead and we're going to torture them with medicine." Annie could only see his eyes and couldn't tell whether he was being compassionate or cold-hearted. His next sentence stopped her in her tracks. He said, "Wouldn't it be kinder to let them 'end the heartaches and the thousand natural shocks the flesh is heir to'?"

Annie went to where St-Onge and Guimond were working together to get the patients settled in their respective rooms. She walked straight up to St-Onge, who was almost a foot taller than she was. She gave him a cold stare and, emphasizing her words with her index finger barely centimeters from his chest, said, "What on earth are you talking about? Saving lives is what we do here. Remember that."

She caught up with Yves, brought the patients' files up to date, and told the doctor on duty about the patients.

Chapter 29

When he got back to his car Gilles called Dr. Lapointe to see if he had a final conclusion regarding the poison that killed Alain Patenaude.

"Pas de question," Dr. Lapointe told him. "It's VX poison. Pretty dangerous stuff. It doesn't take much to kill a person. It's a nerve agent favoured by certain dictators to kill political competitors. It causes paralysis and death by asphyxia. It's always lethal and, depending on dosage, can be fast-acting."

"How would someone get their hands on it?" Gilles asked.

"Haven't got a clue. It's not something that is readily available, that's for sure."

Gilles didn't say anything for a moment. "Could someone make it?"

"If that someone understood chemistry and had access to the chemicals needed, then yes."

"Merci, Docteur," Gilles said. He knew his next step. He had to have another conversation with Jacques Chenier.

The receptionist at Chimie-Vert recognized Gilles. She called Chenier and told him the cop was back. Five minutes later Chenier came to the reception area, and invited Gilles up to his office.

"People are going to think I'm a criminal," he said and chuckled at his joke as they shook hands.

"I'll try not to take up too much more of your time," Gilles said. "I'll get straight to the point. Have you ever heard of a chemical, a poison, called VX?"

"Heard of it, yes. Nasty stuff. Doesn't take much to kill a person and it's not a pleasant way to go."

"Do you collect it? Do you have any on the premises?"

"Hardly. It's a nerve agent with no commercial application that I know of. No reason for us to touch the stuff. And I mean that literally."

"Do you know if any of your people could make a batch of it?"

"Probably most of them could make it. But they'd be fired on the spot if they tried, believe me."

"How would you know?"

"We'd know that one of our employees was up to something if they signed out chemicals they wouldn't normally use in their research or other work. Even if they didn't sign for the stuff we'd notice an imbalance in quantities and all kinds of alarms would go off with the lab supervisor and then with me."

Chenier pulled a manual from a shelf behind his desk and flipped through it. When he found the page he was looking for he showed it to Gilles. "That's the formula," he said, pointing to a sentence that made no sense to Gilles. The only word he could possibly pronounce was "methylphosphonite" and he had no idea what it was.

"We don't have all the chemicals you'd need so the person would have to make substitutions," Chenier explained.

He was willing to bet that Toula had enough basic knowledge of chemistry to whip up a test tube of the nerve agent. But he couldn't figure out why she would. Her connection to Alain Patenaude was tenuous at best. He planned to probe that connection more fully, but first he wanted to figure out how she, or anyone for that matter, could have gotten the poison into him.

Gilles got to his feet. "Would it be possible to talk to the people in your lab before I leave?"

Chenier smiled and walked to the door of his office. Gilles picked up the manual and followed him to the lab on the floor below.

"Detective Sergeant Bellechasse has a question he would like to ask you," Chenier said to the staff. They stopped what they were doing and looked up. Gilles cleared his throat and, reading from the manual, asked, "Do any of you know where to get," he paused not certain how to pronounce the name of the chemical. Slowly sounding out the syllables he continued, "Di-iso-propy-lamino-ethyl?"

Gilles stared at the lab workers in case one betrayed a guilty look. Most of them were repeating the syllables to try and form a word they understood and so he had a room full of blank looks staring back at him. Finally, one of the lab techs spoke up. "Well, Russia, I suppose. Barring that, my guess is the web, the dark web."

The rest of the employees mumbled their agreement.

"Satisfied?" Chenier asked.

"Yes," Gilles said. He used his cellphone to take a snapshot of the page and handed the manual to Chenier.

"If you have no more questions, I'll show you out," Chenier said. The two men shook hands at the door to the building. "Let me know if there is anything else I can do for you. Good luck with your investigation."

Gilles's next stop was the Kathari dry-cleaning plant. He was reluctant to give up on Toula as a suspect.

There was no one in the front of the store. He was about to ring the bell on the counter when he heard Toula and her brother arguing from somewhere in the plant, behind the garment conveyors that looped around the premises.

"Listen," she said, "are you certain it will work? If you're wrong, you're going to ruin a very expensive wedding dress, not to mention the wedding itself."

"No, you listen to me. It's basic chemistry," Iannis replied. "I'm not sure what the stain is, yet, or how it got onto a new dress, but I know what the material is made of. I know what I'm doing."

"You think?" Toula sounded unconvinced.

Gilles was surprised—he'd been unaware that Iannis could do anything other than play computer games. He followed the sounds of the voices and found Toula, her brother, and a couple of employees standing around a table with a wedding dress spread out on it.

"*Theé mou,*" Toula said. "What do you want?"

"A couple of questions," Gilles said. "But finish with your emergency first. What happened?"

The woman Gilles recognized as the one who worked at the counter said, "A bride-to-be and her mother discovered a small stain on the wedding dress. They don't know how it got there or what to do. They brought it to us."

"If I can't figure out how to remove it, they'll have a breakdown, I swear. The wedding is in a couple of days. Thursday."

"You can fix this?" Gilles asked.

"Yeah."

"He'd better," Toula said.

"Don't let me keep you. Go ahead," Gilles said.

Iannis looked at his sister and the employee and bent over the dress. He dipped the tip of an artist's brush into a dish of a liquid he had in front of him and dabbed a little of the chemical on the corner of the stain. The stain darkened and Toula gasped. "Now you've fuckin' done it, Iannis."

Iannis held up his hand but said nothing. He concentrated on the stain. After a couple of minutes, the chemical turned to a powder. He blew it off the dress and that part of the stain disappeared. He repeated the process a couple of times on parts of the stain until it was gone. He held up the dress and said, "Told you."

"You're a genius, Iannis," the employee said. "A true stain whisperer."

"Better living through chemistry," he said.

Toula looked much relieved but only grunted. She turned to Gilles and asked, "What do you want?"

"Interestingly, I wanted to ask you a question about chemistry. But I see that your brother is the one who knows about it." He turned to Iannis. "Did you study it at university?"

"Yeah. I had to take a bunch of other subjects that were of zero interest to me so..."

"So he dropped out," Toula said.

"What do you like about chemistry?" Gilles asked.

"Everything. When you understand it, you understand everything on the planet and everything's relation to everything else."

Gilles showed him the photo of the page he had on his cellphone. "Do you know what this is?"

Iannis looked at it and grinned. "I can read. This is pretty nasty stuff. Don't get within a mile of it. It will kill you."

"So, you've never seen it?"

"Are you kidding me?"

"No," Toula said. "He's trying to pin a murder on you. Someone die, Detective? Poisoned?"

"Yes, as a matter of fact. That's actually what I wanted to talk to you about. Can we talk in your office?"

Toula answered by turning away from Gilles and walking to the stairs that led to her office. Gilles and Iannis followed.

Once seated, Gilles explained that a lawyer by the name of Alain Patenaude had been murdered. "Poisoned."

"What's that got to do with us?" Toula asked.

"You had a lawsuit with his firm. Sevigny, Stein. They sued you."

"Really? I don't remember being sued by them, or anyone else for that matter. In our business, someone brings in something old and tries to blame us when things go wrong. We get threatened but no one actually sues, unless they have more money than brains."

Gilles gave the brother and sister a rundown of the case.

"*Agapité Theé.* That was years ago. I remember now. Some lawyer was threatening my father until I told him to fuck off. And that was that. Hardly worth killing someone over."

Gilles had to admit to himself that he was grasping at straws. Unless he could find some better motive than a dry-cleaning mistake, Toula and her brother were off the hook for the Patenaude murder.

Gilles got to his feet. "Thank you for the chemistry lesson, Iannis. I'll get in touch with one of you if I need any more information."

He drove back to the office to report to Lieutenant Giroux.

Gilles had no idea what changes Lieutenant Giroux had in store for the Division, but she had made a small but significant change to her office. The former occupant, Captain Lacroix, liked to stack files wherever he found an empty space. The clutter gave the office a lived-in but chaotic atmosphere. Stéphanie was significantly neater. Flat surfaces were cleared and dusted. Gilles assumed her file cabinets were well-organized. Her desk held the normal office equipment but was otherwise almost clear. There was a rack on the credenza behind the desk with the current files she was supervising.

She was on the phone when Gilles appeared at her door. She motioned to him to sit down. When she finished her call, she gave the whole of her attention to Gilles. "Quelques progrès?" she asked. She turned and pulled a file from the rack.

"Oui et non," Gilles said. "Let me bring you up to date. I've been investigating the murder of Alain Patenaude. I thought there might be a connection to the Tiddley murder. Both men were poisoned. And I thought there was a connection to the Prodosiakis family, in particular Toula Prodosiakis."

"That would wrap things up neatly," Lieutenant Giroux said. "But things are never that neat, are they?"

"Yeah, no kidding. I actually thought I had found a connection. The Prodosiakis family was involved in a lawsuit, or at least the threat of one, and Patenaude's firm was the plaintiff's lawyer. But it turned out to be nothing. The suit went nowhere."

"And..."

"I talked to Toula and her brother Iannis and realized that I was guilty of tunnel vision. I was trying to fit the evidence to the solution rather than the other way around," Gilles said.

"Better early in the investigation than after arresting and charging the wrong people."

"Of course. But this is where I'm stuck at the moment. I'm certain there is a connection between the murder of Tiddley and L'Étrangleur. Tiddley and the victims of L'Étrangleur lost loved ones to Ian Chambers. And there's also a connection to Patenaude. His mother was the judge at the trial that links all of them to Chambers."

"Are there any other connections?" asked Lieutenant Giroux. "You still may be combining things that have a commonality but no actual connection."

"There's two pieces of evidence that connect, or potentially connect, Patenaude to Tiddley. Blonde hairs found in the bedrooms of the victims and, of course, poison as the cause of death."

"Neither conclusive nor inconclusive."

"I agree. I'm awaiting confirmation on the blonde hairs. They may be from a wig. If they're synthetic it's impossible to connect them to a specific wig, but if I'm right, it is suggestive that they came from the same person for..."

"...an as-yet-unknown reason," Stéphanie said, finishing his sentence.

"Precisely. The other connection is, of course, that both men were poisoned. According to Dr. Lapointe it was the same stuff, VX poison, or at least a version of it. At the moment I have no clear idea how the murderer got Patenaude to ingest the stuff. I'm going to check out his condo again tomorrow. See what I can find."

"Okay. Keep me posted and keep Gaston posted as well for connections to L'Étrangleur. If there doesn't appear to be a connection to Patenaude then I'll assign the case to someone else."

Gilles went to his desk and called Nathalie Gascon in forensics. "Ah, Gilles, j'étais sur le point de t'appeler."

"Great. What've you got?"

"The hairs you found were dyed but not polyester. They're from a person. I extracted DNA from the roots but you'll have to find the head they came from. There's no connection to the blonde hairs from the Tiddley crime scene."

If the blonde hairs weren't from a wig, Gilles guessed that they came from Patenaude's girlfriend. "What about the poison?" he asked.

"I've been in touch with Dr. Lapointe and we agree it's a version of VX."

"How did Patenaude ingest it?"

"We found traces of it in his water bottles. He had a runner's belt, they call them fuel belts, that held six small water bottles. We found traces of the poison in all of them along with something else, a red liquid. I'm pretty certain it was one of those flavouring drops, they come in small plastic containers."

"I'm going to the victim's condo tomorrow. I'll let you know if I find anything. One more question: do you know how long it takes for VX to start to work?"

"That's a question for Lapointe, sorry."

"No problem. I'll call him. Merci, Natalie." They hung up and Gilles called Dr. Lapointe.

"Before you ask, Gilles, I was right about the poison."

"Oui, je sais. I just spoke to Natalie Gascon. I have a question about it. How long would it take to have an effect? For the victim to start showing symptoms?"

"Good question," Dr. Lapointe said. "It would depend on how much he ingested. A small amount would be sufficient to kill him but obviously it would take longer than a large amount. I would say that somewhere between ninety minutes and two hours based on the amount we found in his system. Do you know how the murderer got it into him?"

"Yeah, Natalie told me that she found traces of it in his water bottles. He wore a runner's belt that held small bottles for water."

"That would explain it"

"Thanks," Gilles said. "I'm going back to his condo tomorrow to see what I can find. Natalie thinks it may have been in the flavouring he used for his water. That brings me to questions about the first victim, Tiddley. Assuming for the moment that the same poison was used, why were his symptoms different?"

"The body was undiscovered for a period of time, twelve hours, say, so some of the symptoms, like the sweating, would have dissipated. If the dosage was greater he would have suffered less—death would have come more quickly."

"D'accord, I get it. But there was no diarrhea. That wouldn't have dissipated."

"No, it wouldn't," Dr. Lapointe agreed. "It wouldn't have happened if Tiddley died quickly. It's a symptom of dying, not of being dead. You can hide a lot more poison in a plate of food, especially spicy food, than in a small bottle of water. I'll let you know what we find."

On his way home Gilles called his daughter to see what she wanted for dinner. He would either pick up some takeout or stop at a grocery store.

"Je ne suis pas chez toi, Pa," Émilie said.

"Where are you, Lapin?"

"I'm at Mom's. I'll eat with her."

"Okay. How is she?"

"Still a little upset, nervous, you know."

"Yeah, it will be best if Brigitte can stay with her for the next couple of days. Will you stay the night or are you coming home?" Émilie lived with Gilles as his condo was closer to the UQAM campus.

"I'm coming home," she said. "Will you pick me up?"

"You can take a taxi to the metro, my treat, and I'll pick you up at the Beaudry station. Call me when you're on your way."

Gilles would have liked to have dinner with Annie but he thought it better to be with his daughter. When he got home, he called Annie to see how she was.

"Stressed," she said. "But I'm glad to be home. Pamela and I are going to order a pizza. How about you?"

Gilles told Annie about Émilie and how he thought it important to be home for her. Annie agreed. "I'm off tomorrow and then I'm on nights," she said.

"Then we'll have to get together tomorrow night."

"It's a plan," Annie said.

Chapter 30

Gilles was at the office early on Wednesday morning. He attended the L'Étrangleur briefing and learned that very little progress had been made. As Gilles was leaving the briefing room Detective Sergeant Gaston Lemieux pulled him aside for a quick conversation. "Comment vas-tu sur l'enquête Tiddley?"

"It just got a lot more complicated," Gilles said. "The Patenaude poisoning is connected to it in some way."

"How so?" Gaston asked.

"His mother was the judge in the Chambers trial."

"I see. I knew Judge Patenaude. She and my father were in law school together." "Did you know Alain?"

"No, he was younger than me. She had children, a child, late in life. Other than his mother being the judge in the trial, what's the connection? It's a bit of a stretch, don't you think?"

"It's entirely possible," Gilles said. "But it's my starting point. I thought there was another connection. I thought Toula Prodosiakis was somehow involved, but that turned out not to be the case. Although her brother may be a suspect. I'm going to have a talk with him later today. My first order of business is to take another look at the Patenaude condo. I have to figure out how he ingested the poison."

"I see," Gaston said. "As soon as you clear your cases I want you on the L'Étrangleur investigation."

"If I'm right about Tiddley and Patenaude then when I clear them it may lead to a solution to the L'Étrangleur case."

Gaston gave Gilles a quizzical look but said nothing.

Gilles drove to Patenaude's building on Hutchison, slipped on a pair of latex gloves, and let himself into the condo. He threw his overcoat over the back of a chair. The place was a mess. There was dusting powder on most of the exposed surfaces, bookshelves were in disarray, and cushions were tossed haphazardly on the couch. The bedroom and study also showed signs of being searched. Gilles realized that if there had been anything useful in these rooms the forensics team would have found it. The only room that didn't appear to be disorganized was the kitchen. There were dishes in the drainer and fingerprint powder on the counters. Gilles knew from the photographs of the place where the runner's hydration belt had lain. He checked the fridge for a pitcher or bottled water. Nothing. He checked the cupboards and still came up empty. The pantry yielded what he hoped was the solution to the puzzle: a couple of small bottles of Mio, a flavouring additive for water.

He flipped the lid of the open bottle and sniffed it. There didn't seem to be anything unusual about it. He slipped the bottles into evidence bags and called Nathalie in the Forensics Division. He told her what he had found.

"I sniffed at them," he said, "but I didn't notice anything unusual."

"Gilles!" Natalie said. "If those bottles contain the poison, it's highly toxic. Keep it away from your nose and mouth for God's sake."

"Oui, d'accord, Nat. I know. I'm going to bring them in. Could you put a rush on them?"

"For you, anything."

Gilles drove to police headquarters on St. Urbain Street in downtown Montreal. The area had been the red-light district of Montreal during the pre-Drapeau heyday of Montreal as sin city. It had been reborn as the Quartier des Spectacles, Montreal's entertainment hub, anchored by Place des Arts and any number of music venues to its east.

Gilles hopped over a slush puddle that had formed on the sidewalk, showed his badge at the entrance, and found his way to the floor that housed the forensics labs. He didn't have to wait long for Natalie. They two-cheeked kissed and Gilles presented her with his evidence bags.

"How long do you figure?" he asked.

Natalie stood close enough to Gilles so he could smell her shampoo. She looked up at him and smiled. "Not long to determine if they contain poison. A little longer for a more detailed analysis."

"Thanks, Nat. I really appreciate it. Call me when you've got something."

"No time for a coffee, Gilles?"

"No. Sorry. I spent the morning poking around the crime scene and now I want to interview a possible suspect. Next time."

"I'll hold you to that," Natalie said

Gilles left headquarters, careful to avoid the snow bank that had been plowed to the curb, and headed for the Prodosiakis house in the Town of Mont Royal. He wanted to find Iannis alone and he was certain that Toula would be at work. He had to take the small chance that Iannis was still at the dry-cleaning plant.

Gilles rang the doorbell and received no answer; he tried again after a minute or two. He did this three times and was about to give up when Iannis answered the door. He was dressed in the uniform of the layabout: sweatpants, a zippered hoodie, and white sweat socks. He held a can of Red Bull.

"What now?" he asked by way of a greeting.

"A few questions. May I come in?"

Iannis turned and walked down the hall. Gilles stomped the snow off his shoes, tested one of them on the inside doormat to ensure that it was clean and dry, and followed him.

In the kitchen there was a breakfast nook in an alcove on the left. It held a table with two chairs on one side and an upholstered bench on the other. Iannis slid onto the bench. Gilles slung his coat on one of the chairs and occupied the other. Iannis played with the can of Red Bull he had in front of him. "What now?" he asked.

"I'd like to follow up on something you said when I saw you at the dry-cleaning plant."

"You got a stubborn stain or something?"

"No, but in a way that's what I wanted to ask you about. You said something to the effect that chemistry connects everything. Remember?"

"Actually, no. But it is something I believe. Chemistry connects everything to everything else," Iannis said.

"Fair enough. I had no idea you were interested in the subject. Did you major in it at university?"

Iannis took a slug of his drink, swallowed, and gave a snort, which Gilles took to be a derisive laugh.

"Yeah, like I told you. I found university at the "for dummies" level. And they got mad when I tried to move ahead of where the class was at. We, that is the university and I, agreed to a parting of the ways."

"Do you have access to a lab?"

"Why would I need a lab?"

"Well," Gilles paused. He couldn't very well ask Iannis if he could whip up a batch of poison. "Well, if you needed to make some sort of chemical for dry cleaning. To remove a stain like you were talking about the other day."

Iannis smiled. "It doesn't take a lab. You can make solutions in a reasonably well-equipped kitchen. Since *Breaking*

Bad people have had a naïve idea of what you needed to mix chemicals."

"How would you acquire the chemicals you'd need to mix a stain remover, say?"

"I can't," Iannis said. "My sister does that through the plant. She—well, it—has licenses for what they purchase. It's not hard to get any sort of benign chemical, but anything potentially dangerous is not a possibility without filling out a lot of paperwork."

"Okay, I get that. Is there some way you can follow your interests by working with chemicals?"

"I wish," Iannis said. "Making stain removers is not my ideal."

"You know," Gilles said, "there might be a way for you to work in chemistry at a level that you'll find interesting."

For the first time since they met, Iannis showed a less sullen side of himself. "Really?" He said the word without his usual chip-on-the-shoulder edge.

"I met a guy, Jacques Chenier, who has a business that employs chemists," Gilles said as he scrolled through his cellphone. "He might have a job for you. I'll give you his phone number."

"Oh, thank you. What does he do?"

"His company recycles chemicals. Your company's drycleaning chemicals for one. He's trying to work out a way of turning them into something less dangerous. Something useful."

"You mean Chimie-Vert? I thought they just disposed of the stuff."

"But that's not the ultimate goal, I gather. The company is looking for ways to turn the chemicals into something that can be used again. Do you want his phone number?"

"Yes, please." Gilles dictated Jacques Chenier's name and phone number and Iannis put it in his cellphone.

Gilles got to his feet. "I don't need anything else for the moment." As he and Iannis walked to the door he added, "I'll call Chenier and tell him about you. Give me an hour and then call him. Mention my name."

"I will, thanks," Iannis said. He held the door open for Gilles and just before closing it he said, "You know, I always keep the front door locked. Always."

"Got it," Gilles said.

Gilles drove back to the shopping centre where he had had lunch and bought a coffee, then called Jacques Chenier to tell him that he had given his name to Iannis. Jacques didn't answer so Gilles left a message. While he sipped his coffee, he thought about what Iannis had said as he was leaving.

Of more immediate concern, though, was to find out who poisoned two people who didn't know one another and whose only connection went back a generation.

While he mulled over his next steps his cellphone rang. It was Natalie Gascon from the forensics unit. "Nat," Gilles said. "Don't tell me you have news already."

"You know you're my favourite customer."

Gilles smiled. "You found something?"

"Both of the little Mio bottles were full of the VX poison. Enough to drop an army in its tracks," Natalie said.

"Really? So why didn't Patenaude drop dead in his kitchen or while running?"

"Because he probably only put a couple of drops into his water bottles and we don't know when he ingested it. My guess is that it was when he got home that he was most dehydrated, and he drank most of his water then. It would take time for the poison to take effect."

"Thus, keeling over at the bus stop."

"Exactly."

"Merci, Nat. Tu es super," Gilles said.

Gilles decided that the next person he wanted to see was Dr. Mary Russell at the Gursky. He had to get a handle on the complexity of making poison. He checked the time and realized it was too late to call her.

Gilles went to the SAQ in the shopping centre to buy a bottle of wine to bring to Annie's, then returned to the office and wrote up his notes on the events of the day. He had gathered a lot of information and he didn't want to forget any of it. As much as he disliked the tedious work of typing up the notes of his day's work, he knew it was important to do so as soon as possible.

After dinner, the table cleared and the dishes in the dishwasher, Gilles poured the last of the wine into their glasses. Annie hadn't talked much about her day at work and Gilles knew that this meant that she was internalizing the stress. He asked her if the new strain of flu she had mentioned had abated. Annie sighed then said, "The new strain of the flu. It's actually more than that. Or worse than that, I guess, is a better way of putting it. And it's both highly contagious and no way to prevent it."

Gilles had the medical knowledge of a person who almost never got sick and when he did it was only a cold. He was of the opinion that for things like the flu there were vaccines, so it came as a surprise to him that a flu-like disease could exist without a preventative. "No vaccine?" Gilles said. "Doesn't that mean that anyone and everyone can get it?"

Annie swirled the wine in her glass. "Absolutely. And when a person gets it there is a strong possibility of death."

"There's no treatment?"

"Yeah, if you call being intubated and attached to a ventilator a treatment. There's no medicine we can give patients at this point. We know almost nothing about Covid."

Gilles imagined Annie or Émilie lying sick and helpless in a hospital bed, tubes and machines helping them breathe. He found the image horrifying. He moved his chair so he was closer to Annie. He put his arm around her. "And you're seeing an increase in cases?"

She snuggled into his embrace and said, "The worst possible increase in cases. Just about everyone we're seeing comes from the homes for the elderly we service. It's spreading at an alarming rate."

"Why at old peoples' homes more than anywhere else?"

Annie sat up. Gilles could see the anger in her eyes. "It's partly because they're a more vulnerable population. But it's also because of the way we treat the elderly. They're warehoused in these facilities with comforting names such as Sunset Manor or Lakeview Gardens. Many of these places are awful, with residents confined to their beds or a day room where they spend hours virtually unattended, usually immobile. If they're incontinent they're left in their dirty diapers for hours, sometimes for days. Those places, because they are crowded and without sufficient staff, are breeding grounds for the transmission of a deadly virus. We have patients arriving at the hospital doubled over in the foetal position, undernourished, emaciated, often with their hands curled into claws, one fist under their chins."

Gilles's throat constricted involuntarily at the horrible picture Annie's words painted. He thought about his own parents, both now dead, and how their lives ended. His mother suffered from Alzheimer's and although his father, Gilles, and his siblings did their best to care for her, in the end she had to be placed in a facility. The Bellechasse family was lucky in that they had enough money to afford a home where there was enough staff who were also compassionate, and his mother didn't suffer from neglect. She died in her sleep at the age of eighty. His father died of a heart attack not long after. He was happy that his parents, after working hard all their lives, did not have to suffer unduly as their lives drew to a close. He inhaled and exhaled a couple of times and said, "And you're able to help these poor souls?"

"We do our best, but in a lot of cases there's only so much we can do."

"It seems so sad that through the use of technology and pharmacology we do our best to keep these old folks alive and do so little to provide any kind of quality of life. It's hard to see the elderly suffer. I understand why you're so stressed. It must be hard on all of you. Do you ever wish you could just pull the plug or withhold medication and end their suffering?"

Annie gave Gilles a hard look. Her eyes squinted and she paused before she spoke. "I'm a healer. I won't, I can't, make a decision that must be made by the individual and their family. But you made me remember something. One of the orderlies I work with said the strangest thing."

"How do you mean?"

"He said something weird. He's pretty good most of the time but I had to remind him what we do is save lives. We're not in the business of torturing our patients."

"He said saving lives was torture?" Gilles asked. He could hardly believe a health care worker could be so callous. He understood perfectly Annie's reaction.

"He said it in a funny kind of way. He said something like it's better to end the thousand shocks to the flesh—or something like that."

"Crisse. I'm surprised you didn't report him. Get him fired." But he knew Annie wasn't that type of person. She would handle the orderly in her own way.

Gilles stood and gently raised Annie to her feet so he could give her a full-body embrace. He said softly, "Your patients are very lucky to have you. What can I do to help you?"

Annie kissed her boyfriend and said, "Just do what you've been doing. Be a good listener. Let's find something to watch that will take my mind off the misery."

Once they went to bed, Gilles lay on his back so Annie could fall asleep with his arm around her, her head on his shoulder, her breasts pressed against his body. Annie fell asleep quickly and it didn't take Gilles much longer. Two hours later he woke up with a jolt. Annie rolled away from him but didn't wake up. He must have been thinking in his sleep, on a subconscious level, about what Annie had told him. He realized that the phrase, "end the heartaches and the thousand natural shocks the flesh is heir to," was familiar to him. He couldn't place it but he knew he knew it from somewhere. It was an odd way of speaking so he was certain that no one had said it to him.

He stared at the ceiling, unable to sleep, as he thought about what the orderly had said. After almost an hour, just as he was dozing off again, he remembered where he thought he had seen the sentence. He was determined to check his hunch as soon as he got to the office the next morning.

Chapter 31

Toula Prodosiakis, wearing a loose-fitting sweatshirt and pyjama bottoms, walked into the kitchen at seven on Thursday to make herself a coffee before she left for work. She was surprised to find her brother there having breakfast. He usually didn't put in an appearance much before noon. Even more surprising was that he was neatly dressed in a freshly dry-cleaned button-down shirt and slacks. He was shaved and his hair was combed.

"Iannis, my God, what are you doing here?"

"Huh, having breakfast. What does it look like?"

"I mean early in the morning. Is the coffee fresh?"

"Yeah." Toula poured herself a cup and joined her brother at the table. "I have a job interview at nine," Iannis said.

"What? A job interview? You have a job at the plant."

"Not my thing."

"It's our family business. It built this house and puts food on the table and, I might add, allows you to spend all your waking hours playing games online. So, I'm glad to see that you're ready to work. You can drive to the plant with me."

"*Àkou me adherfi.* I have zero interest in being your gofer. This is something for me."

"Really? And what would that be?" Toula drummed her fingernails on the table.

"Research. Something in chemistry research. In a lab."

Toula couldn't believe that her brother, with virtually no education, could land a job in a research lab. "Whose lab?"

"Chimie-Vert, that's who."

Toula almost choked on her coffee. "How on earth did you get an interview with them? They collect our chemicals."

"Yeah. The cop gave me the lead. He even called and made an introduction."

"The cop?" It took Toula a moment to grasp to whom her brother was referring. "Bellechasse? When did you see him?"

"He was here yesterday and he offered."

Toula couldn't remember when she had had so much surprising information thrown at her. It was hard to process all of it.

"The company disposes of chemical waste. It's like being a garbageman with chemicals. That's what you want?"

"Fuck, Toula, that's not really what they do. The company does research. They're trying to find a way to turn the chemicals into something useful. That's the research part."

Toula knew full well what the company did. "That's all very nice, but you can't work there. It's a conflict of interest. Sorry."

Iannis stared at his sister. He'd long ago gotten used to her controlling behavior. It only bothered him periodically. But she had crossed a line. "Conflict of interest? How do you figure? You don't own shares in the company."

"We're a customer," Toula replied weakly.

"So what? I'm not likely to divulge a trade secret. They know you use dangerous chemicals."

"Nevertheless."

Iannis got to his feet and placed his empty cup and cereal bowl in the sink. "Nevertheless, nothing."

Iannis left his sister in the kitchen drinking a cup of lukewarm coffee. After a couple of minutes, she emptied her cup into the sink and went to her room to shower and get dressed for work.

Gilles awoke before Annie Thursday morning. He quietly slipped out of bed so as not to disturb her. She didn't have to be at work until three and he wanted her to sleep in if at all possible. He was surprised to find Pamela, wearing an old pair of Annie's scrubs, having a coffee in the kitchen while she read one of her medical textbooks. Pamela was a medical student at McGill University. She spent almost every waking hour on her studies. Annie worried that her daughter was sacrificing a social life to her studies but Pamela seemed to enjoy what she did.

"Gilles, hi. I hope I didn't wake you," she said.

"No, not at all. I don't want to wake your mother if at all possible. She's on evenings starting today."

Gilles went to the counter and poured himself a cup of coffee. "I'm going to make some toast. Can I make some for you?"

Pamela held up her plate, empty save for some bread crumbs. "All done, thanks anyway."

Gilles ate his toast and drank his coffee silently. Pamela obviously preferred her textbook to morning small talk.

Gilles rinsed his cup and plate and said, "As soon as I shower I'm heading to the office. Can I give you a lift?"

Before she could answer, Annie came into the kitchen wearing a bathrobe. "Morning, you two," she said. She gave her daughter a hug.

"Can I get you something before I jump into the shower?" Gilles asked.

Annie poured herself a coffee. "Thanks, no. Coffee is all I want at the moment."

Gilles went to shower and returned to the kitchen twenty minutes later dressed and ready to leave for work. "I guess you don't need a lift to campus," Gilles said to Pamela.

“No thanks. I don’t have a class until this afternoon so I’ll study here and keep Mum company.”

Gilles kissed Annie goodbye and headed to the office. Luckily it hadn’t snowed overnight so his car was cold but not snowed in.

The streets of NDG hadn’t been cleared since the last storm and were still snow clogged, and it took Gilles forever to snake through them to the entrance to highway 720, the fastest way to get from the west end of the city to the Major Crimes Division. The drive exhausted Gilles and he bought a restorative cappuccino on his way up to the office. Stéphanie Giroux was in her office and Gaston Lemieux was talking to some of the cops on the L’Étrangleur task force. Gilles hung his coat in his cubicle and thought about joining Lemieux and the task force to report that he might have some helpful information. He decided against it. Lemieux, Gilles knew, wasn’t interested in what might be. If there was information, he wanted it. If not, not.

Gilles sipped as his cappuccino as his computer came to life. He opened the transcript of the sentencing part of the Chambers trial. Gilles was less familiar with Adobe pdf files than with Word files and it took him a bit of time to navigate to the search area. If his memory was accurate, it would be a simple matter to find the phrase he was looking for. He typed the phrase, “flesh is heir” into the search bar. A second later he was reading the phrase that Annie had recalled. In this case, the accused, Ian Chambers, was responding to the judge’s question asking if he had anything to say before she passed sentence. He said, “‘We end the heartaches and the thousand natural shocks the flesh is heir to. This is a consummation devoutly to be wished.’ “

Gilles slapped his desk. “Got it!” He spoke more loudly than he intended and Lemieux and the other cops looked up from their meeting.

"Je m'excuse," Gilles said. "I think I've got something. Give me a minute to print this."

The transcript didn't record Chambers' tone of voice, which, given the context and the odd syntax, Gilles imagined as arrogant. Nor was there any way of telling if the judge paused before responding to what Chambers had said. Her words clearly demonstrated her anger at his lack of remorse. "Don't think for a moment, Mr. Chambers, that a clever quote will in any way mitigate the seriousness of your crimes." She then went on to pass sentence, following which Ian Chambers was led out of the courtroom.

Gilles Googled the quote and discovered it was from *Hamlet.* Chambers had turned the part of the quotation that was a question into a statement, but other than that he had lifted it whole from the Shakespearean play. Gilles guessed that Chambers had looked it up and memorized it in preparation for his courtroom statement.

Gilles made several copies of the page with the sentence he had found, and joined the meeting. He handed a copy of the printout to Lemieux and pointed to the sentence he thought important. Lemieux directed Gilles to pass out copies to the rest of the cops assembled and asked him to explain. While Gilles spoke, Gaston did a quick search on his computer.

"Cette page est tirée de la transcription du procès Chambers," Gilles said. "It comes from the sentencing portion of the trial." He directed his colleagues to the important sentence and continued, "My girlfriend heard one of the orderlies in the ER at the hospital say virtually, if not exactly, the same thing." Everyone in the Major Crimes Division knew that Gilles's girlfriend was a nurse in the ER at the Gursky Memorial Hospital. "The task force has determined that there's a connection between the crimes of L'trangleur and the crimes of Ian Chambers. We now have a suspect and if not that certainly a person of interest. It can't be a coincidence that two people, decades apart, said the same thing. There's got to be some kind of connection."

The cops on the task force looked to Lemieux for comment. "Gilles is right," he said. "It's the kind of thing a person would look up if they wanted something clever about death. I agree, it's unlikely that two people who have the same job over two decades apart would say the same thing. It stretches credulity to think it's a coincidence. There must be some connection. The question is: what is the connection?"

Gaston patted Gilles on the shoulder and said, "Good work, Bellechasse. Or should I say that to Annie?" Gaston was aware that Annie had provided invaluable insights to other crimes Gilles had investigated.

Gilles smiled. "As usual, Annie deserves a lot of the credit."

"Okay," Gaston said. "We have another path to investigate, but that doesn't mean we stop doing what we've been doing until this bears fruit. Let's get back to work." The meeting ended and the cops returned to their cubicles and got back to doing as instructed. "You and I are going to see the boss," Gaston said to Gilles.

They went to Stéphanie's office. After they were seated Gaston explained what Gilles had uncovered. "The point is," Gaston concluded, "we have no real evidence that this guy has anything to do with the crimes."

"D'accord," Lieutenant Giroux said. "But the next step is clear. Gilles will investigate this aspect of the case."

"Oui, absolument," Gaston agreed. "Find out all you can about this guy."

"Do you want me to bring him in for questioning?" Gilles asked.

"It's probably too early for that. If he's connected to the crimes, I don't want you to tip him off that we're looking at him," Gaston said.

"But we want to make certain that he doesn't strike again," Gilles said.

"Once you identify him and get the information back to me, I'll make sure we keep an eye on him until we get something more conclusive," Lieutenant Giroux said.

The meeting ended. Gilles wanted to see Annie before she started work. If at all possible, he wanted to have a discreet look at Jean-Guy St-Onge before approaching him. After all, he had nothing on the man other than a quote that anyone could have looked up.

He called Annie and proposed meeting for lunch before the start of her shift. Without being specific, he explained that he needed her help with something. "I'll put that in the pleasant surprise column," Annie said.

Gilles smiled and suggested that they meet at the Café Briki, located on Queen Mary at the corner of Gatineau, in the shadow of St. Joseph's Oratory and the Cormier-designed tower of the Université de Montréal.

Gilles and Annie had been to the Café Briki several times when they wanted a pleasant place to meet that was far enough away from the hospital that they were unlikely to have to interrupt their conversation to exchange greetings with other people from the Gursky. The waitress, Denise, whose section of the café they favoured, greeted Gilles warmly when he arrived and placed a coffee in front of him almost as soon as he sat down. "A cappuccino for Annie?" she asked.

"She shouldn't be long."

“Okay, I’ll wait,” Denise said.

Annie arrived about five minutes later and she and Denise two-cheeked before she joined Gilles.

The menu at the Café Briki was restricted to salads, burgers, and sandwiches. Annie ordered an avocado salad and Gilles opted for a cheeseburger. He was about to order fries with it but Annie’s look changed his mind and he asked for a small side salad.

They sipped their coffees and chatted casually while they waited for their food to be delivered. When it arrived, Annie speared a slice of avocado with her fork and asked, “What is it that you need my help with?”

Gilles swallowed a bite of cheeseburger and said, “When you told me what the orderly had said, I realized that I had heard it somewhere.”

“Really?”

“I couldn’t place it, but in the middle of the night it came to me. I hadn’t heard it—I’d read it. You’ll never guess where I read those words,” Gilles said.

“You’re right … and I can see you’re bursting to tell me.”

Gilles smiled. “In the transcript of the trial of Ian Chambers.”

“In the what?” Annie, in spite of herself, was surprised. She’d expected Gilles to name a book or maybe some poem, something he found on the web. She didn’t expect it to come from a trial transcript of a long-ago court case. “The Chambers trial?”

“Yes. When the judge asked Chambers if he had anything to say he made some rambling comment about being merciful to the patients and he finished by saying,” Gilles consulted his notebook to make certain he got the quote right, “the full quote is: ‘To die—to sleep—no more; and by a sleep, to say we end the heartache, and the thousand natural shocks the flesh is heir to. "'Tis a consummation devoutly to be wished.' Almost word for word what the orderly said."

"How odd," Annie said.

"My question exactly," Gilles said. "And that's why I need your help. I'd like to find some unobtrusive way for you to point him out to me."

"Why? There have been no unexplained deaths in the ED."

"Right. But that doesn't mean there won't be, and I'd like to be in a position to prevent any. But that's not my real reason. There's been a series of strangulations that are connected to the Chambers case. The victims are descendants of victims of Chambers."

"Like Ruth Ettinger," Annie said.

"Exactly."

"And you think Jean-Guy had something to do with the attacks?" Annie felt a chill run through her body. She hugged herself.

"I don't know. I can't very well accuse him because of something he said in an unguarded moment. But I do want to keep an eye on him. I don't believe in coincidences where murder is concerned. He must have known what Chambers said. I want to know the why and how of it."

Annie considered what Gilles had told her. They ate in silence for a moment or two. "It's unnerving to think we have a killer in emerg. But yeah, I can find a way to point him out to you. No problem there. What are you going to do?"

"Once I can identify him, I can keep an eye on him. Set up surveillance, that kind of thing. If he tries something, we'll grab him. And that brings me to the second part of what I'd like."

"There's more?"

"Unfortunately, yes. The only witness to the crimes so far is Pamela. I'd like to see if she can identify St-Onge as the perpetrator."

Annie pushed her empty plate aside and stared at her boyfriend. “That is so not going to happen. Even if there is only one chance in a thousand that you are right, I’m not going to put Pam at risk. You can’t be surprised. Really.”

Gilles covered Annie’s hand with his and said, “I understand, chérie. I don’t expect her to do it in some obvious way. I don’t want St-Onge to know we’ve got an eye on him. Is there some surreptitious way of doing it? Maybe when Pamela meets you at work? I’ll talk to her so she knows what I’m looking for.”

“I don’t know. If Pam and I agree you bet you’ll talk to her first. I don’t know that she’ll do it at all but she certainly won’t do it without knowing what she’s getting into.”

“That’s all I ask,” Gilles said. He stroked Annie’s hand. He knew he was close to crossing a line. Annie was very protective of her child and would not put her at risk. “But first things first. I’d like to get a look at the fellow and talk to him if at all possible. Do you know if he works this afternoon?”

“No. I won’t know until I get to work.”

Denise cleared the empty plates and asked if they wanted another coffee. Annie looked at her watch and declined. Gilles asked for another. “How about this for a plan? I’ll wait here while you head to work and you text me if St-Onge is working. If he’s there I’ll come to the hospital and...”

“And what?” Annie asked.

“Give me a minute to think of something.” Annie watched Gilles with a slight smile on her lips as he considered the possibilities.

“Okay, how about this. You call me to say you forgot something and ask me to bring it to the hospital. Then you get busy with something and ask St-Onge to get it from me when I bring it to the hospital. Will that work?”

“Yeah, I suppose so. What did I forget?”

"How about your wallet?"

Annie took her wallet out of her purse, handed it to Gilles and said, "It'll work so long as I don't get stopped by a cop on my way back to work. My driver's licence is in it."

"Take it. He doesn't have to know it's not in your wallet."

Annie slipped her licence and registration into the pocket of her scrubs. Gilles walked her to the door of the café and they kissed goodbye. "Don't think we've dropped the subject of Pam identifying St-Onge as your suspect. We'll talk about that later."

Forty-five minutes later, barely seconds before Gilles was ready to give up hope, Annie called. "Gilles honey, I forgot my wallet somewhere. Did I leave it in your car?" She spoke a little more loudly than usual and she never called him honey.

"I'll check," Gilles said and after a couple of seconds continued. "Yes, I have it."

"Can you bring it to the hospital? I need it."

"Will do," Gilles said. He played along despite the fact that he was pretty certain that no one could hear his side of the conversation.

Fifteen minutes later he walked into the Emergency Department and looked around for Annie as he donned the face mask the security guard handed him. Tasso, one of the people who worked in Registration, spotted Gilles and asked, "Hi Gilles, looking for Annie?"

"Yeah." Gilles worried that Tasso was about to ask if he could help in some way. "She forgot her wallet. I've got it."

"Right," Tasso said, "she got called to Resus. She asked me to get Jean-Guy to bring it to her. I'll page him."

A couple of minutes later a tall slim man with blonde hair approached Gilles. "Sergeant Bellechasse?" he asked. Gilles realized that he had seen the fellow once or twice when he met Annie at the Gursky.

"Oui," Gilles said. "You're...?"

"Jean-Guy St-Onge." He and Gilles shook hands. "Annie asked me to bring her her wallet. She was called to a patient."

Gilles didn't know if he had accomplished much but he would be able to give the task force a good description of St-Onge. That might help them in their investigation—and St-Onge now knew that at least one cop knew who he was.

As Gilles was driving back to the office Annie called to tell him that she had received her wallet.

"What time do you get off?" Gilles asked.

"Late, not till eleven."

"I want to talk to you and Pamela. Maybe she can give me a description that won't necessitate her actually seeing St-Onge. How about if I take you both to breakfast tomorrow morning?"

"I'll have to confirm with Pam. I'll call you later."

◎

Gilles looked forward to a quiet evening at home with his daughter. It had been a long time since they had spent time talking. Émilie was spending as much time as she could with her mother, providing support and solace after the attack. Gilles was proud of Émilie for stepping up with very little prodding. He was aware that it meant that she had given up precious friend time.

When he got home, Gilles was surprised to be greeted by smells he associated with Indian or Asian restaurants. "Lapin," he called.

"Dans la cuisine, Pa."

He found his daughter in the kitchen standing over a wok, an item he'd forgotten he had. It was something he purchased after his divorce with the intention of learning how to cook Chinese food. He used it once to reheat leftovers from a meal he had had delivered from a local Chinese restaurant.

"Wow, quelque chose sent bon, Lapin." He and Émilie exchanged kisses on both cheeks. "I didn't know you could cook."

"Oui, Pa, j'apprends," she said and showed him the cookbook open on the counter. "I thought I would try a vegetable stir-fry. It will be ready in about fifteen minutes. I'm waiting for the rice to be done."

"Can't wait," Gilles said. "I'm going to wash up."

Gilles changed into jeans and a sweatshirt, washed his hands, and returned to the kitchen. Émilie was scooping the stir-fry over steaming white rice on two plates. Gilles took knives and forks from a drawer and set the table.

"Les baguettes, Pa, it's Chinese food."

Gilles retrieved a couple of sets of chopsticks from the cutlery drawer where he had a small stockpile of them from takeout orders. He struggled with them, but was pleased to see how adept his daughter was.

While they ate Émilie chatted happily about her courses. She was working on a Molière play. It was the senior production and she, as a second-year student, was thrilled to be a part of it.

Gilles was of two minds concerning Emilie's chosen profession. On the one hand, he had never seen her happier and more motivated. On the other, he was aware that it was very hard to make a living in that line of work. He knew full well that the world was full of unhappy people in professions they chose in order to have some kind of financial security, so he had convinced himself that she was better off being a happy actor than an unhappy accountant.

"Do you know what you and your classmates will do for your senior production next year?"

"We haven't decided yet. We have time. But I'm pushing for *Hernani*."

"Her and what? Her and I?" Gilles had a smattering of knowledge of the classics of French theatre, but had never heard of this one.

"Non, Pa," Emilie laughed. "It's one word, *Hernani*. It's by Victor Hugo."

"He wrote plays?"

"Yeah. Obviously, that's not what he's best known for. *Hernani* was very controversial when it was first performed in 1830. It violated the five rules of classical French theatre. That's why I want to do it. To honour rebellion."

Gilles had given up on the chopsticks and was using a knife and fork. The meal was spicy and delicious. "Do you have any plans for the weekend?"

"Oui, Pa, a bunch of us are going skiing. We have a chalet."

Again, Gilles was a little surprised and envisioned his novice daughter with a broken leg. "Skiing? I didn't know you had equipment."

"Cross-country skiing, I should have said. I don't have equipment; I'll rent some at the trail."

Much relieved, Gilles said, "That's wonderful, Lapin."

"There's only one problem."

"Is it money? I don't mind helping out, not at all."

"Non, Pa, it's not money. It's Maman."

As if on cue, Gilles's cellphone rang. It was his ex. Gilles sighed.

"Oui, Yvonne."

"As-tu parlé à ta fille?"

"She's right here. Why?"

Émilie picked up the empty plates and brought them to the kitchen.

"Why? Because she's going skiing this weekend."

"Yes, she just told me."

"And you have no problem with that?"

Gilles inhaled through his nose and exhaled slowly. He knew that Yvonne was wound up about something, but he couldn't see why it would be a weekend ski trip.

"Non, bien sûr que non."

"So, you don't care that she's leaving her mother completely alone? After what just happened?"

"Okay, Yvonne, I know you're upset, but Genest has been arrested and he's unlikely to bother you again. And the Longueuil cops are going to keep an eye on your place just in case. Still, I understand why you're worried and I think it would be best if you and Brigitte could continue to stay together. Step by step, life has to get back to normal."

"Normal for you and Émilie, maybe, but not for me. You weren't attacked. I was. There's a word for what I have, you know, post-traumatic stress disorder."

"Oui, Yvonne. That's possible. But for that you need to see a professional, a therapist. There's not much Émilie can do."

"She can spend time with me."

"Yes, of course. I think she's spent as much time as she can with you since the attack. But she has school and it's important for her to spend time with her friends. She has to get over the shock as well."

Yvonne sighed and said, "I agree. Émilie has been terrific. But I'm still a bundle of nerves. I jump whenever I hear a loud noise."

"Oui, je comprends," Gilles said. "It will take some time for your life to get back to normal and you know you can count on Émilie and me. But for this weekend I'm sure you'll agree that Émilie needs time to unwind."

"I suppose. But if I catch sight of Genest you'll be the first person I call."

"The second. Call the Longueuil cops first."

Émilie returned to the dining room with a couple of pastries on a plate. "That was your mother," Gilles said. "Did you know she was going to call?"

"Should I cancel, Pa? I don't want her to think I don't care."

"Non, Lapin. You go ahead with your plans. You've been wonderful. I'll call her over the weekend to ensure she doesn't feel abandoned. She agreed to stay with Brigitte."

Émilie gave her father a big hug.

Chapter 32

Gilles arrived at Âllo! Mon Coco before Annie and Pamela. When they got there, they found him at a large table next to a window, nursing a coffee and flipping through a copy of *Le Journal de Montréal* he'd found on the bench next to him. He half rose when Annie and Pam slid into the bench opposite.

Annie looked serious, her normally warm smile absent. After they ordered their breakfasts, Gilles was about to tell Pamela why he wanted to see her, but she beat him to it. "Mom said you wanted to ask me something," she said.

"Yes. I'd like your help with an investigation."

"Wow, sounds serious." Annie put her hand on her daughter's forearm but said nothing.

"It may turn out to be nothing, but you're the only one who has seen L'Étrangleur, and I was hoping you would recognize him if you saw him again."

"You caught the guy?"

"No, darling," Annie said. "Gilles wants you to take a look at a potential suspect. Am I right? I think it's too risky, dangerous."

Pamela looked from her mother to Gilles and was about to ask for an explanation when the waitress arrived with their food. After a bite or two of his omelette, Gilles said, "There's a guy who works as an orderly in emergency who said something that makes me suspect him. It's kind of a long shot but we have to investigate every lead."

"What do you want me to do?" Pam had ordered toast and coffee. She took a bite of her toast.

"I'd appreciate it if you could somehow arrange to take a look at him. Nothing obvious. Pretend to be meeting your mother for something. And let me know if you recognize him."

"I only saw him run away so I don't know that I'll be much help. But yeah, I don't see the danger."

Annie put her utensils on her plate and turned to her daughter. "The danger is that if he is the guy they're looking for then he'll know you'll know who he is. And he's killed already. What's to stop him from coming after you?"

"Mum, if he's the guy then aren't you at more risk than me? You work with him. I haven't even asked what makes you think an orderly would go around killing people. That's insane."

"It may very well be insane. Insane things happen. My real worry is that Jean-Guy is the killer. You may not recognize him but what if he recognizes you? The guy who attacked Ruth Ettinger saw you, and he had a better look at you than you did of him. Get it?"

Gilles understood perfectly the look Annie directed at him but continued, "Your mother makes a very good point. Ideally, she'll be able to point him out to you without him noticing. Would it be possible for you to accompany your mother to work after breakfast? If he's on, Annie will give you a sign or something. I'll be parked outside so when you leave, I'll give you a drive to campus. The whole thing should take less than five minutes."

Pamela and Gilles turned to Annie. She sighed and said, "I'm not pleased, but if I spot him, I'll say something like, 'Thanks for breakfast, honey.'"

"It's a plan," Pamela agreed.

"That's great. Thanks," Gilles said.

"If she makes a positive ID, I expect you to arrest him. Get it?" Annie told Gilles.

"Absolutely."

The rest of the meal passed in silence. It was only over coffee, once the table was cleared, that conversation became normal, thanks mostly to Pamela. She talked about her medical school courses and how much she was looking forward to her first hospital rotation. Annie still looked worried.

Instead of parking in the corner of the curved road that served the entrance to the Emergency Department, Gilles parked on the street. He didn't want Annie and Pamela to be seen getting out of his car by any of the staff.

He didn't have to wait long. Pamela was back in less than ten minutes. She got in the passenger's side and said, "Follow that car. 'The game is afoot.'"

"Very funny," Gilles said. "Did you see him?"

"Yes, he was busy with a patient so he didn't see me. So mum is happy."

"So am I. Was he the guy who attacked Mrs. Ettinger?"

"I can't say for certain. He had the same body type but it was dark and his face was covered."

"I was afraid of that. I'll have to find some other way of getting some kind of identification."

Gilles dropped Pamela off at McGill University. His next stop was another visit to the Kathari dry-cleaning plant. He had given Iannis's remark about the unlocked front door a lot of thought and concluded that Toula may have discovered a way to commit the perfect crime of murder.

Family dynamics were complicated and often unfathomable. Iannis may have resented his sister for being the dominant sibling. There were any number of other possibilities and Gilles decided not to speculate.

As he drove he called the office and asked that a cop be assigned to do some research on Jean-Guy St-Onge. He provided what little he had in the way of information.

He pulled into the Kathari parking area and, as he had several times before, asked the woman at the counter if Toula Prodosiakis was available.

After a brief telephone conversation, the woman at the counter motioned to the door to the stairs. "You know the way," she said.

"*Oh Theé mou.* Don't you have anything better to do?" Toula said by way of greeting.

"I had an interesting conversation with your brother."

"Yeah. I know. I'll thank you to keep your nose out of my family's business."

"Meaning...?" Gilles said.

"Meaning, my family has a business and I expect my brother to take an interest in it. To work here. He doesn't need to be sent to some lab to wash test tubes."

"He seemed happy enough to have the opportunity to meet Monsieur Chenier."

"Like I said, keep your nose out of my family's business. Are we done?"

"We haven't begun," Gilles said. "While we're on the subject of your family's company, I was wondering what it was like for you to work with your father. It can't have been easy to be both his caretaker and business partner. How were you able to handle that?"

"I don't see it's any of your business but you're right. It was difficult. And the worse my father became, the harder it was. But he was my father and family sticks together."

"Did he continue to come into the office?" Gilles asked.

Toula sighed. "Yes, in spite of the fact that he was no longer able to...to, well, get anything, I mean...make a contribution to the running of the company. I hate to say it but sometimes he was in the way. As much as I loved him, that's a fact, a sad fact."

"You must miss him."

"Yes, yes, I do. I miss him as the father he was, but I'd be lying if I didn't say that running Kathari is much easier since his passing."

Toula's comment didn't surprise Gilles in the slightest.

"Your brother told me that he unfailingly locks the front door. Probably because he's in the basement and couldn't hear if someone came in. He can barely hear the doorbell," Gilles said.

Toula rearranged some of the implements on her desk. She picked up a promotional stress ball in the shape of a light bulb and squeezed it in her left hand. "This is of concern because..."

"Because on the night your father wandered off, the door was unlocked. That means someone had to unlock it. It wasn't your brother and it certainly wasn't your father, so that leaves you."

Toula got to her feet. "Are you accusing me of something?"

Gilles stood and looked her straight in the eyes but said nothing.

"Get out of my office."

"On my way. But just so you know, I'm investigating two other murders, and the perpetrator of those crimes may not have luck on their side."

Gilles heard Toula's office door slam behind him.

Chapter 33

When Gilles got back to the Major Crimes Division office, he found a thin file on his desk. It contained the research on Jean-Guy St-Onge. There wasn't much but the cop who did it had had the foresight to request his personnel file from the Gursky. Gilles flipped through it. The file provided St-Onge's home address and basic employment information. St-Onge had worked as a pharmacy technician after he graduated from CEGEP. After three years at that job, he took the training course for orderlies. He worked at a hospital in Quebec City until moving to Montreal a year previously, when he got a job at the Gursky. He didn't provide his father's name for his file. He listed him as deceased. He gave his mother's name as Arlette St-Onge.

The Post-it Note on the cover of the file indicated that the research had been done by Constable Marie Rousseau. Gilles called her and asked if she had any more information. She explained that she was still working on it and would bring him additional details as soon as she had them.

Gilles walked the file over to Gaston Lemieux's office and explained what he had so far unearthed and that it wasn't much. Gaston flipped through the file and said, "Tu as raison, Gilles, there's not a lot here. What makes you think this guy has anything to do with the murders?"

"All I have is the fact that he said pretty much the same thing that Chambers said at his trial and the victims are all connected to the Chambers vics."

"What about your two poisoning cases?"

"Them too. Both connected to Chambers."

"Do you suspect the St-Onge fellow for them as well?"

"I don't know. At this point, no, but I have to keep an open mind."

Gaston was sitting at his desk and Gilles was leaning on the door frame while they talked. Gaston got to his feet and said, "Let's talk to the rest of the team."

Gaston walked out of his office with Gilles a pace or two behind him. They went to the area that had been reserved for the Étrangleur unit. Most of the team were working at a long table or scattered around the area engaged in private conversations.

Gaston stood at the front of the room at a whiteboard and called for everyone to gather around. He wrote the name, Jean-Guy St-Onge, on the whiteboard and explained that Gilles suspected, so far without much in the way of evidence, that he was L'Étrangleur. Gaston held up the file and told the team what it contained.

"Je veux que vous regardiez de plus près ce gars. Discreetly. I don't want him to know we're looking at him. If he's our guy I don't want him to disappear." Gaston went on to explain that Gilles would be able to give them a description of St-Onge. Gaston wrote St-Onge's address on the whiteboard.

While Gaston was instructing his team, Constable Rousseau appeared at the back of the room and waved the papers she was carrying at Gilles. He went to her; they had a whispered conference and she handed him the paperwork. Gilles flipped through the file as he walked back to the front of the room. He stopped for a moment, a smile on his lips, and quickened his pace. He interrupted Gaston's instructions and showed him one of the sheets. Gaston nodded and said to the team, "Gilles and Constable Rousseau just came up with something which makes St-Onge our main suspect. Gilles."

Gilles held up the papers and said, "Marie found his birth record. It gives us the information missing from his hospital file. Now we know the name of his father. Ian Chambers."

A chorus of congratulatory comments greeted the news. Gaston called for order and said, "It's important to have eyes on this guy. We don't want him to kill again. Do you know if he's at work, Gilles?"

"Oui. A witness to one of the attacks saw him there. I can find out when he leaves."

"What's the best way to put eyes on him?" Gaston asked.

"Give me a minute to get some information and I'll let you know." Gilles called Annie and walked to a quiet corner of the room while he spoke.

Gilles gave a description of St-Onge to the assembled cops and told them that he was at work, but that he would be finished in an hour. Gaston assigned two cops to the first surveillance shift. He chose a man and a woman and told them, "Get over to the Gursky and go to the Emergency Department and blend in with the people in the waiting room. Gilles will show up and find a way to indicate the St-Onge guy. You know what to do. Keep me posted."

The two plainclothes cops headed for the Gursky.

Gaston went to the whiteboard and wrote the names of cops in teams of two. He turned to those assembled and said, "You know what this is. It's a surveillance rotation. Take note of your place in it and be certain to communicate with the team you're replacing so you'll know where to pick up your shift. Gilles and I will be on call all weekend. If St-Onge does anything remotely suspicious, call us and we'll get you the backup you need. With any luck we'll have enough to make an arrest. We don't want any more attacks. Clear?"

"At what point do we bring him in for questioning?" one of the cops asked.

"That will have to wait on events," Gaston said.

Gilles drove to the hospital. He parked in his usual spot in the corner near the entrance of the Emergency Department. He spotted the two cops in the waiting room and looked around for Annie. She was busy with a patient in Triage. She nodded at Gilles without taking her eyes off her patient. He leaned against the wall at the far end of the waiting room but in full view of the glassed-in triage area. She completed her examination and flipped on the mic and said, "Jean-Guy to Triage with a wheelchair, please." The patient started to rise from her chair but Annie put her hand on the patient's forearm. A moment later Jean-Guy St-Onge appeared with a wheelchair. Annie had left the mic on so everyone in the waiting room heard their conversation.

"Last one for the day, Jean-Guy. Please take Miss Sullivan to Blue."

He held the wheelchair while the patient got into it. He turned and wheeled her down the corridor to the Blue section.

Annie called for the next patient, turned off the mic, and smiled at Gilles. He nodded to the two cops who nodded back.

Gilles was certain that St-Onge had not noticed him; he left the hospital before St-Onge returned from delivering the patient. He waited in his car and ten minutes later he saw St-Onge leave the hospital wearing a bright blue puffy jacket. The two cops were on his tail at a discreet distance.

A couple of minutes later his cellphone rang. It was Annie. "Did you get him? I saw him leave and a couple walked out just after him. Your people I assume."

"You assume correctly. You did great. Leaving the mic on was brilliant."

"You'd be surprised how often that happens. See you later?"

"You bet. What time do you get off?"

Chapter 34

The first report from the cops tailing St-Onge came in just as Gilles was pulling away from the Gursky. Detective Constable Monique Larose called Gilles to tell him that she was in an unmarked car parked a block or so west of the Gursky on Côte-Sainte-Catherine and her partner, André Côté, was following the suspect on foot. She had her partner in view. She called again about fifteen minutes later to report that they had followed St-Onge to his home, a duplex on Bradford Place. "On ne peut pas stationner devant la maison," she said. "It's odd – really only sidewalk with houses on both sides. You can't drive on it, only walk. There are two other streets just like it on either side."

"That's bad for us. Do you have eyes on St-Onge's house?"

"Oui. Luckily, it's on the corner so we can see it clearly. No problem," Larose said.

"Okay. Can one of you do a quick check of the area? Is there any way he can leave his house without being seen?"

"André's freezing. I'll do it on foot."

Monique Larose kept Gilles on the phone while she walked. She reported that there was an alley behind the houses that ran from Côte-Sainte-Catherine to Dupuis Avenue. That made it possible for St-Onge to leave his house by a back door or through the garage, which opened to the alley without being seen. Monique risked being spotted and walked into the alley to peek in the window of the garage under St-Onge's house. A dark-coloured Corolla was parked there.

"We can't assign more teams to the surveillance. Watch the front of the house and maybe check the alley from time to time if you can do it without being spotted."

"D'accord, Gilles."

Annie had to work both days of the weekend but they had a late dinner on Saturday night and spent Sunday morning together until Annie had to report to work. The only interruptions were the frequent phone calls from the cops surveilling Jean-Guy St-Onge, reporting that nothing much was happening. On Saturday they followed him grocery shopping with his mother, who lived with him. This confirmed that the Corolla belonged to him. Other than that, he barely set foot out of doors. On Sunday at one o'clock an unidentified woman showed up at the house. She stayed for a couple of hours, presumably having lunch with Jean-Guy and his mother.

Bradford Place was one of three neighbouring streets. The other two were Beaminister Place to the east and Campden Place to the west, built in the British mews style, nineteen duplexes on each. The three streets were built in 1936 and called Cotswold Village, named after the area in the south of England. Because automobile traffic was not possible between the houses, only foot traffic, the area was peaceful and quiet—a delight to the residents and a problem only for police on a stakeout and delivery people.

Chapter 35

Gilles got to the office early on Monday morning. He found a thick file of research on his desk. Constable Rousseau had managed to fill in a lot of blanks on St-Onge. She had found someone in the nursing office of the Emergency Department at the Gursky who provided St-Onge's work schedule. He was not at work at the times of the attacks attributed to L'Étrangleur.

In addition to the birth certificate, Constable Rousseau found documents that his mother had filed with the Directeur de l'état civil changing the family name from Chambers to St-Onge. The reason she gave the court for wanting a name change was that the father had deserted the family. Gilles supposed this was literally true as he had been in prison. Arlette failed to mention this in the documents.

Gilles tapped the papers back into the file and went in search of Constable Rousseau. "Travail fantastique," he told her. "It connects the suspect to the crimes in a way we never would have discovered without your digging."

He then went to Gaston Lemieux's office and explained what Constable Rousseau had dug up.

"Okay, I get it," Gaston said. "But the information links him to the victims. What makes you think he's the perpetrator? He himself may be at risk."

"Right. But I think the fact that he said almost the same thing that his father used in his defence tells me that he has the same opinions as his father."

“Does that explain four murders and an attempted murder?”

“I don’t know for certain, but I do know that he’s definitely worth questioning.”

“D’accord,” Gaston said.

The two men went to Lieutenant Giroux’s office and told her of their progress on the L’Étrangleur case.

“We don’t have any hard evidence,” Gilles said. “I want to invite St-Onge to come in for questioning.” He emphasized the word “invite”.

“And if he refuses?”

“I’d like to have a warrant in my back pocket. I’d rather talk to him informally, without having to read him his rights, to start.”

“Hold off on the warrant. Once you have it you have to advise him that he’s a suspect. If you can’t get him to come in voluntarily then get the warrant. Tell Manon you may need it.”

“D’accord, boss,” Gilles said.

He returned to his desk and called Manon Tremblay and explained the situation.

“Keep me posted,” she said.

He headed out to find Jean-Guy St-Onge.

Larose and Côté were again the cops on duty when Gilles parked next to their car. “I’m going to talk to St-Onge. Pull into the alley so he doesn’t run when he sees me.”

Gilles waited until Larose had pulled into the alley and rang the doorbell at the duplex on Bedford Place.

A short woman about sixty years old with short grey hair answered the door. She wore a housecoat over a nightgown, which she held closed with one arm across the middle of her slim frame. She bore the remnants of a suntan, which indicated that she was recently returned from escaping the

Montreal winter. "Madame St-Onge?" Gilles asked and showed his ID. "Je suis Sergent-détective Gilles Bellechasse. I'd like to have a word with Jean-Guy St-Onge. May I come in?"

Madame St-Onge stood aside to admit Gilles to the vestibule but she stood in the doorway that opened to the house proper. Gilles stamped the snow off his boots but made no move to remove them. Madame St-Onge looked up at him and said, "Il n'est pas ici." She crossed her arms over her chest and remained in the doorway.

Gilles rushed out of the house and ran to the alley. He asked Larose if she saw St-Onge drive away. He didn't wait for an answer but checked the garage. It was empty. He returned to the unmarked car and said, "He's not at home. I'm going to check the hospital." Gilles had a very bad feeling that St-Onge had made one of the surveillance teams and taken off. He called the Emergency Department of the Gursky, identified himself to the person who answered the phone, and asked if Jean-Guy St-Onge was at work.

"I haven't seen him but I'll page him," the person in reception said. A moment later she came back on the line and said, "I was just told that he's not on the schedule today, Gilles."

Gilles turned his attention to Larose and Côté and asked, "Is there a possibility that St-Onge spotted you?"

The two cops were silent for a moment. Côté looked embarrassed. Larose was thoughtful. "Well," she said. "Just after we arrived a woman spent a great deal of time looking out the window in our direction. We slid down. We were out of sight but she may have been suspicious of the car for some reason."

"His mother saw you and told him," Gilles said. He instructed them to go to the house and keep an eye on her. "If she won't let you in, camp on the doorstep." Then he ran back to his car. He wanted to be out of the cold, his fingers were freezing even though he was wearing gloves and his nose was running. He called the office and explained that a suspect had taken off. He wanted the licence plate number of the car and an all-points bulletin issued for it. "Call me as soon as you get some—any—information. I'm going to question the suspect's mother."

He returned to the St-Onge house to find Larose and Côté in the vestibule with Madame St-Onge still blocking entry to her house. Gilles didn't know whether to be touched or angered by her maternal protective instinct. The cops wouldn't enter without her permission.

"Madame St-Onge," Gilles said. "I have to question you. We can do it here or we can take you to headquarters as a material witness. Which do you prefer?"

Most people, including experienced and hardened criminals, capitulate at this point, but not Madame St-Onge. She stared up at Gilles and considered her options.

"You'd pull an old woman out of her house in her nightgown?" she asked.

"Constable Larose will accompany you to your bedroom if you want to change."

"Never mind," she said. "Take off your boots and come in." She turned and walked down a hallway. Gilles told André Côté to stay in the vestibule while Monique Larose accompanied him.

He followed Madame St-Onge to the kitchen. It was large enough to accommodate the normal kitchen appliances along with a table next to a window that looked out on the back alley. The kitchen was spotless.

Now that there were two cops seated at her kitchen table Madame St-Onge's mood warmed a little and she offered them coffee. She didn't wait for them to answer and poured them each a cup from a Keurig carafe.

"Merci, madame," Gilles said and pulled out his notebook. "When did Jean-Guy leave?"

"Why do you want him? He hasn't done anything."

"We have some questions for him," Gilles said. "Just routine. I'll ask you again: do you know when he left and where he was going?"

"He's gone. That's all I know." She sat at the table with her own cup of coffee.

"Do you know where he went?"

"No. I told you."

"Did he tell you where he was going?

Madame St-Onge was silent for a minute. She clearly felt uncomfortable giving the police information about her son. Finally, she said, "I'm only going to say again that he's gone." She folded her arms across her chest. Gilles understood that she didn't want to tell an outright lie to the cops.

Gilles tapped his pen against his notepad and was about to say something when his cellphone rang. He took the call. It was the office providing him with the plate number of St-Onge's car and to confirm that an APB had been issued.

"Bien," Gilles said. "Get someone to call Air Canada and WestJet security to see if he's on a flight out of Montreal. Check the other airlines, alert the TSA, and you may as well check with Via Rail as well. If he's leaving the city I want to know where he's going. And when." He ended the call and returned his attention to Madame St-Onge. "You heard all that. If your son thinks he can elude us he's very badly mistaken. And if you think you can help him in any way, so are you. You're risking arrest as an accessory after the fact."

Madame St-Onge's lower lip trembled but she didn't say anything. She regained her composure and said, "I told you. He was gone when I woke up."

Gilles was silent for a moment. Monique covered Madame St-Onge's hand with hers and said, "It's natural for us to want to protect our children. But sometimes the best thing we can do for them, the hardest, is to help the authorities when necessary."

Tears welled up in Arlette St-Onge's eyes. "Constable Larose is right," Gilles said. There were times when I had to make difficult decisions concerning my daughter. When I made the tough decisions, things worked out for the better, I can assure you."

"He's a good boy. I don't know what you think he's done, but there must be a mistake. Tell me."

"We want to question him about a series of attacks. As I said, routine." Gilles did not want to give away too much information. He sensed that Madame St-Onge was in a fragile state and he didn't want to risk her health. "Tell us something about him. We know that his father was convicted of serious crimes and that you did your best to protect your child."

"Children. I also have a daughter," Madame St-Onge said. "I moved to Quebec City where no one knew us and probably didn't know what my husband had done. I changed our name. In the end I gave them as good a life as I could."

"You chose your maiden name, St-Onge, right?" Gilles asked.

"Oui. Ian was a loving father. He was wonderful with his children, so I wanted to remember that part of him. Selfish I suppose, but that's the way I felt."

"They, your children, didn't know anything about your husband's crimes?"

"They were very young, so no; they only knew that their father had done something wrong and he couldn't live with us anymore."

"Did they ask about him, about what he had done?" Monique asked. Gilles made some notes about what Madame St-Onge had so far told them.

"Not at first. But when Jean-Guy was in high school he started to ask questions and by the time he was in CEGEP he started to do research on his own. His father was dead, himself a murder victim, at that time."

"Do you know what your son thought about his father?" Gilles asked.

"Oui. He thought his father was some kind of innocent victim, a man who sought to end suffering as God intended. He didn't talk much about it but I could tell from what little he said that he thought life was a journey that had a beginning and an end. That making people suffer to prolong the journey when the person couldn't enjoy it made no sense."

Gilles didn't want to get into a theological or philosophical debate with Madame St-Onge. He wanted to catch a killer. "Did he express anger at what happened to his father?"

"When he talked about it at all, yes. Absolutely. And I agreed with him. Jean-Guy was denied a loving father who's only purpose was to end suffering. Maybe I was wrong but I felt that Ian was heroic and time has proved me correct, non?"

"Now there are laws to allow people to decide when it's time to bring an end to their suffering. Do you think my children are unaware of this? Do you think they don't understand that their father was taken from them for caring about people before the law came to the same conclusion he did?" Madame St. Onge was talking about events that occurred twenty-five years previously. They were still fresh wounds for her and her family.

"Did your feelings fuel the anger of Jean-Guy?" Gilles asked.

"Yes, I suppose it did but what was I supposed to do? Lie to my children?" Madame St-Onge said. "I gave them the facts. The people who spoke at my husband's trial made it sound like their relatives were killed in the prime of life. In fact, they were lingering at death's door, barely in their right minds and my Ian gave them a dignified end."

"Even if it led to feelings for revenge?"

Madame waved her hand in the air as if she could wave away Gilles's last sentence. "You don't know that." She said.

Gilles was silent for a moment to give Madame St-Onge a moment to bring her feelings under control.

"Do you have a photo of your son?" he asked. St-Onge did not have much of a head start and he wanted to get his photo out as an APB.

Madame St-Onge got up from the table and went to the living room. Gilles followed her. The room was sparsely furnished. There was a sofa with a coffee table in front of it. A bay window behind the sofa looked out on the front area of the mews. There was a large flat-screen TV on the wall opposite the sofa and a comfortable-looking leather chair and ottoman placed at an angle that indicated it was where Jean-Guy sat to watch TV. An unused fireplace took up most of the wall adjacent to the sofa. There were some bookshelves full of books and some photographs on the wall opposite it. The room looked functionally comfortable but Gilles could see that other than some family photos there was very little of a personal nature in the room, no souvenirs or other mementos from Jean-Guy's life.

Madame St-Onge went to one of the bookshelves and returned with a photograph of Jean-Guy, smiling, in his scrubs. He was standing between two women with his arms around them. The woman on left of the photo was obviously his mother. The younger woman on the right side in the photograph, her left shoulder outside the camera's range, was, Gilles assumed, St-Onge's sister. Mother and sister were a little out of focus. "The young woman," Gilles said. "Who is she?"

"My daughter, Jacqueline," Madame St-Onge said.

As they walked back to the kitchen Gilles asked Madame St-Onge how long she had lived with her son.

"I don't live here. I live in Quebec City. I was in Florida but had to leave. My insurance won't cover me for this corona thing. Stupid. I decided to visit my kids before facing a Quebec winter."

Another small mystery solved.

Gilles propped the photo up and took a picture of it with his cellphone, making certain to get St-Onge in clear focus. He emailed it to the Major Crimes Division with a note to circulate it as an update to the APB.

Madame St-Onge retrieved the photo from Gilles and held it close to her chest.

"I'm going to ask you again, Madame, do you know where your son is headed?"

"No. He just said that he might leave and not to worry. He sent me a message." She pulled her cellphone from a pocket of her housecoat and showed the cops the message from her son. It said that he had to leave for a while and not to worry. The time stamp was 6:43 that morning. Madame St-Onge construed this as proof of his innocence. Gilles had Madame St-Onge forward the message to his cellphone and he took the extra precaution of recording Jean-Guy St-Onge's cellphone number in his notepad.

Gilles believed her when she said she had no knowledge of his whereabouts.

He gave Madame St-Onge his card and told her to call him if she heard from her son. "Je vous en supplie, Madame, pas d'héroïsme. I don't want harm to come to any more people." Gilles got to his feet and he and Monique left the St-Onge home.

Gilles was about to assign tasks to the two cops when he received a call from the office. Gilles listened to the report and rang off. He told Monique and André that St-Onge was not booked on any flights out of Montreal and the same was true for Via Rail. "He's had a head start but not a big one," Gilles said. "I'm going to go back to the office and coordinate the search from there. Let's hope the APB turns something up."

Back at the office Gilles told Gaston Lemieux and Lieutenant Giroux what had transpired and checked to see if any sightings of St-Onge's car had been made. No luck. Gilles went to the food court in the shopping centre below the Major Crime Division offices and had an early lunch. He was nervous at not having had any news, and the sandwich he had eaten didn't sit well in his stomach.

He paced around the shopping centre, hoping to walk off his nervous energy. After twenty minutes he gave up. Still feeling queasy he returned to the office.

"Gilles," the receptionist said as soon as Gilles emerged from the elevator, "we're looking for you. Why didn't you answer your phone?"

He took his phone out of his pocket and saw that there were a number of missed calls. He had set his phone to silent when he was interviewing Madame St-Onge and had forgotten to change it back.

"Merde," he said. "What is it?"

"I think they found the car you're looking for. Sergeant Lemieux has the details."

Gilles rushed to Gaston's office and apologized for having missed the calls. "The car's been found?"

"Oui, a couple of cops in Laval found it near the Montmorency metro station."

"Laval? He ditched his car there?"

"Yeah," Gaston said.

Gilles fell into the visitor's chair in Gaston's office. "That makes no sense. I can see him heading south or east, but why get rid of the car? How would he get another one?" Gilles thought for a minute and realized what St-Onge had done. He quickly got to his feet and said, "C'est une ruse. He's hoping we'll look for him in Laval or maybe the north. I'll bet he jumped on the metro and headed for the bus terminal. I'm on my way."

Gilles sped to the Voyageur Bus Terminal on Berri with his siren blaring. It took him less than fifteen minutes.

Gilles fast-walked into the terminal and saw that there was a lineup at the ticket windows. He walked around the building looking for St-Onge and noticed machines where travellers could buy tickets to their destinations. No trace of his quarry. If St-Onge had bought a ticket to somewhere, Gilles hoped he had used one of the machines, as he was certain there were closed-circuit TV cameras at each one. It didn't take long to find a uniformed security agent. Gilles identified himself and asked to see the head of security.

The agent spoke into his walkie-talkie and brought Gilles to the office of Pierre Beliveau, the head of security. Beliveau, tall and broad with white hair and a white moustache, a former cop, stood to shake hands with Gilles and invited him to sit down in his cramped office. Gilles got right down to business. He asked if there was CCTV at the terminal, especially in the area of the ticket machines.

"Il y a des caméras partout," Beliveau said. "What do you need?"

"I'm looking for this guy." He showed Beliveau the photo he had. He used his thumb and index finger to expand the image of Jean-Guy St-Onge. "I think he bought a ticket to somewhere this morning. Probably after seven."

Beliveau took Gilles to the operations room, next door to his office. There were security personnel working on computers. A large electronic map of North America showed where buses were moving across the continent. Beliveau spoke to one of the technicians. Gilles sat next to the technician so he could get a clear look at the CCTV from four ticket machines, arranged in quadrants on the screen.

"Don't you have face-matching technology?" Gilles asked without taking his eyes off the screen.

"Not here. For that we send the tapes to the cops."

Gilles hoped it wouldn't be necessary to take that step. St-Onge would be long gone if that were necessary. The technician brought up the second batch of four machines and started to scroll. "Wait," Gilles said, pointing to the screen. "That's our guy. Slow down."

Gilles watched St-Onge operate the ticket machine, pick up his ticket from the dispenser and walk away.

"Where is he going?"

The technician noted the time and machine ID and rolled his chair to another computer terminal. He typed the information into it, waited a second or two, and said, "Quebec City. He was on the eleven o'clock bus. It gets into the terminus at two fifteen."

"It stops in Sainte-Foy, right?" Gilles said, naming a suburb of Quebec City.

"Oui," the technician replied.

Gilles called his boss and reported what he had found. "The bus should be at the Gare Sainte-Foy in about fifteen minutes. If the Quebec City police meet the bus there they should be able to apprehend our guy," Gilles said.

Gilles returned to the office to await news from the Quebec City police.

He didn't have to wait long. Thirty minutes later he received a call from the Quebec City police informing him that they had Jean-Guy St-Onge in custody. Gilles arranged for the Sûreté du Québec to transfer St-Onge to Montreal the next day with its scheduled transfer of prisoners.

Back at the office he called Suzanne Rigaud at the Computer Crimes Division and asked her to check Jean-Guy St-Onge's cellphone records. He gave her the dates and times of the crimes of L'Étrangleur, including the attempt on the life of Ruth Ettinger. He added that he needed the information by the next day if possible.

"You don't ask for much, do you, Gilles?" Rigaud said.

"Not more than you can handle."

"You have no idea how hard it is to get information out of the phone companies. They have the annoying habit of asking for warrants. Protecting the privacy of their subscribers, they claim."

Gilles sighed. He didn't want to wait for the crown prosecutor to find a judge to sign a warrant—a procedure that could take a couple of hours or a day. He wanted the information for when he interviewed St-Onge. "I'll call Tremblay," he said.

"Let me give it a try. I can tell by the telephone number prefix that it's a Quebec cellphone company. I have a friend there. I'll let you know if I get anywhere."

"You're the best, Suzanne. I owe you."

"You certainly do. I'm running a tab for you. The problem is that you never come to Ville St. Laurent so I can collect. Do I have to wait for someone to be murdered out here to see you?"

"I'll get there. Promise," Gilles said.

The last thing he did before leaving for the day was to call Manon Tremblay to request two warrants. One to search the St-Onge home on Bedford Place and another to get cellphone location records for St-Onge's phone in case Rigaud struck out.

"I suppose there's a rush," Manon said.

"Of course. When isn't there? If for any reason I'm not available when you get them, please give them to Gaston or Lieutenant Giroux."

Chapter 36

Gilles didn't expect the Sûreté to get St-Onge to Montreal much before ten. He got to the office at nine in order to consult with Gaston and Lieutenant Giroux and prepare for St-Onge's interrogation. The two men occupied chairs in the lieutenant's office. She slid coasters to the two men for their coffee cups. "Are you prepared to make an arrest, Gilles?" she asked. "What have you got in the way of evidence?"

"Frankly, not much. As I explained, it was something that Annie overheard him say that raised my suspicions. I wanted to question him at his home. The fact that he took off is to me evidence that he's guilty of something. Or else why run? I think he was planning to hide out at his mother's house. She lives in Sainte-Foy. At the very least he's a material witness who fled the jurisdiction."

"Gaston?" Lieutenant Giroux said.

"Oui, d'accord. I think Gilles is right. I'm not saying that innocent people look forward to being interviewed by the cops, and they may do what they can to avoid it, but they don't try to throw us off with a false trail. Either they make themselves scarce or they get it over with as quickly as possible. So, yeah, I think St-Onge is our man. Getting him to confess is quite another problem."

"What's your plan?" Lieutenant Giroux asked.

Gilles sipped his coffee, placed the cup on the coaster, and said, "We know he has no alibi for the times of the murders. That in itself is not proof of anything unless we have more, a weapon, something. He knows we're on to him. After talking to his mother I have a pretty clear idea how he felt about his father and what motivates him. He doesn't know what I know so I'll start by letting him guide the conversation and see where we end up."

"I'm hopeful that we'll have at least enough for a search warrant," Gaston added.

"It's in the works. I spoke to Manon yesterday," Gilles said.

"Okay. Gilles in the interview room, Gaston watching," Lieutenant Giroux said.

While they waited for their prisoner to be delivered, they spent time in Gaston's office reviewing their tactics and chatting.

Shortly after ten the Sûreté transferred custody of St-Onge to Gilles. Gilles brought him to an interview room and offered him a coffee, which he gratefully accepted.

After a couple of minutes Gilles said, "Let me lay my cards on the table. You're a smart guy and I'd rather not play games." St-Onge raised his head and stared at Gilles. "I wanted to talk to you because something you said about death, about it being 'a consummation devoutly to be wished,' rang a bell for me. I checked and discovered it was what Ian Chambers said at his sentencing. I then discovered that you're his son."

St-Onge sipped at his coffee. He needed a moment to collect his thoughts. He didn't expect to be interrogated about his father.

"Do you have any memories of your father?" Gilles asked.

"Yes, some. Not many. He was taken from his family when I was a child. But the memories I do have are happy ones."

Gilles leaned forward and said, "But he had done some terrible things. He was a murderer."

St-Onge was silent for a couple of seconds and then slapped the table. "He wasn't a murderer. He was a caring, compassionate man who didn't want his patients to suffer needlessly. We all die. Why add suffering into the bargain?"

"Neither you nor your father have the right to make that decision for the patients under your care."

"I never did anything other than follow the instructions of the nurses or the doctors," St-Onge said, doing his best to bring his anger under control.

"There were four murders and one attempted murder. All the victims were people connected with your father's trial, with people who made victim impact statements."

"You mean people who did their best to deny me my father?"

"So, you know about them, that they were murdered?"

"I read the newspapers," St-Onge said.

"How do you feel about them?"

"What an odd question. Why should I feel anything?"

"They were human beings who hadn't done anything to anyone and they were murdered. You'd think you would feel a little of that compassion you spoke of earlier."

"For people who had my father incarcerated for trying to ease the suffering of their relations. Hardly."

Gilles didn't say anything for a moment.

St-Onge took Gilles's silence for an indication that the interview was over and that he was free to go. He got to his feet and said, "If that's all, then I think I'll be on my way."

Gilles didn't move. "We're not done. Sit down," he commanded.

St-Onge sat back down and glared at Gilles. Gilles went to the door of the interview room and asked the uniformed cop at the door to keep an eye on his prisoner while he consulted with Gaston.

He returned to the interrogation room and said, "Do you know or have you heard of Marcus Tiddley or Alain Patenaude?"

"I think Tiddley is at the hospital. I never heard of the other guy."

"Tiddley's father was killed by your father and Patenaude's mother was the judge at his trial. They're both dead. Murdered."

"Now you think I'm a strangler and a poisoner." St-Onge.

"I didn't say anything about poison," Gilles said.

"Like I said, I read the papers."

"The interview is over for the moment but not at an end. I'd like you to remain. I can get you something to eat if you like. Or more coffee."

"Do I have a choice?" St-Onge asked.

"Not really."

"Then I'd like a lawyer," St-Onge said.

"You can make a phone call if you like. You haven't been charged with anything. As far as we're concerned, you're a co-operating citizen."

"Still, I'd like a lawyer to make certain that my co-operation," St-Onge emphasized the word, "doesn't get me in trouble. I don't know any lawyers, though."

"I'll have someone sent up from Legal Aid," Gilles said and left the room.

He called Legal Aid and arranged for a lawyer to be present for the rest of the interrogation. Gilles then held a brief consultation with Gaston who informed him that a warrant had been issued and Larose and Côté had been sent to the St-Onge house to search it.

Gilles and Gaston decided that they would let St-Onge stew in the interrogation room while they grabbed a sandwich for lunch. There wasn't much they could do until the lawyer from Legal Aid arrived. Experience had taught both cops that when a suspect was left alone for a while, they tended to be more co-operative when the questioning resumed.

They returned from lunch to find an angry woman waiting for them in the reception area. The woman, short and slim with mouse-coloured hair cut short, dressed in a blue skirt and matching jacket, got to her feet and introduced herself as Pierrette Lavoie, the lawyer from Legal Aid.

"Je ne suis pas impressionnée par vos jeux," she said. "I want to see my client. You know damn well making him wait is a violation of his rights."

"Je suis desolé," Gilles said. "We didn't expect you to get here so quickly. The receptionist should have called us. We were just downstairs."

"Yeah, I'll bet," Pierrette Lavoie said.

Gilles and Gaston led her into the squad area. As they passed the receptionist Gilles winked at her. She made the motion of drinking a coffee, communicating the cost of blaming her for keeping the lawyer waiting.

Gilles accompanied the lawyer to the interrogation room and Gaston wandered off to take up his position in the viewing room. At the threshold to the interrogation room Lavoie turned to Gilles and said, "I want time alone with my client. And make sure our conversation is private." She nodded at the two-way mirror and gently pushed Gilles out of the room.

Five or so minutes later she opened the door and said, "Okay. We're ready. But first my client needs the bathroom. If you had kept him waiting five more minutes he'd have pissed in the corner."

When St-Onge returned he sat on one side of the table with his lawyer beside him, facing Gilles and the mirror. Gilles turned on the tape recorder, gave the date and time, and asked St-Onge and Lavoie to identify themselves for the purpose of the recording.

Before Gilles could ask a question Pierrette Lavoie spoke up. "Why exactly are we here? Why was my client arrested in Quebec City and brought back to Montreal? What exactly is he charged with?"

"To answer your last question first: nothing. Why was he arrested in Quebec? We went to his house to talk to him. He fled. Ditched his car and made his way to Quebec where he probably intended to hide out at his mother's house and then head God knows where. He'd be less than two hours from the American border. Pretty suspicious behaviour, wouldn't you say?"

"I'd say it's the behaviour of someone who was under no obligation to talk to you and went to Quebec to prepare his mother's house for her. She'd been in Florida for a couple of months and he wanted to air out her house and stock the fridge. It's a lot to ask of an elderly woman. She stayed at his place in Montreal."

Gilles was barely able to supress a smile. It wasn't much of a story but a pretty good effort, nevertheless. He looked at Lavoie respectfully. "Good try. Please explain why he parked his car in Laval. There's plenty of parking at the bus terminal."

"Where my client parked his car is not germane. It's not illegal to park in Laval. And if it is, the Laval police will ticket him. We'll be on our way." She got to her feet and motioned for St-Onge to do the same. Before they could move toward the door there was a knock on it and Marie Rousseau walked in with a file folder in her hand. She showed Gilles the contents of the file, two pieces of paper, one with writing and the other a map. Gilles thanked her and returned to where he was seated. He told Lavoie and St-Onge to sit down.

"I'm not done," he said. "The reason we wanted to question your client had to do with a series of murders, strangulations." Gilles opened the file and continued, "I have a report from the phone company. It puts Jean-Guy St-Onge at the exact spot where an attempt was made on the life of Ruth

Ettinger." He flipped the file folder around so lawyer and client could look at the map which showed cell towers and a series of numbers and times.

Lavoie, still standing, placed her hands on the table and leaned forward in order to look at the map, which was full of swirls and x's on a street grid. "Am I supposed to understand this?"

"Sit down and I'll explain," Gilles said. The lawyer sighed. She and St-Onge sat down. Using his pen as a pointer and reading from the first sheet he'd pulled from the file he said, "These are pings from the cell towers closest to where the attack on Mrs. Ettinger occurred. One of the cellphones in the area belongs to your client." Gilles tapped his pen on one of the series of numbers.

"And the others? Maybe they're guilty of something."

Gilles waited a second before answering. "Not possible. One of the other cellphones belonged to the victim, Ruth Ettinger, and another to the young woman who happened on the scene and saved her life. We have her statement. No, the attacker was your client. So..."

Gilles was interrupted by another knock at the door and again Marie Rousseau entered. She showed Gilles something on her cellphone and left. Again, Gilles returned to the table and said, "My colleague just showed me some photographs of the kind of rope used in the murders of the other four victims. She'll be forwarding them to me. While we've been here a search was made of St-Onge's home, with a warrant, and that's where we found the rope."

Gilles's cellphone beeped and he showed Lavoie and St-Onge the photos of the yellow rope the search had turned up.

"You mean rope that anyone could buy anywhere and use for any number of reasons. You'll be hauling in people by the busload if that's your evidence. I'll bet every garage in the city has that rope," Lavoie said.

"You may be right, Maître, but that's not where we found it. This rope was hidden in the hassock in the suspect's living room. How many people would you say stash something like this," Gilles waved his cellphone, "in a place like that?"

The room was silent while Gilles let the information sink in. He got to his feet and said, "Jean-Guy St-Onge, I'm arresting you for the attempted murder of Ruth Ettinger. You may be charged with additional crimes as the investigation progresses."

He walked around the table to where St-Onge was seated, pulled him to his feet and placed him in handcuffs.

"I'm instructing my client not to answer another question unless a lawyer is present," Lavoie declared.

"So far he hasn't answered any questions," Gilles said as St-Onge was led away.

Pierrette Lavoie turned to leave but Gilles stopped her. "It's the other way," he said and led her to the reception area. She retrieved her coat from the closet and while she waited for the elevator, she told Gilles, "I won't be representing St-Onge in the future. He has a good job and doesn't qualify for legal aid. Had I known that when you called, I wouldn't have come. Be careful about that in the future." The elevator arrived and just before the doors slid closed on her she added, "At St-Onge's request, I'll call his mother and tell her where he is."

Gilles shrugged at his reflection in the elevator doors and went to his desk to complete the paperwork necessary for the arrest and booking of Jean-Guy St-Onge.

About thirty minutes later he was told that there were two women in the reception area who insisted on speaking to him. He was confronted by Madame St-Onge and a young woman. She was dressed in jeans, a burgundy-coloured sweatshirt and a dark green puffy jacket.

"Où est mon fils?" Madame St-Onge demanded.

"He's been taken to jail," Gilles said. "You'll probably be able to see him tomorrow."

Madame St-Onge went white and almost collapsed into one of the chairs. She was supported by the young woman. "Assieds-toi, Maman," she said and helped her mother to a chair. She turned to Gilles and said, "I don't know what you're playing at, but you have no right to arrest my brother." Gilles recognized the woman from the photograph of Madame St-Onge and her son.

"You're Jacqueline, right?" Gilles said. "His sister? Your brother is charged with a very serious crime and possibly crimes. So yeah, he's under arrest."

Jacqueline took a step closer to Gilles. They were standing almost toe to toe. "You have no right. My brother hasn't done anything. Where is he? Is he here?"

This was not the first time a relative of a perp had got into Gilles's face, and it didn't bother him. He did feel sorry for Madame St-Onge.

He looked down at Jacqueline who was almost a foot shorter than he. Now that he saw her close up, he was certain that he'd seen her somewhere before.

"Look," he said, "there's nothing to be done today. Take your mother home and see she gets some rest. This is obviously very hard on her. You should be able to see your brother tomorrow."

Jacqueline held her ground. "And what about bail?"

"Tomorrow at the earliest. A judge decides that. I've told you all that I can for the moment." Gilles turned and walked through the door that led to the squad room.

The last thing he did before he left for the day was to give the dates, times, and locations of the other L'Étrangleur crimes to Suzanne Rigaud so she could determine if St-Onge's cellphone was at the scene of any of them.

That night at his condo he and Annie talked about their days as they finished dinner. Annie looked stressed, more affected by the day in the Emergency Department than usual. He wanted to tell her about the arrest he had made but understood that she obviously had a lot on her mind and wanted to talk about it. "Was today very rough?" he asked.

"One of the worst in my career. This epidemic, pandemic really, is very bad. We had three more cases today." Annie shook her head slowly and continued. "It's awful, very contagious, we've had more than a dozen patients with it in the last week or so. All elderly from old people's homes. It spreads like fire and is fatal to the aged. We lost five and the others are on the edge."

"Where did it come from?"

"It came from China and the only thing you can do is shut everything down. Stay home. We're wearing N95 masks and protective gear and God knows how long our supplies will last. Many of the old people's homes don't have enough masks and other equipment—or staff, for that matter. The way we treat the elderly is shameful. Now they're the first victims of this new epidemic and it's killing them. Just imagine what would happen if we treated some other part of the population that way?"

Gilles and Annie moved to the living room sofa. Gilles held Annie in a close embrace while she sipped at her wine and let the day drain away from her. "Thank God I'm off tomorrow," she said and snuggled closer to her boyfriend.

They sat in silence. Instead of telling Annie about the events of his day, he went over them in his mind. He replayed the scene with Madame St-Onge and her daughter several times, hoping to remember where he had seen her before.

"Damn," he said aloud, waking Annie from a dozy nap.

"What?" she said. She placed her empty wine glass on the coffee table.

"Did you know Jean-Guy St-Onge had a sister?"

"No, how would I?"

"Well, we arrested him today and his mother and sister came to the station. I knew I had seen her, the sister, before but I couldn't place her. I just realized where."

"Wait. What? You arrested Jean-Guy? What for?"

"At the moment for the attack on Mrs. Ettinger. There will very likely be more charges."

Talking about the attack on Mrs. Ettinger brought back the memory of the risk her daughter had taken in defending the woman and another jolt of stress shot through Annie.

"She has a different last name, though. She's one of the researchers in Tiddley's lab. She was at the meeting I had with Dr. Russell."

Wide awake and happy to have something to occupy her mind that was not the coronavirus, Annie said, "Tell me everything."

Chapter 37

Gilles's first order of business the next morning was to make another visit to the St-Onge home, this time to talk to Jacqui. He drove to Bedford Place and rang the doorbell. Jacqui, dressed in pyjama bottoms and a McGill University sweatshirt, answered the door. She had opened it wide but when she saw who was on the doorstep, she closed it halfway and placed her foot against it to prevent Gilles from pushing it open. "What?" she asked.

"I'd like to talk to you and your mother for a couple of minutes."

"Not unless you have a warrant. Haven't you done enough?"

"Listen to me," Gilles said. "If you insist that I get a warrant to talk to you and your mother I'll do it. But in that case, we'll be talking at my office. A squad car will come with the warrant and bring you in. Is that what you want?"

Before Jacqui could answer, Madame St-Onge called from the back of the house, "C'est qui, Jacqui?"

"The cops."

Madame St-Onge came out of the kitchen, tightening the tie of her bathrobe as she walked toward the door. "What do you want now? Haven't you done enough?"

"He wants to talk to us," Jacqui answered. "He'll bring us to the police station if we don't let him in."

Madame St-Onge stood next to her daughter and glared at Gilles. "For God's sake, the only reason to go back to the police station will be to bring Jean-Guy home. Let him in."

She turned and walked back to the kitchen. Jacqui shrugged and opened the door wide enough to admit Gilles.

They sat at the kitchen table. Madame St-Onge poured coffee for herself and her daughter and pointedly did not offer Gilles one.

"I know this is hard. First your husband is jailed and now your son is in custody. I have a daughter and I know how I would feel if she was in trouble." Madame St-Onge's glare softened a bit but she still didn't offer Gilles a coffee. "Your son is charged with serious crimes. . ."

"Without evidence," Jacqui put in.

"With evidence and more to come. Once we know who the perpetrator of a series of crimes is, the evidence tends to fall into place."

"And if not?"

"Then we know we have the wrong person and we follow the evidence wherever it leads. That's why I'm here. If you co-operate, it will go easier on Jean-Guy."

"Evidence? What evidence? The cops have already searched the place."

Gilles looked Jacqui in the eyes and said, "I'm not talking about physical evidence, at least not at the moment. And my questions are for you."

"Me? I don't know anything."

"We'll see. You're a chemist in Dr. Tiddley's lab, right?"

"Yes," Jacqui said.

"You have a degree in chemistry?"

"A master's."

"Okay," Gilles said. "Did you in any way provide your brother with a poison that could be used as murder weapon?"

Jacqui didn't answer immediately. She continued to stare at Gilles and he detected a slight smile on her lips. "No," she said, finally.

Gilles took his notepad from his jacket pocket. He flipped it open and asked, "I'd like your address, please.

"As if I have a poison-making lab in the basement. It's an apartment." She gave Gilles her address on Vendôme. "It's near the corner of Sherbrooke," she added. "I'm in apartment seven."

"I'd like to head over there now, if that's okay with you?"

"Not without a..." Jacqui paused for a moment and continued. "Not now. I'm with my mother and I want to stay with her a little longer. How about this afternoon, after lunch? I'll be home."

Gilles was about to object. He didn't want to give Jacqui the opportunity to head home and clean up any incriminating evidence. But he had a better idea and readily agreed. "If you give me your cell number I'll call when I'm on the way. And one more thing. Why is your last name different from your mother's and your brother's?"

"I was married. I kept my ex-husband's name," Jacqui said. "How is that your business? It's hardly illegal. It's not even unusual." She provided Gilles with her cellphone number and walked him to the front door.

Back in his car he called the division and arranged for an unmarked police car to keep Jacqui's apartment under surveillance. If she returned home and removed evidence, he wanted to know about it. He gave instructions to photograph anything Jacqui did if at all possible.

He drove to the address on Vendôme to await the surveillance car, just in case Jacqui got home before it arrived. As soon as the unmarked car was in position, Gilles returned to the office. He reported to Lieutenant Giroux and Gaston and called Suzanne Rigaud in the Computer Crimes Division to see if she'd had any luck with the information he'd given her.

"I'll need paper," Suzanne said. "I can call in one favour, that flies below the radar. But four, that will be a problem."

"I'll call the crown and have her get in touch with you. It will be Manon Tremblay."

Gilles called Manon Tremblay, explained what he needed and gave her Suzanne Rigaud's email and phone number. By the time he had finished all of this it was eleven-thirty. He knew that Annie could probably use a decompression break, so he called her and suggested a lunch in the area. It would get her out of the hospital for a while.

He picked her up at noon and headed to one of the cafés on Côte-des-Neiges.

"Would you like a glass of wine?" Gilles asked when they were settled at a table.

"More than you realize, but no, I need all my faculties."

"More coronavirus?" Gilles asked.

"Two more cases this morning. Tell me about your morning, I don't want to talk about mine."

They ordered sandwiches and cappuccinos and Gilles told Annie about his meeting with Madame St-Onge and Jacqui.

"You're assuming that she helped her brother poison two people?" Annie asked.

"Hypothetically."

"It's possible, I suppose. But there is another possibility," Annie said.

"She had the skill to make the poisons to kill Tiddley and Patenaude."

"I'm sure she did. But it seems to me that you are solving three sets, if I can use the term, of murders." Annie said. "How about this as a possibility? There are times when patients present with multiple symptoms that may indicate that they have two or more conditions which share symptoms. We have to differentiate between the conditions to know which symptoms belong to which condition."

Gilles thought for a couple of minutes and said, "I hadn't thought of it in quite that way, but you're right. I have three murder methods, so three murderers. The hardest one to figure out is the death of Mr. Prodosiakis. Was there something in the meds Tiddley gave him? Is his daughter somehow involved? Or was it the result of an unfortunate accident, his wandering around unprotected in the cold?"

Annie smiled and the conversation turned to other topics.

After Gilles dropped Annie off at the hospital, he called the surveillance car and asked if there had been any activity.

"Oui. Elle est revenue il y a environ une heure."

"And," Gilles prompted.

"She brought a bag of garbage down and threw it in one of the recycling bins. We have the bag in the trunk. It was the only one in the bin. The pickup had already taken place. We have photos, before and after, to prove it."

"Excellent. I'm on my way." He called Jacqui as promised and headed to her apartment. His original idea was to motivate her to try to hide evidence which the cops on stakeout would witness, then grab the evidence. It worked.

Gilles found the surveillance car in the alley next to Jacqui's apartment building. It was parked far enough back so the cops could keep an eye on the street and the area behind the building. "What've you got?" he asked. The driver popped the trunk and Gilles retrieved the see-through blue recycling bag. He climbed into the back seat of the car to go through it. She had stuffed the bag with shredded paper including some bills on which, although torn, Gilles could make out her name. At the bottom of the bag he found evidentiary gold – a blonde wig and a hairnet. With a gloved hand he slid the wig into an evidence bag. He used his thumb and forefinger to carefully lift the hairnet and place it in an evidence bag. He poked around and found an N95 mask. It, too, went into an evidence bag.

Gilles got out of the car and walked to the front door of the building with the two uniformed cops. He briefed them on what he wanted and mounted the stairs to Jacqui's apartment. She had changed her pyjama bottoms for a pair of tight-fitting jeans, but still wore the McGill sweatshirt.

"Do your thing," she said by way of a greeting.

Gilles told her that the two uniformed cops were there to see that she didn't interfere in the search and asked her where she wanted to wait. She chose to sit at the kitchen table.

He was pretty certain that he had as much evidence as his search would turn up, along with evidence of Jacqui trying to dispose of it. He didn't want to miss anything, though.

He started in the living room and then moved to the dining alcove. Nothing out of the ordinary. There was a small room that Jacqui used as a home office. The computer was on a table and there was a two-drawer file cabinet that contained bills and other papers.

The bedroom was large and comfortable. There was a queen size bed, neatly made, a dresser, a night table and a comfortable chair with clothing folded on it. Gilles checked the dresser and night table drawers and then turned his attention to the closet. There were four lab coats on hangers. They all bore the logo and name of the Gursky Memorial Hospital stitched onto the chest pocket. He placed each of the lab coats in an evidence bag. He joined Jacqui and the cops in the kitchen.

She and the two cops, both male, were having coffee and an animated conversation. The cops fell silent when Gilles appeared.

"I'm done. I'll give you a receipt for these," Gilles said, indicating the lab coats. He put them down and scrawled a receipt on a page from his notepad.

"That's it? My lab coats? I could have brought them to you," Jacqui said.

"That's not quite it. I need you to come to the station. I have some questions. These officers will drive you."

Jacqui started to complain but Gilles had walked out of the kitchen. He left it to the two uniformed cops to get Jacqui to the division office. Gilles had a stop to make on his way.

He picked up the evidence bags from the stakeout car and was careful to have the cops sign the bags over to him to ensure the chain of evidence was respected.

He brought all that he had collected to the Forensics Division at police headquarters. This was an unusual step. Normally the forensics team collected evidence and retained it until it was examined. Gilles gave the forensics technicians the details of the crimes he was investigating. He didn't provide any more than the basic information but his hope was that the Law of Exchange would turn up something incriminating. When two objects, a human and an object or two humans come into contact with each other something of each of them rubs off on the other. Fingerprints are and obvious example of this but it could be anything, clothing fibres, material from shoes, anything.

As he drove, he had to pay attention to avoid the perils of Montreal winter driving, ice patches and snow banks. Luckily, he only ended up in a skid once and he managed to pull out of it before hitting a snow bank on the side of the road

When he arrived at the office, he checked the interrogation room and saw that Jacqui was there, guarded this time by a woman cop. He told her he would be with her in a couple of minutes. He reported to Gaston and Lieutenant

Giroux on what he had discovered and his next steps. He asked that Jean-Guy St-Onge be brought from jail and kept in another of the interrogation rooms. Gilles had questions for both siblings.

He brought Jacqui a glass of water and sat opposite her. He looked straight into her eyes. He expected to see a look that suggested she was a lot less cocky than when in her apartment or with her mother. Gilles was wrong. Jacqui was looking daggers at him.

"For the purposes of the recording," Gilles pointed to the mic hanging from the ceiling, "I'm Detective Sergeant Gilles Bellechasse." He looked at Jacqui and said, "Please state your name for the record."

She gave her name and added, "For the record, I have no idea why I'm here. If you've brought me here because you think I stole some lab coats you're very much mistaken." She took a sip of water. She held the glass aloft for a moment and put it back on the table without spilling a drop.

"I'm not here to play games," Gilles said.

"Great. Neither am I."

"I want to talk about poison and two deaths. Those of your boss, Dr. Marcus Tiddley, and Alain Patenaude," Gilles said.

"Don't know anything about the first and don't even know the second guy."

"No?" Gilles said. It was not really a question. "Both of them had a connection to your father. Tiddley's father was a victim of your dad's and his mother testified at the trial. Patenaude was the son of the trial judge."

Jacqui said nothing.

"At first I thought that your brother, who attacked and murdered others connected with the trial in totally crazy revenge mode, got you to make some poisons for him so he could kill two guys that might not be so easy to attack on the street, or maybe because he wanted to throw us off the trail by using different methods. But as I thought about it, I formed a different conclusion."

"Really, sounds fascinating. It couldn't be more off the mark than your original idea," Jacqui said.

"I think you worked with your brother. I think he strangled people and you poisoned them. To be blunt, I think you poisoned Tiddley and Patenaude. And you'll soon..."

A knock at the door stopped Gilles from completing his sentence. Marie Rousseau opened the door and handed Gilles a thick file. He ignored Jacqui as he went through it page by page. He took out a photograph of the empty recycling bin and showed it to Jacqui. He then placed two other photos beside it and said, "The first photo is of the recycling bin in front of your apartment building. As you can see, it's empty. The second photo is of you placing a bag of recycling in the bin, and the third photo is the cop who had your building under surveillance removing the bag."

Gilles flipped to another page in the file. "We found the blonde wig you disposed of and identified the hairs as the same type as those found at one of the crime scenes."

Jacqui interrupted Gilles's explanation with a laugh, "You know that these things have no identifying markers. All polyester is pretty much the same. You thought you found something incriminating in my garbage? Laughable."

"Actually, you're right. I did find something incriminating in your garbage."

Gilles showed her the photos of the N95 mask and her lab coat that someone in the forensics division had taken. He pulled out a sheet of paper and read from it, "The mask and lab coat have traces of the poison used to kill Patenaude. Take a look." The report contained the formula of VX poison which was a series of letters and subscripts, $C_{11}H_{26}NO_{2}PS$, meaningless to Gilles but something Jacqui understood. "I can think of no reason why you would be working with..." Gilles paused and silently sounded out the term in the report before he spoke, "...a thiophosphonate, a nerve agent, other than to kill someone. Can you?"

"I have nothing to say. I want a lawyer," Jacqui said.

"You'll have the opportunity to make a phone call soon enough. You don't have to say anything, but I have something to say to you. Did you, or your brother, think for a minute what this revenge crime would do to your mother? She suffered the disaster of having her husband convicted of murder and she did her best to rebuild a life for the three of you. She succeeded. What's more, she didn't deny you the memory of your father's good points. Saying nice things about the man who destroyed her life must have been terribly difficult for her. And this is the way you repay her? By making her relive the trauma? Now losing her children as well as her husband? This is a level of thoughtlessness that I've never seen. You want to stay silent. Good for you. I don't know if I have the stomach to hear anything else from you."

Gilles got to his feet and opened the door to admit Marie Rousseau. Gilles turned to Jacqui and said, "Stand up. You're under arrest for the murders of Dr. Marcus Tiddley and Alain Patenaude. Cuff her and take her."

Marie Rousseau put the cuffs on Jacqui and led her out of the room. "She'll want to make a phone call before you put her in," Gilles said.

"I changed my mind," Jacqui called from the hallway. She turned to Marie and said, "I want to talk to him."

Marie turned to see if Gilles agreed. He nodded and said, "Oui, ça va."

"What is it you want?" he asked once Jacqui was again seated at the table in the interrogation room.

She leaned forward, looked straight at Gilles, and said, this time in a softer voice bereft of anger, "You're right. I did a stupid thing. I allowed my brother to convince me to help him. I should have known his insane plan for revenge would blow up in our faces."

"Are you ready to confess without a lawyer present?" Gilles asked. "This conversation is being recorded, so if you agree there's no backing out later."

"There's no point in putting off the inevitable. I want to get this over with."

"Okay," Gilles said.

Gilles opened the door and beckoned for Marie Rousseau to enter and he pointed to the mic hanging from the ceiling. She said, "Constable Marie Rousseau also present." She and Gilles sat down.

Gilles asked Jacqui to identify herself for the recording as well, and said, "Ms. Di Camera is being questioned with regard to the murders of Marcus Tiddley and Alain Patenaude. She has waived her right to counsel. Is that correct?"

"Yes, yes, it is," Jacqui said.

"Fine. You were about to tell us how you helped your brother Jean-Guy St-Onge to poison Tiddley and Patenaude."

There was silence for a brief moment before Jacqui spoke. "My brother, Jean-Guy, wanted to get revenge for the imprisonment of our father Ian Chambers. Jean-Guy believed he wasn't guilty of murder but of helping sick and suffering old people by bringing an end to their pain and restoring to them a certain amount of dignity."

"You agreed with him?" Gilles asked.

"I can't say I agreed with him but I didn't really disagree with him either. I thought revenge was foolish. I just wanted to leave events where they belong. In the past."

"Yet..." Gilles prompted.

"Yet, I foolishly allowed him to convince me to make a poison that would prove fatal to two innocent people. I'm ashamed to say that I didn't think so much about the victims. My concern was my mother, should Jean-Guy be caught, and of course I was concerned for Jean-Guy as well. I hoped that when it came time to administer the poisons, he would have a change of heart and the whole thing would come to an end. I didn't know that he planned to strangle five people and the poisoning was intended to throw the police off his track. I'm sorry, very sorry."

Jacqui put her face in her hands, her elbows on the table.

"That's it?" Gilles asked.

From behind her hands Jacqui answered, "Yes."

"To be clear. You're saying that the whole idea for the murders was your brother's and you only helped him in the hopes that he *wouldn't* go through with them?"

"Yes," Jacqui said. Her hands now flat on the table.

"That's it for now," Gilles said. "I'll have more questions about details later." He nodded to Marie and said, "You can take her to jail now."

Marie got to her feet and put the handcuffs on Jacqui again. As she was being led out, she turned to Gilles and asked, "I co-operated, so how about bail?"

"That's for a lawyer to handle at your arraignment. You can make a phone call."

"Interview over," Gilles said and gave the time for the recording.

Gilles went down the hall to the interrogation room that held Jean-Guy St-Onge. He was surprised to see that Pierrette Lavoie, the Legal Aid lawyer, was with him.

She noticed his surprise and said, "He hasn't had time to arrange for private counsel so you're stuck with me until he does."

Gilles placed the file he carried from his questioning of Jacqui Di Camera on the table. "More refutable evidence?" Pierrette asked.

"Hardly," Gilles said. He identified himself for the recording as did Pierrette Lavoie and Jean-Guy St-Onge when prompted.

Gilles placed his hand flat on the file and said, "I've just finished interviewing your sister and I'll play back the recording of what she told me." Gilles fiddled with the buttons on the console and his and Jacqui's voices filled the room.

St-Onge listened silently but his face became redder and redder as he heard his sister blame him for all the murders. The vein in his neck throbbed. "She what? She what?" St-Onge said, almost shouting.

Lavoie put a restraining hand on his forearm and leaned in close for a whispered conversation.

"Is she prepared to testify to that in court?" Lavoie asked.

"You heard. I didn't ask her specifically but that's obvious, no? Or why confess?"

Another whispered conversation ensued. While it took place, a cop brought Gilles another file which he flipped through. "If it will help your consultations, I can tell you that I've just received confirmation that his cellphone was present at the scenes of the other four strangulations."

St-Onge nodded in agreement to something his lawyer whispered and said aloud, "Jacqui means to stick everything on me, right? She thinks she can get away with that?"

"Apparently," Gilles said.

"Yeah, well, that's not going to happen. She was my partner, not an innocent victim forced into my plot." St-Onge did his best to bring himself under control. "She's the one who suggested that she poison the two guys, to divert suspicion in the event that someone saw the connection among the victims."

"Do you know how she got the victims to ingest the poison?"

"Yeah, you'd be surprised at how easy it is. Tiddley was easy. He was her boss and it wasn't hard to engineer an invitation to his house, slip the poison into something in his fridge and leave. She told me she dosed his chutney that he would use with Indian food. Everyone in the lab knew he liked spicy food. She also thought it would be a good idea to plant blonde hairs in his bed, to further confuse things. Quite the mastermind, my sister."

"And Patenaude?"

St-Onge grimaced. "Almost as easy. She staked him out, saw that he was a runner and even joined him for a couple of kilometers on the mountain. Once he had left for work it was a simple matter to break into his place and inject the poison into the Mio flavouring he put in his water bottles. Sooner or later he would drink it and that would be that."

Gilles had the confession he needed but couldn't resist asking the next question. "You gave no consideration to how this would affect your mother?"

"We asked all kinds of questions about our father. Our mother was hesitant at first to answer our questions. But we, and especially me, insisted on knowing what our father had done. What memories we had were of a loving father. He played with us, took us places, did all the things that dads do. Our mother did nothing to paint a different picture of the man. We grew up believing that our father was accused of things that weren't really crimes. That the truly guilty people were the ones who made our father a victim in order to assuage their own guilt. They had to pay for denying us our father."

Gilles shook his head slowly. "Revenge never solves anything. Didn't that occur to you?"

"My, our, anger was stronger than that realization," Jean-Guy said.

"Do you still feel that way?" Gilles asked.

Jean-Guy was quiet for several minutes. He sighed and Gilles could see he looked deflated. Finally Jean-Guy, "Now that it's over. I have to say, 'no.' Murder didn't solve anything. I'm still angry and I have the guilt for what I did added to that. I'll never be free."

Chapter 38

"Tell me everything," Annie said. Dinner was over and they were relaxing with coffees in her living room. She shifted her position so that she was sitting against the armrest of the sofa. Gilles twisted so that he was facing her and said, "From what you told me about Jean-Guy St-Onge's reaction to patients in distress I formed the opinion that he merited a closer look for the L'Étrangleur killings."

"You didn't consider a random quote to be evidence of guilt, did you?"

"Hardly," Gilles said. "It just made me think that he was worth a closer look. When he made a run for it, I became convinced that he was involved in the murders. At first I wondered why he strangled some victims and poisoned others. That made no sense. My experience is that once a murderer finds a way of committing their crimes, they stick to it. When I discovered that he had a sister who was a chemist I concluded that either she helped him or she too was a murderer."

"In other words, the crimes weren't committed by the same person. You have two sets of murders."

"Exactly," Gilles said. "When I applied the diagnosis process you told me about it became clear that I was dealing with one plot and two murderers."

"What about the third?"

"The third?" Gilles asked.

"The death that started your investigation, that of George Prodosiakis."

“Right,” Gilles said. “I’m convinced that Toula Prodosiakis left the front door of her house open, knowing her father was likely to wander off. The night was cold and he’d be unlikely to survive. In fact, I think she knew a lot more about the drugs Tiddley gave her father. She figured out who he really was when she started dating him. It’s possible that she knew or suspected the drugs Tiddley gave her father might be contributing factors, but there’s no law against forgetting to lock a door, and we’d never be able to prove intent.”

“The poor man,” Annie said softly. “The poor, poor man.”

Epilogue

Charging Jean-Guy St-Onge and Jacqui Di Camera for multiple murders was the end of one process and the beginning of another. The police had to gather enough evidence so that the crown, in the person of the Crown Prosecutor Manon Tremblay, could make the charges stick at trial.

The resources of the department were deployed in order to accomplish this. A large part of the work fell to the Computer Crimes Division which was able to trace the whereabouts of Jean-Guy St-Onge by tracking his cellphone on the nights of the L'Étrangleur murders. The Forensics Division demonstrated how Jacqui was able to create the poisons she used on Marcus Tiddley and Alain Patenaude. Moreover, forensics was able to prove how the murderer gained access to Patenaude's condo using CCTV footage from cameras in the neighbourhood—one of the merchants on Park Avenue had a camera in the alley to protect the back door. There was clear footage of Jacqui Di Camera lurking around the rear of Patenaude's condo.

She worked with Tiddley and it was easy to prove that she had been at his house a number of times for a variety of reasons, most recently the Friday before he died. It was a simple matter to get the poison into the jar of chutney.

Even when presented with overwhelming evidence of their crimes neither Jacqui Di Camera nor her brother pleaded guilty. They each wanted their day in court. Jacqui at first tried to blame her brother for instigating the crimes, depicting herself as an unwitting accomplice. She couldn't sustain this defense at trial as she made and planted the poison that killed two people. She did this on her own, without any help from Jean-Guy, proving that she was equally culpable.

Their trial ended with guilty verdicts for both of them which meant that they would be spending the next twenty-five years in prison.

The arrest and trial proved devastating to Madame St-Onge. She suffered a heart attack which would have killed a person with less of a will to live. The defence attorneys for her children wanted her to be in the courtroom for the trials to show that in spite of everything she supported them. Madame St-Onge agreed, not because she supported their actions but because she felt some guilt at blaming others for what her husband did.

She made a statement at the time of sentencing, however. She apologized and explained that she hated the crimes that her children committed but loved them—they were her children, after all. She promised to devote whatever time she had left to working toward improving the care of the elderly.

She began to live up to her promise by volunteering to work with a group who made up Personal Protection Equipment kits for those who cared for the elderly as the spread of Covid became worse.

Acknowledgements

I am thankful to Maggie Quinsey, a nurse in the Emergency Department of the Jewish General Hospital. She is not only an excellent and compassionate nurse but is also a close personal friend to me. She has taken the time and the trouble to provide support during a very difficult time in my life and I am grateful for that as well as for allowing me to use her as the role model for Annie Linton, R.N.

Deirdre O'Donnell King read an early draft of Serving Life and made valuable suggestions for its improvement. Deirdre is a brilliant reader and I was pleased to incorporate all her editorial ideas as I revised the novel.

I benefited from Elise Moser's excellent and insightful editorial skills she applied to Serving Life for which I thank her. I count my and Elise's many years of working together as a blessing.

I also want to thank Blossom Thom for her work on copy editing *Serving Life*. No error or typo was too small to escape her notice.

I want to thank my friend Jacques Chenier for allowing me to use his name and to model a character on him.

I am fortunate to have Robin Philpot and Baraka Books as a publisher. Working with Robin is a delight that every writer should have with their publisher. Robin is straight forward in his comments, decisive and insightful. All in all, the best qualities a publisher can have.

Friendships mean a lot to me and I am lucky to have John Aylen as a close friend. He provides encouragement and sound advice when needed—which in my case is frequently.

Mary Reinhold provides support in ways too numerous to count. She has played and continues to play an important role in my life and I doubt that I'll ever be able to repay her for her many acts of help and encouragement.

Without the love of my brothers Joel and Norman and their families and of my son Nicholas my life would be empty. I am blessed to have them in my life and I hope that I am in some small way able to repay them for all that they have done for me.

Richard King passed away on January 4, 2022 without seeing the final edition of this third instalment to the Nurse Linton, Detective Bellechasse Mystery Series. Richard had half completed the fourth book in the series. The first book, *A Stab at Life* appeared on April 1, 2020, two weeks after the Covid-19 pandemic was declared. Baraka Books is proud to have published the series, which is Richard's glowing tribute to nurses, healthcare workers in general, and to Montreal, the city he loved and knew so well.

Robin Philpot, Publisher

MIX
Paper
FSC® C100212

Printed by Imprimerie Gauvin
Gatineau, Québec